BE YOUR BEST SELF

MAXINE MORREY

Boldwood

First published in Great Britain in 2024 by Boldwood Books Ltd.

Copyright © Maxine Morrey, 2024

Cover Design by Leah Jacobs-Gordon

Cover Photography: Shutterstock

A CIP catalogue record for this book is available from the British Library.

Paperback ISBN 978-1-83751-129-7

Large Print ISBN 978-1-83751-128-0

Hardback ISBN 978-1-83751-127-3

Ebook ISBN 978-1-83751-130-3

Kindle ISBN 978-1-83751-131-0

Audio CD ISBN 978-1-83751-122-8

MP3 CD ISBN 978-1-83751-123-5

Digital audio download ISBN 978-1-83751-125-9

Boldwood Books Ltd
23 Bowerdean Street
London SW6 3TN
www.boldwoodbooks.com

To my fabulous cousin, Heidi.
A book about one strong woman dedicated to another.
Thank you for all the love and belief you've shown. You are amazing. I
love you.

1

I hadn't always been a witch. The thought had never really occurred to me before I moved back to the village I grew up in. I lived in a semi-detached Victorian cottage with a wonderfully long garden backing onto a paddock, and had been happily growing ingredients for ointments, teas and tinctures for years, each season bringing with it a further appreciation of the nature around me than the one before. I was what is called a green witch. Or so my friend, Crystal, who runs the local alternative therapies shop, told me. It's all about the peace and tranquillity for me.

'What the hell are you doing?' I yelled.

Spud and I were just returning from our early-morning walk in air that had a hint of early spring warmth. Above us birds chirped and cheeped in the trees, the leaves of some tentatively unfurling as though testing the air to decide whether to continue just yet. The grass was vibrant and green beneath our feet and the sun sparkled on the surface of the nearby stream, making it glitter and shimmer as it ambled its way along. Heading back into the village, I'd smiled as Spud's toenails clicked rhythmically on the pavement as he trotted along beside me and turned towards home. And that's when I'd seen it. The mini digger sinking its sharp metal teeth into my neighbour's front garden.

The operator ignored me, the noise of the machine drowning my words. I waved my arms to catch his attention and repeated my question as he turned off the engine.

'What are you doing?'

'What I'm paid to.' He gave a shrug and made to start the machine up again.

'But you can't!' I said. 'Some of these roses are prime specimens!'

'Looks like a bit of a wilderness to me.' The machine rumbled to life once more.

'Well... yes. Yes, it is. I agree. At the moment,' I shouted, trying to make myself heard above the din. 'But the answer isn't just ripping everything out with a digger! It can be restored.'

'Is there a problem?' A deep voice cut across the noise, followed a moment later by its owner, who strode out from behind the huge skip that was slowly being filled with the contents of the garden.

The digger's jaw turned away from me and scooped out the roots of a once beautiful, but now admittedly overgrown, cherry tree that was just beginning to bud with flower. It toppled and fell to the ground.

'Oh!' I cried out, an almost physical pain scything through me at the destruction.

'I asked if there was a problem.' The man was close to the gate now, where I was standing. Spud had found a warm spot on the ground and was sunning himself, unaware of the tumult going on around him.

'Yes! There is. This!' I spread my arms to encompass the machinery and the garden.

He didn't even take a moment to glance back. 'What about it?'

'You're destroying it!'

'No. I'm having an overgrown disaster zone cleared.'

'It's not that bad!'

He fixed me with a steady look, his deep green eyes almost daring me to quantify that statement.

'OK, fine. It is. But it doesn't have to be!'

'I know. That's rather the point of having the work done.'

'That's like using a sledgehammer to crack a pistachio.'

'Nut.'

'Pardon?'

'The expression is to crack a nut.'

'I know what the bloody expression is! Which is exactly why I chose something smaller that you can open with your fingers.'

Was I really standing here debating nuts with this stranger?

'Oh, I see. Fair enough.'

'The point is,' I emphasised, 'that you're taking an overly heavy-handed approach!'

'I see.' He cleared his throat. 'Forgive me, but may I ask something?'

'Yes.'

'What exactly does any of this have to do with you? My name is Henry Darcy and, as far as memory serves, I paid a good deal of my own money to buy this house and was under the impression it was then mine to do with as I wished. I must have missed the part where I had to run everything past any random person walking by for approval.'

'There's no need to be sarcastic.'

'I'm just stating facts.'

'Sarcastically. And I'm not some random person. I happen to live next door!' I pointed at my side of the house.

The man's head turned slowly to where I was indicating the

sunshine-yellow-painted front door, surrounded with terracotta flowerpots of various sizes bursting with crocuses, hellebores, primroses and some early daffodils. These would soon be followed by another wave of daffodils and narcissi, their flowers ranging from egg yolk yellow to ghostly white and everything in between. After that would come the tulips.

'Oh. How wonderful.' His eyes returned to meet mine once more, his tone entirely flat.

'Yes, well, I'm not thrilled either.'

'Morning, Willow!' Jerry the postie wandered along and handed me three letters and a small package. 'All right, Doc. Hope you're not getting on the wrong side of Willow here. You know she's a witch, right?' He gave a chuckle as we both just looked at him. 'The good kind, obviously, but I reckon she wouldn't be past turning the odd bloke into a frog if he gets on her wick too much. Ta-ta!' And off he went, whistling slightly off key.

Henry was staring after him.

'Some of these plants are decades old,' I prompted, seemingly jolting him out of his daze.

'Then it's probably about time to freshen things up, isn't it?'

'That's not how a garden works!'

'It may not be how your garden works, Ms…?'

'Haines. Willow Haines.'

He nodded. 'Ms Haines, and that's your prerogative. What I do in and on my own property is my business and I'd thank you to respect that. Now, if you don't mind, I have things to do.' He gave a sharp nod, turned around and strode back through the side passage to where, craning my neck, I saw the back garden was being subjected to the same rough treatment. The whine of a chainsaw began to screech and I winced, both from the sound and the thought of what it might be attacking.

'Come on, Spud,' I called to the dog who was still chilling on the pavement. 'Time to go home.' He looked up, pushed himself up onto his short stubby legs, gave a stretch and then trotted on and through the garden gate up to the yellow door.

I closed the front door behind me, but it did little to drown out the sound of the destruction. I'd have to fish out the noise-cancelling headphones. Having worn them nearly all the time in London, I really only used them now when I travelled. It was a rare occurrence to have to dig them out here in the village, let alone in my own home. Ugh! Dreadful man. When I'd seen the removals van outside a few weeks ago, I'd been excited at the prospect of having neighbours again. I loved peace and quiet, but Mill Cottage was situated towards the edge of the village and a little apart from the rest of the houses. I'd adored my previous neighbour and we'd become good friends over the years, but time had ticked on and, after her husband had passed a few years ago, Edie finally took the decision to move into a modern retirement flat nearer to her family. I totally understood that. The house was bigger than she needed and was getting too much to look after on her own, especially in the winter with fuel bills going up and up.

And the garden... well, my new neighbour was right – not that I'd admit that to his face. It had become a bit of a wilderness. They were long gardens, over one hundred feet, typical of the period and it did take work to keep on top of them. For me, my garden was a sanctuary; for Edie, I knew hers had become a burden. With Ted gone, she lost the will to continue with something they had once always done together. Gradually nature had begun to reclaim its territory. But still, surely there was a less drastic solution than this?

From outside I heard the unmistakeable sharp crack of a tree trunk splitting and rushed to the window just in time to see the large sycamore that had stood close to our boundary fence crash to the ground. Turning, I grabbed my phone and pressed the contact for my best friend.

'He's a monster!' I said by way of a greeting.

'Good morning to you too,' Abby replied. 'And who exactly is a monster?'

'Sorry, hi. My new neighbour from hell!'

'Mmm, I hear he's more like heaven. Apparently, he's got the face of an angel and a body made for sin.'

'Well, yes. I suppose he is quite good-looking. I wasn't paying much attention, but his personality doesn't match up to it. Appearances can be deceptive. He's most definitely not heavenly.'

'You know he's called Darcy, right? Dr Henry Darcy. He's joined the clinic as a new doctor. I bumped into Steve in the village and he was over the moon about it. Very skilled and well respected apparently.'

'Yes, I did know and I can assure you he's definitely no romantic hero in my eyes!'

'So what exactly has he done to earn this defamation of character?'

'He's ripping out Edie's garden! I mean, not just cutting it back. Literally ripping it out. There are diggers and everything. And that lovely big sycamore has just been felled!'

'The one in the middle?'

'Yes!'

'The one you used to moan about because it kept dropping seedlings, sucked all the moisture from the ground and shaded a good part of your border?'

I paused. 'That's not the point.'

'Maybe he's done you a favour. You never wanted to risk upsetting Edie by asking to have it trimmed, although I don't think it would have bothered her at all. I'm not sure she really cared by then, to be honest. Now it's gone, so the problem's solved.'

'You're supposed to be on my side.'

Abby laughed. 'I am, my lovely. But I think you're overreacting a bit.'

'Did you hear me? He's literally ripping *everything* out!'

'Wils, relax. Maybe he just wants to redo the garden to his own design. It was kind of a mess, and it is his house now.'

'Ugh. I hate it when you're rational.'

'I know. Sorry about that. I do get why you're upset. But the truth is, neither of us can do anything about it. And who knows, it might end up being even better than before if he's having it professionally landscaped.'

I let out a sigh as I pondered. 'That's true. I hadn't really thought of it that way.'

'OK, I'd better get on, but I'll speak to you later.'

'Yep, thanks, Abs.'

'You're welcome. Talk to you later.'

* * *

Hopes for a more beautiful outdoor space than before were scuppered entirely when I returned from Spud's walk a few days later.

'You have got to be kidding!' I said, as I halted in shock.

Henry Darcy appeared from behind the van that was now parked outside the house.

'Good morning. I'm guessing from your exclamation that you have an opinion on this too.'

'On smothering the earth with plastic? Yes, I do actually.'

'I thought you might,' he replied, turning away.

'You do know how appalling this fake grass stuff is for wildlife and, well, the planet in general? It's effectively single-use plastic!'

'It's also convenient for my lifestyle.'

'You can hire people to mow real grass if you didn't want to do it yourself.'

'I do know that but that's not the path I chose in the end. As you can see.'

'We starting round the back then, mate?' A solid-looking chap hefted a roll up onto his shoulder and was followed by a lanky, wiry lad carrying a bucket of tools.

'Yes. Just down there.' Henry pointed to the side passage. 'I'll be there in a minute. Was there anything else?' He turned back to me, looking down from his substantial height advantage. There was a detached air about him. No warmth in his eyes, his expression unreadable. If I'd have had to pick an emotion, I'd have said bored.

'Would it matter if there was?'

He shifted his weight. 'Right. I'll get on then, if you don't mind.'

'It doesn't really matter if I do mind, does it?' I replied, petulantly.

'No, I'm afraid it doesn't.' With that, he strode off, following the same path the workmen had taken, and disappeared from sight.

'Hateful man!' I hissed between gritted teeth and stomped back to my side of the house, closed the door, unclipped Spud's lead and attempted to calm down by doing some breathing exercises. These were not made any easier by the disco hits blaring out from the turf fitters' radio deafening all wildlife – including me – within the vicinity.

'Oh, that's just perfect!' I seethed, stomping over to the kettle. As I reached for my mug everything went quiet. Sort of. The back garden no longer sounded like a 1980s roller disco, which was something. I peered out of the French doors, careful to keep myself in the shadows of the curtain.

My new neighbour was out there, talking to the turf bloke and… wait, was that a smile? No, it couldn't have been! It must have been a trick of the light. An actual smile would probably crack that annoyingly attractive strong jaw. But either way, the radio was turned down to a much more bearable level, which I, and likely anything in the locality with ears, appreciated.

Switching on the retro-design radio in my work room, the soothing sounds of Classic FM drifted around the room, drowning out the last remnants of the competing music in next door's garden.

I picked up my current project and sat down in the squashy, cosy lemon-yellow armchair by the window. Light streamed in through the glass and birdsong drifted through the open window. Actually, now that the tree had gone it was even brighter in this back room. Not that it wasn't just fine before. I tuned my brain in to the classical piece playing and set about gently repairing a well-loved teddy bear named Harold who had recently been admitted to Willow's Hospital for Teddy Bears and Poorly Dollies.

It had never been my greatest wish in life to set up the teddy hospital and had in fact come about entirely by accident.

Although I'd grown up in the village, I, like many when they leave school or university, thought the place was stifling me. Moving to the big, bad city was the only way I was going to find the space to spread my wings and live my dream. The fact I had no idea what that dream was was neither here nor there at the time. I had a degree in business studies – also because I'd had no idea what I wanted to do and that seemed like a good grounding for most things – and I was ready to conquer the world!

It rarely works like that, though, does it? Don't get me wrong. I had a good time. For a while. I got a job as a business analyst for a large corporation, made friends, went out and did all the things I felt like I was supposed to do. I even met The One. At least, I'd thought he was The One.

2

Seven years later it had become unerringly obvious that neither of us were the right one for the other. Life in London grated on my nerves. I loved the museums and parks and architecture, but I could no longer bear the noise, the unending swarm of people, packing myself in on the Tube every day like a sardine only more smelly – especially in summer.

It was just all too much.

Mark didn't see it that way. Gradually the things we'd thought we had in common became less and less. A good night for me was tucking myself into a cosy spot with a herbal tea and a good book. A good night for him was heading out to a bar and drinking. I no longer wanted that, and as it turned out, he no longer wanted someone who didn't want that. Amazingly, and luckily, both of us stayed reasonable enough for the split to be amicable. So amicable, in fact, that I wasn't actually divorced yet. We'd filled in all the paperwork, split everything down the middle and done everything we needed. But somehow we'd never quite got around to processing that final step.

'Done it yet?' Abby asked, the next time I saw her.

'Nope,' I replied, sliding in behind the table at our favoured local café.

'Why not?'

'Just haven't had time. Like I told you last week. And the week before. And the week before that.'

She shook her head.

'It's not like there's any rush. I never meet anyone anyway.'

'Maybe you don't want to.' She took a sip of her Spring Sunshine smoothie. 'Ooh, yum!'

I leant over and took a drag on her straw. 'Oooh! I think I'm having smoothie envy.' I went back to my own drink. 'Although this Wheatgrass Wonder is pretty good.'

Abby wrinkled her nose, having known me long enough to spot a fib – even a teeny one.

The truth was, it wasn't bad but not a patch on hers. But it was doing me good. That was the important thing. I could always have a slice of their salted toffee cake to make up for how much good it was doing me.

'You really should get it sorted. I'm amazed Mark hasn't wanted to already either.'

'He told me he wouldn't marry again, so I guess he's not so bothered.'

'Why not?'

'Get married again? I don't know. He just said he didn't think he was cut out for it.'

'But you are.'

I pulled a face as I sucked my straw.

'You are,' my friend reiterated.

'I'm happy as I am.'

'Are you, though?'

I opened my mouth to reply.

'Truly?' Abby interrupted. 'Swear on Spud's life that you wouldn't want to meet someone.'

Spud looked up at hearing his name. 'It's all right, boy,' I said, fishing out an emergency treat from my pocket. He took it gently and crunched away happily before resting his nose back on his paws then returned to watching the world go by the window. Not that there was a lot to watch in the village, but he seemed content. I smiled down at him, ran my hand down his fluffy back before getting back to Abby's question. Was I happy on my own, with Spud?

'Ugh, OK. Fine. Yes, it would be nice. But let's face it, I'm hardly likely to meet someone, am I? Spud is the only man I can see in my life for the foreseeable future.'

'Excepting the fact that you do, of course, live next door to the most eligible bachelor in the region.'

'Dr Grumpy? Ha! Yeah, that's never going to happen.'

'Why not? He can't be that bad. Actually, he seemed really nice when I went to see him.'

'What's wrong? You didn't tell me you were ill.'

'I'm not. Ed was getting antsy about that aching back I've had. I knew it wasn't anything to worry about, but you know what he's like.'

I did know what he was like. Ed had worshipped the ground Abby walked on for as long as I could remember. He'd been watching that day she'd had the fall and wouldn't leave the hospital until he knew she was going to be OK.

'But everything was all right? You're all right, aren't you?' I heard my voice pitch up.

'I'm fine!' Abby said, laughter in her voice. 'You're as bad as Ed! Dr Darcy was soooooooo nice and really reassuring. He scheduled a scan just to put our minds at rest.'

'When is the scan?'

'I've had it.'

I opened my mouth but Abby was there before me. 'And yes, everything is fine. He just told me to take it a little easier.'

'I said you shouldn't try to wrestle that mattress out on your own!'

'I know, I know, and I promise I won't go overboard like that again.'

'That was pretty quick to get the scan then? I know the clinic here is good, but still.'

'Yeah.' Abby pulled a face. 'I kind of blabbed about Ed being worried and so far away and started getting a bit upset, so Dr Darcy managed to put a rush on it. He was really sweet and funny actually.' She gave a slightly-too-dreamy smile.

'Erm, excuse me. Whilst I am grateful to him for getting you checked over double quick, I cannot sit by and listen to other praises being sung. In my experience, he is neither sweet nor funny. He's rude and a garden wrecker and you're supposed to be on my side. I did tell you about the fake grass, right?'

'Yes. You did. And I do agree. That does seem a shame for nature and stuff, but—' she gave a shrug '—it is his house.'

'He could have been a bit more polite about it,' I grumped.

'He did seem a bit short from what you said. But then I suppose if someone asked you what the hell you were doing on your own property, you might be a bit uppity too.'

I gave a long draw on my smoothie before raising my eyes to my friend's. 'Do you mind not being so intensely reasonable all the time?'

'Sorry. I used to be a primary teacher, remember? I dealt with children all the time.'

'Thanks.'

Abby giggled. 'Sorry, that came out wrong. Although...'

'Ha ha. Very funny.'

'Penny-lope said he'd moved here from London. Bought it for cash, apparently.' Penny-lope was another from our nursery school alma mater. One of us had mispronounced her name way back when and, decades later, the nickname was still firmly in play.

I thought of my mortgage and sniffed. 'All right for some.'

'Yeah, I know.' Abby gave a flick of her eyebrows in agreement. 'But I guess property prices in London are so bonkers now, it's hardly surprising either.'

'Hmm, shame I was renting when I lived there. Even back then we couldn't afford to get on the ladder.'

'Probably a bit of a culture shock for him, moving down here. London – any city – is so anonymous. Nobody talks to each other. Now he's landed somewhere where everyone knows everyone's business. People actually talk to their neighbours. It must all feel a bit alien.'

'Well, nobody made him move here and frankly I'm quite happy not to talk to him.'

Abby gave me one of the looks she had honed during her teacher days.

I looked up at her through my lashes and stuck my bottom lip out in a massive sulky face.

'Perfect!' Abby laughed and, before I knew it, snapped a photo.

'If that goes on the village chat thread, I will dig up Dr Grumpy's fake turf and bury you under it.'

'I'll just keep it as a bargaining chip for something like... hmm, I don't know. Finalising your divorce, for example?'

'Ugh!' I let my shoulders go slack and slumped forward, taking a slurp of my drink. 'It's in process! Why are you so hung up on that? It's not a big deal.'

'It's a huge deal! It's like telling the universe that you're not interested in finding someone else because you're still techni-cally, and legally, bound to your husband.'

'I'm sure the universe has much bigger things to worry about than the state of my love life.'

'You know what I mean.'

'I know, I know…'

'There was something on breakfast telly the other day about manifesting. Have you ever thought about giving it a try?'

'Not in a definitive way. I do try and keep my focus on the good stuff, but as for vision boards and stuff, no. I've never really dived into it that deeply.' I slurped the last of my smoothie and pondered.

'You've got that look on your face.'

'What look?'

'That drifting off look. You get it when you have an idea for the house, or the garden, or another miracle way of fixing a bear that looks like it's had its last cuddle.'

I let out a gasp, my hand to my chest. 'Wash your mouth out! No bear has ever had its last cuddle. There is always a way.'

Abby grinned. 'Thanks to you and your magic skills.'

I smiled back, part of my mind drifting, just as my bestie had said.

'Do you think I should do it?'

'What's that?' Abby said.

'Manifest my perfect man.'

Abby sat up straight, her wide, slightly gap-toothed grin lighting up her softly freckled face. 'You're going to try it?'

I gave a shrug, my smile matching hers as enthusiasm fizzed between us. 'Why not? But why stop at manifestation? I've already got some crystals in the house for good energy but maybe I'm just doing everything a bit half-arsed. If it's going to work, I need to throw myself into it utterly. Manifest the life I truly want.'

'It's going to work. I know it!'

'Got time for another drink to celebrate?'

Abby checked her phone for the time and said that she had. A few minutes later, we were clinking together our ginger, lemon and turmeric teas and toasting my new endeavour.

Once I'd hugged Abby goodbye, I plopped Spud into the special basket I'd had made for him that attached to the front of my bicycle. It was like one of those old-fashioned butcher's or grocer's delivery baskets but a little smaller, divided into two. One side was for shopping, library books and so on and the other, with its cosy blanket, was my dog's personal transportation. He absolutely revelled in it, his tongue hanging out tasting the wind, his little ears flapping as I propelled us along, friends and neighbours waving as we scooted past. Thoughts percolated in my mind as I pedalled in the warm sunshine. Crocuses smothered the verges, planted years ago by the residents in a huge planting drive and now naturally multiplying, the purples, whites and yellows vibrant among the verdant grass. There were certain parts of my life, like this, that were already perfect. I loved living here, with Spud. The loud melodic song of a robin reached my ears and I turned my head briefly to see him perched on a thick yew hedge bordering a garden, giving us a private concert. Yes, certain parts of my life were already more than I could wish for.

As we came around the bend near Mill Cottage, I was reminded of the areas of life that were most definitely less than perfect. I began slowing on the approach and saw Dr Grumpy getting into his swanky sports car, the gate closing behind him on his plastic, sterile garden. I slowed my bike even more, hoping to avoid any interaction, but as if sensing something, he looked up and, after a brief pause, raised a hand in a greeting so brief I wasn't entirely sure it had happened. He then slid behind the wheel and switched on the engine, which burbled for a moment or two before he put the car into gear and pulled out, driving smoothly past me, a brief nod the only other acknowledgement. He was already gone before I got a chance to give a cursory nod back.

As he turned the corner I dismounted my bike while still in motion. (It took me ages to get the hang of that. Believe me, it's not so easy as they make it look in films! Ask me how I know.) I wheeled it up the side passage of the house and parked it under the little lean-to I'd made there, before lifting Spud out and putting him down on the ground to go and do his usual circuit of the garden, checking for intruders, while I let myself in the back door and put the fresh bread I'd bought into the bread bin. After a few more rounds, Spud trotted in and started lapping noisily at his water bowl while I made myself a cuppa.

'All clear out there then?' I asked, as I added milk into my oversize bone china mug of Darjeeling tea.

Spud looked up at me, gave an enthusiastic wag of his tail and trotted back out of the open door, turning his head once to make sure I was following.

We walked to the bottom of the garden, stopping every so often to admire and smell flowers and stroke tactile leaves. Admittedly, that was mostly me, but Spud did a fair amount of his own sniffing, undoubtedly for different reasons.

Once at the bottom, I took a seat on an old Lutyens-style bench I'd got from an online marketplace. It had been in a bit of a state when I'd gone to take a look at it, but there was no sign of woodworm and the structure of it looked pretty sound, so I'd snapped it up. I'd even managed to get the chap to bring it over to my place in his van for an extra fiver. After a sand down and a bit of filler, I'd prepped and painted it a soft, pale green that helped it blend into the landscape. After that, I'd run up a cushion and covered some foam I'd had cut to size for the seat. I loved the look and shape of the bench, but you've got to admit, they're not the most comfortable things to sit on for any length of time. With that and a few more weatherproof scatter cushions I'd sewn up after finding some deadstock designer fabric on sale, it was now a lovely place to sit and look out over the millpond and paddock that lay behind the house.

Hanging high in an almost cloudless blue sky, the sun shone down its warming rays. Spring was revving up to burst onto the scene in triumph. After a few minutes soaking them up, I leant over and wound the handle of the nearby parasol until Spud, who'd hopped up onto the cushion and snuggled against me, and I were shaded and my brain could stop getting in a flap about my Celtic colouring.

I inhaled deeply then let out it out, soft and slow, before repeating the exercise, feeling my entire body relax and soften as I did so. The only sounds around us were the sounds of nature. The soft splosh of a duck diving in the pond, bottom up, its tail feathers on display, the birds singing and calling in the trees, and in front of us the horse and donkeys in the field, who would occasionally let out a whinny or race each other up and down the paddock, their hooves thundering on the ground.

Currently they were happily chewing the grass on the far side. A trail of disturbed water on the pond fanned out as a moorhen paddled out to the centre then turned and chugged back into the reeds. A robin gave out a cheerful song every so often, the strength of it defying the bird's size. Sparrows chirped and dashed back and forth between the shrubs and trees in my own garden and the various bird feeders dotted about, while Mr and Mrs Blackbird found goodies in the lawn and borders. Everything was so peaceful. It really was perfect.

Squeeeeeeeeeeeeeeeeeeeeeeeeeeeal!

3

The sudden ear-piercing screech made us both jump. Spud sniffed the air and looked both sleepy and discombobulated as I twisted on the bench and peered back up towards the house. The new folding doors to next door's kitchen were wide open, the noise of power tools whining shrill and loud through them.

'Great.' I returned to the bucolic landscape in front of me, sat back with a thump and tried, unsuccessfully, to block out the sound. After another five minutes, I headed inside, Spud at my heels. I found my noise-cancelling headphones and rammed them onto my head once again, glaring at the party wall between me and my neighbour as I did so.

It was dusk when I took Spud out for his evening walk. The warmth of the day still lingered and the light jacket I wore was plenty to keep any hint of chill away. The birds had roosted for the evening and the only sound was the occasional haunting hoot of an owl, now awake and looking for its supper. We did our usual evening loop, and I was busy chatting to Spud as we came up to the front of the house. I fished in my pocket for my key and, as I looked up, a tall shadow close by shifted.

I halted, my heart suddenly hammering.

Henry Darcy stepped from behind his car into the moonlight.

'Sorry, I didn't mean to startle you.'

I put my hand to my chest. 'What are you doing, hiding down there?'

'I wasn't hiding. I was checking my tyre.'

'For what?'

'A puncture.'

'Oh. Is it all right?'

'No. I have a puncture.' His tone was short.

'Oh. Right.' A thought flew into my mind. 'It wasn't me!'

Was that a smile? No, of course it wasn't. Shame, though. I was willing to bet he had a great smile…

Clearly, I hadn't put my parasol up soon enough earlier in the day and the sun had gone to my head. This was my grouchy, insensitive, nature-hating neighbour we were talking about.

'I didn't suspect you for a moment. Until now.' He paused. 'Should you be walking around in the dark?'

I stood straighter. 'I do it every night.'

'That's not what I asked. Just because people do things doesn't always mean they're safe.'

'You're not in London now, Dr Darcy.'

'It would be hard not to notice that.'

'I can't work out whether you think that's a good thing or you're regretting having moved.'

We'd made our way to my gate, and the porch light, combined with various fairy lights I had wound around the trunk of a flowering cherry and a mature plum tree, dispelled the shadows, throwing a gentle light onto my neighbour's features.

'How do you know I moved from London?'

'Tammy told Penny, who told Abby, who in turn told me.'

He looked back at me, his face blank. 'Tammy?'

'The estate agent you dealt with here? The one you got the keys from?'

'Oh, right.'

Tammy was not going to be pleased she had been so easily forgotten.

'Nothing like client confidentiality when you're conducting business.'

'Oh, for goodness' sake,' I snapped back, stepping through the waist-high wrought-iron gate with its peeling paint. I waited for Spud to follow me, but he was busy sniffing along the bottom edge of the garden wall. 'She's an estate agent, not a criminal defence solicitor, and it's hardly something any "normal neighbour" wouldn't have told me themselves.'

'There's not a lot of privacy in this village, is there?'

'I think you're confusing privacy with anonymity. And if that's what you wanted, then you probably should have stayed in the city.'

He let out a short breath which, with anyone else, I might have classified as a laugh, but this was Henry Darcy we were talking about. 'No, thanks. Definitely had more than enough of that.'

I felt a smile touch my lips. 'You're rather hard to please, aren't you, Dr Darcy?'

He looked down at me, his expression neutral. I guess that came in handy in his profession.

'So what are you going to do about your puncture?'

He glanced back at the car. 'Hope I can find someone to change it first thing tomorrow, I guess. I'm assisting a colleague with surgery at Exeter in the afternoon. Failing that, I assume there's a good, reliable taxi firm here somewhere.'

'Give me your phone.' I held out my hand.

'I beg your pardon?'

'Please give me your phone.'

'Why?'

'God, you're the suspicious type, are you? Don't worry. I have no intention of calling you. What I do have is the name of both a very good mechanic, who will know how to solve your problem quickly, and also a local taxi firm who, yes, are extremely reliable. If I put my number in your phone, you can send me a blank message and I can then reply with their contact information.'

'Oh. I see,' he replied, his voice quiet as he handed over his phone.

'It's locked.'

'Oh, right. Yes.' He leant over me and pressed his thumb against the image of a fingerprint and the device unlocked.

'Great. OK. So this... is my number.' I handed it back to him. 'Now you send me a blank message and I can send those contacts on to you. When you speak to them, tell them Willow sent you.'

My phone gave a little tinkle like a tiny bell. I'd pulled it from my pocket and was already scrolling my contacts when I opened his text. He literally had sent a blank one. I mean, I know I said to do that, but most people would have said hi or thanks or sent an emoji, just something, wouldn't they? I would. My eyes drifted past him to his plastic garden. Yes, *I* might but, as he'd continuously proved since he moved here, he and I had absolutely nothing in common.

'There. Done.'

His phone gave two generic beeps. He didn't even glance at it. 'Thanks. I appreciate that.'

Could have fooled me!

'Not a problem. I hope you get everything sorted. Come on, Spud.'

Spud was engrossed.

I pulled a treat from my pocket. 'Spuddy! What's this?'

His ears perked up as I crouched down, biscuit in hand.

'Bribery?'

'Needs must. He's very good normally but occasionally he gets a whiff of a really good smell.' Kind of like I had when my new neighbour had leant over me to unlock his phone. I pushed the thought out of my mind.

'Goodnight then, Willow.'

'Night,' I said, scooping Spud up and walking up the garden path.

'I hope the noise didn't bother you too much today,' Henry called once I was a few steps away. I turned back to face him.

'I know that Edie and Ted hadn't updated things for some time. It was probably due a refurb.'

'You're very good at not answering the actual question you're asked, aren't you?'

I gave a shrug as I shuffled Spud under the other arm to get my front door key from my pocket.

'Still, I'm sorry if it did.' His Eton tones were clipped and banal, and if he'd actually sounded sorry, I'd have appreciated the comment more.

'Thanks. Goodnight.' I closed the door behind me, plopped the dog down on the floor and leant heavily against the solid oak, breathing out a sigh.

The problem with living next door to the good doctor was that, despite the fact that everything he did annoyed me and that he looked at me like he'd be first in the queue to suggest I have a ride on the old village ducking stool, he was really, really good-looking. I mean, like, unfairly so.

Seriously, what the hell was the universe thinking when it landed him next door? Was it a test of some kind, or did the Power That Be just think it would be a great jape to have what, on first glance, would seem the perfect chance to meet the perfect man, and then throw a spanner the size of Pluto into the works by making us so entirely different in our outlooks that even the thought of us getting together was ridiculous?

On the surface, he seemed great – the village grapevine had reliably informed me that he'd been working as a trauma doctor in London for years as well as several stints with Médecins Sans Frontières. Staff and patients alike down here were raving about him – such a polite, empathetic, and brilliant surgeon. I couldn't comment on the last one, but I'd been surprised at the first two as both those qualities had seemed thin on the ground on the few occasions we'd met. But it seemed I'd been outvoted on those aspects and, like I said earlier, he smelled like heaven. It was all going so well. But then what happened? Did the universe get distracted or something? It's like it was dead on track and then did a massive, random swerve off course.

Not only did he rip out all of the wonderful plants in the garden next door but, from what I'd seen, there was barely a jot of colour in his house either. Not that I was looking on purpose. I couldn't help it if he left the lights on when I took Spud out for his nightly walk. Seriously, the universe couldn't have got it more wrong.

I thought back to my conversation with Abby. Perhaps she was right. Perhaps my signals had been a bit mixed, even if it was unintentional. I picked up my phone and scrolled through until I found Mark's contact. Tapping out a quick message, I pressed Send. There. Step one complete!

* * *

The longer I'd stayed in London, the more detached I'd become from it. I'd realised that I missed the countryside I'd grown up in and the daily walks I'd begun to take in the parks weren't really cutting it. It had been at that point that I'd started reading about alternative medicines and connecting with nature more. Now, don't get me wrong, if you have something dire wrong with you or have an accident, you need to take the advice of people who know what they're doing and have expertise in the area. People like Dr Henry Darcy, by all accounts. But since returning to the village I'd become a big proponent of looking to the earth for help too. I had a 'tea border' in my garden that was purely for growing plants for making teas and tinctures. Rosemary and feverfew for headaches, German chamomile for calm and, of course, mint, among others. A cup of fresh mint tea in the morning picked from my garden set me up for the day like nothing else ever had. Over in my sage-coloured Victorian-style greenhouse, there were trays of calendula seedlings, collected from last year's flowers, for making a soothing balm, and around my back door, as well as over a wrought-iron arch I'd rescued from a skip, grew beautiful fluffy-headed climbing roses for making rosewater and soaps. The scent on a warm summer's evening was wonderfully intoxicating and I looked forward to seeing the fat buds full of promise develop each year. Then, of course, lining the meandering path that led down to the bench, swathes of lavender grew and would be swarming with bees once they flowered. I left a lot for the pollinators but did cut some to dry for using in soaps and pillow sprays, not to mention my delicious speciality, lavender biscuits.

Some of the older villagers would tell me I was just like my nan, whose footsteps I was following in. There had still been so much to learn from her. But when I'd had the opportunity, I hadn't been interested. How I wished I could ask her all the questions now. Unfortunately I'd never come across a potion for that. If I had, I knew she would have said things like that should be left well alone. Nan was always on the side of the light, so it must have taken quite some patience to see me though my Goth phase growing up. Thankfully it had been a very short one. Apparently I was 'too cheery' to be a Goth. But I did hope that Nan was looking down on me, happy with how I was treading the same path, tending my garden the same as she had done years ago.

Nan had passed away sitting on her garden bench in the evening sunshine. I like to think she knew she was going and decided where it was going to happen. I still didn't know how I'd found a voice to speak at her funeral, but when something is important enough, you make it happen, don't you? And I'd stood up there, in front of what felt like the whole village and more, thanking her for raising me. She'd been a force of nature but carefully wrapped in a soft soul full of love, wisdom and kindness. There wasn't a day I didn't miss her or think about her. I hoped that, wherever she was, whatever plane she was on, she thought about me too.

I'd always believed in a deep connection with the earth and nature, probably again influenced by my nan, but somewhere along the way, I'd lost myself. Nan had passed away unexpectedly during my first year of uni. Suddenly she was gone, and I wasn't entirely sure where that left me. I'd switched from studying English Literature to a business degree, and as soon as I'd graduated, I'd gone to London to find myself, kick some arse and discover who I really was. Years of false trails led me nowhere, and it was only when I came home to the village that the Willow I knew, the one I recognised from deep down, began to emerge and bloom. And I was, finally, happy. I had a beautiful house – yes, it always needed something doing, but that's the way with old houses. The walls were solid and it was gorgeous. The Victorians really knew how to build stuff to last. I enjoyed doing it up, as much as possible learning and using my own skills so as to save money. Of course it would have been nice to be able to afford to have it all done in one go like my neighbour, but not all of us had those resources. I certainly didn't. Another difference between us. Another slip-up by the higher power. And actually I got a lot of satisfaction from the work I put into my house and garden. Would Dr Darcy be able to say that? Did he even care?

I pottered into the kitchen and took the milk bottle from the fridge. Having poured some into a pan, I set it to heat on the Aga – it came with the house and was a right state when I moved in, but she was a beauty now – then walked through to the cosy living room and ran my fingers gently along the spines of my books, stopping occasionally to pull one out. Heading back into the kitchen, I melted a couple of squares of chocolate into the pan and then poured the mixture into a mug with Spud's face on. Abby had had it painted for me as a birthday present when I'd got him. It was my favourite and I always saved it for my bedtime drink.

'I'm heading up, Spud.' I opened the French doors to let him out to do what he needed to do and waited as he wiped his feet on the mat – one of his most impressive, not to mention useful, tricks. I locked up behind him and made my way to the foot of the stairs. Spud headed up in front of me, having stopped only to collect Colin the Cabbage, a squeaky plush cabbage with a cheery face that Ed had bought for him and which, for reasons best known to Spud, immediately became his favourite toy. By the time I got up the stairs with my drink and books, Spud was curled up in his bed beside mine, his paws around Colin and his head resting gently on top of him. Warmth flooded through me, swelling my heart with joy. How had I ever lived without this dog? He had not only made me fitter but had made me smile and laugh every single day since I'd picked him up as a pup from the shelter. In that compact, fuzzy little parcel was everything I needed. Well, almost everything.

'So, Spud,' I said, tucking myself in under the duvet and picking up one of the books. 'Let's see just how I'm supposed to go about manifesting the perfect man.'

Spud looked at me.

'OK, the second most perfect.'

4

I sat bolt upright in bed and swore. Snatching the clock from the bedside table, I swore again but this time the sound of a drill plunging into a wall next door drowned it out.

'So much for the perfect man! The first thing I need to manifest is some bloody ear defenders!' Throwing back the duvet, I marched grumpily downstairs to where Spud was waiting patiently on the mat for me to open the French doors and allow him to go and do his morning ablutions.

I boiled the kettle, scooped out some dried camomile buds from one of the jars that lined the nearby shelf into a mug in the hope it might calm me a little, and followed the dog out into the garden to get my daily dose of morning light. This normally peaceful start to my day was now accompanied by the sound of someone apparently drilling to the centre of the earth. I felt all my nerves tightening like strings on a bow. I sipped the tea but I'd probably need a barrelful to have any impact whatsoever. Striding down the path to the bench at the furthest extent of the property, I stopped at the sound of my name.

'Willow!'

My neighbour was approaching the end of his own garden, frowning across at me.

'Bloody hell!' I wrapped my robe tighter around me. 'You frightened the life out of me. Again.'

'Sorry.' He did actually look it this time. 'I wanted to apologise. About the noise, I mean.' He waved at the house.

'Right. Well, it is a little early,' I said, clearly throwing my hat into the ring for the title 'mistress of the understatement'.

'It is. I totally agree. I had no idea they'd be starting this early. I mean, they asked if it was OK to start early and I said yes, but apparently we have differing ideas of the term's exact definition. Six thirty does seem a bit much, but they assured me no one else would hear, being out this side of the village.'

'You live in a semi-detached house! I'm not bloody deaf!' I swung a black look at his house. 'Not yet, anyway.'

'Yes, I did try to explain that, but they said if they didn't get started today, it would mean the job will take several days longer. Apparently, they're rather in demand. And I... well, I'd really rather get it done and over with and have my house back.'

I could understand that. When I decorated just one room, the entire house seemed to somehow get involved in the mess. I couldn't imagine the state of next door right then.

'Are you staying there when all this work is being done?'

He nodded. 'Yes. I want to oversee it as much as possible.'

'The hotel in the village is very good and I'm sure they've probably got space as the season hasn't started yet. It might give you somewhere a bit less chaotic to stay for a few days.'

'Thanks, but I'll stay here. I'm sure it will be done soon.'

The drill began again, this time as a duet with something that sounded like a tile cutter, judging by its high-pitched, whining squeal.

'I hope,' Henry added darkly, frowning back up the garden at his house.

Even right down here, the noise was hard to avoid. I turned back to face my own house. 'Thanks for the apology. I think I'm going to take Spud for a walk.' My voice was raised above the noise.

'Unusual name,' he replied in a momentary lull.

'It suited him at the time, and he likes it now.'

'I see. Right. Not really a dog person myself.'

Not really a dog person!

I knew there was a reason I didn't like him. Apart from the snobby, aloof manner, fake turf and the early-morning power tool alarm clock.

'Right. Well, *I* am,' I said, picking up Spud and cuddling him to me. In his innocence, his little tail wagged enthusiastically at my neighbour, not understanding in the slightest that he wasn't a fan. I dropped a kiss on the top of Spud's fuzzy head, offended on his behalf. 'Come on, darling,' I said, popping him down on the grass. 'Let's go for a walk.'

At the sound of these magic words, the dog spun around in a circle, and lifted his front paws off the ground, tottering for a moment on his back legs. His antics, as always, brought a smile to my face, pushing away the negative feelings of a moment ago. 'I know! It is exciting, isn't it?'

I took a couple of steps back in the direction of the house only to be halted as Henry spoke again.

'He's obviously very fond of his walks.'

'He certainly is,' I replied, the smile still in place as Spud danced about me. 'Come on then, go and find your lead.'

With that, the dog zoomed up the garden and disappeared into the house. Now what was I supposed to do? Should I just walk off? Was that rude? But on the other hand, my neighbour had just said he didn't like dogs – in front of my dog! I don't know about you, but I thought *that* was pretty rude.

'I'd better let you go then,' he said, unwittingly solving the problem.

'Thanks.' I walked quickly up the garden. Spud appeared at the back door, his lead in his mouth and trailing behind him, his tail wagging at such a speed it was a blur.

'I'm coming!' I said, laughing, and began to jog.

* * *

When we returned from the walk over an hour and a half later, Dr not-really-a-dog-person Grumpy's car was gone but the noise inside remained. Hammering and banging was interrupted only by that high-pitched whine of whatever it was they were cutting.

'Be careful what you wish for,' I said on a sigh as I unlocked the door and bent down to unclip Spud's lead. I'd been so eager for a new neighbour. Edie, Ted and I had spent many happy hours over the years chatting over the fence and in each other's gardens, whiling away the time nattering about anything and everything. More often than not, it would end in them insisting I came round for tea and, despite my protests, somehow they'd always managed to win. And, of course, they'd loved Spud.

'Oh!' I stopped mid-step and looked down at the dog, who was looking up at my exclamation. 'Did I manifest a neighbour?' I asked him. Spud gave a small whine in reply. Plopping down into a baby-pink squishy armchair, I thought about it all. I'd hoped for a new neighbour for ages, but I hadn't been specific about what kind of neighbour. That was the key, from what I'd read last night. When we'd chatted about it, Abby had suggested, only half joking, that it should be someone tall, dark and handsome. Had the universe taken that on board without me realising? My new neighbour was certainly all three of those things to a tee and, I mean, it sounded good, didn't it? In fact, it sounded perfect. Except it wasn't. Because although my neighbour appeared exactly that, he also appeared to be anti everything I valued.

'Abby!'

'Wils? You OK?' Her soft Devonian accent – something I'd left behind back in London – like her face, was full of concern.

'We did it!' I waved my arms at the phone screen.

'Great! That's excellent news. Yay us! What exactly is it that we did?'

'No, it's not excellent news. It's terrible news, the worst! We manifested Dr Grumpy!'

'Oh. Right. We did?'

'We must have! We spent all that time talking about how great it would be for someone to move in, and then wouldn't it be fab if it was a gorgeous man.'

'I knew you thought he was gorgeous!' She grinned.

'Missing the point!' I said, waving some more.

'Yes. Right. OK. Yes, we did.'

'And now look!'

'So isn't that... good?'

'No! Not good at all.'

'OK, I'm officially lost.'

'We only focused on the superficial stuff, Abs. Not the things that really matter! Like, for example, do you know what he told me this morning? Having woken me up far too early, I might add.'

'Oooh! He woke you up?' Abby was suddenly far more interested, leaning closer to the screen, her eyes widening.

'Not like that. Not content with ripping out the garden, he's been ripping out the interior and the builders started at half past six.'

'Oh. Although it was a bit dated in there, you said so yourself. But that does seem ungodly early. So what else did he say then?'

'That he's, and I quote, "not really a dog person".'

Abby's shocked intake of breath was enormously satisfying.

'I know, right.'

'Has he met Spud?'

'Spud was right there!'

'Noooo!'

'I know!'

'So he just randomly said that?'

'No, he came down the garden to apologise for the noise.'

'Well, I guess that was something.'

'Yeah, it's just a shame he didn't stop there rather than continuing and ruining the moment.'

'Oooh!' she said again, leaning in once more. 'There was a moment?'

'No, of course not. You know what I mean. My point is that I think we did it! We manifested him. Accidentally. So now I'm stuck with Dr Grumpy and his sterile house and garden. Do you know he hasn't got an ounce of colour in that house?'

'Have you been in?'

'No, but I can't help it if my eyes drift that way when I'm out walking the dog because he hasn't put any curtains up.'

'Of course not. Anyone's would. That's just human nature.'

This was exactly why Abby had been my best friend since nursery school. She knew these things and what was important.

'So, I was thinking that if we accidentally did this, then if I really focused, did it properly, manifesting really could work and bring me The One.'

'Anything's possible. Although there's just one thing.'

'What?'

'You're still married. Maybe that's why the universe brought Dr Grumpy. Maybe it's saying, "Look what I can do, but there's no point making him right for you because you're still married to someone else."'

I was silent for a moment. Was Abby right? Had I had the opportunity and missed it?

'Right. That's it. I'm going to do it. No half-arsed or accidental attempts.'

'Great!'

'I'm going to call Mark right now and get the divorce finalised. I sent him a message the other day, but he didn't reply and then with one thing and another I forgot. But I'm going to get it done.'

'Wow. OK. And how do you feel about that?'

How did I feel about that? 'Surprisingly OK, now I think about it. I don't think I was at the beginning. I'm still sad it didn't work out, but in the end we wanted totally different things.'

'Funny he hasn't completed things either.'

I gave a short laugh. 'I wouldn't read too much into that. You know Mark's never been a details person. He only looks at the big picture and misses the fact that a lot goes into making up that picture.'

'Sounds about right.'

'OK, I'll give him a call. Speak to you later.'

'OK, hon. Let me know how you get on.'

* * *

I got Mark's answerphone. He never picked his messages up, so I sent another text, more detailed this time. Quickly I reread it.

> Hi Mark, hope you're well. I was just thinking
> that it's probably about time we completed the
> divorce, don't you think? As we've had the
> Conditional Order, we just need to apply for the
> Final Order. I can do it alone but I think it would
> be easier to do it as a joint application, if that's
> OK? There's a form to fill in, of course.

That should do it. Send!

His message came back surprisingly quickly.

> Hi Willow, good to hear from you. Interesting that
> you bring this up. Have you met someone? I'm
> still footloose and fancy free (*smiley face*) Well
> apart from being married to you of course!

He always did have a way with words. A soft tinkle signalled another message.

> Just read that back. Sorry. I didn't mean that like
> you're a ball and chain. And yes, if that's what
> you want. Shall I come down to you to do it?

If that's what I want? Mark had been the first one to suggest splitting up, although at that point it was obvious to everyone that things weren't working.

> I just think it's time, don't you? And you don't
> need to come down just for this. I'm sure we can
> do it separately.

> It'd be nice to see you...

Oh.

Umm, OK. If you don't mind. It's a bit of a hike down here to Devon.

That's fine. It'd be nice to get out of the city for a bit. Perhaps we could work something out?

Sounds good.

That'd be great. I'll get back to you when I've checked my diary.

OK. Thanks.

Looking forward to seeing you.

* * *

'Do you think he wants to get back together?' Abby asked, handing the phone back to me having read the messages.

'Mark?' I said, with a laugh. 'Most definitely not. He's a nice bloke but we've been there and done that and it didn't work. I'm just glad we could work it out without things getting acrimonious.'

'OK.'

I pulled a face. 'That was a very loaded OK.'

'Well, the whole "be nice to get out of the city" thing? That doesn't sound like the Mark we know! To him, anything other than London may as well be Middle Earth.'

'I'm sure it was just a turn of phrase.'

'I guess we'll see.'

'When's Ed back?'

Abby let out a sigh. 'Another two weeks yet. It feels like forever.'

I reached across the table and laid my hand on her arm. 'I'm sure. But then he'll be home and under your feet all the time and you might regret it.'

Abby smiled, her eyes filling with tears. 'Honestly, I can't think of anything better.'

I stood up from the table and went round to give my bestie a massive hug.

'I know it's going to be an adjustment. He's been in the Air Force since he was eighteen, but he's got some interviews lined up. One sounds pretty promising, too, working with another ex-RAF engineer.'

'That's great.' I almost hated to ask the next question. 'Are they local?'

'That one is.' Abby crossed her fingers and we left the rest unsaid. Ed *had* to get that local job. After years and years of deployments and separation, Abby and Ed would finally have time together, without having to count the days until he was away again.

'I know it's selfish, but I really don't want to move.'

'I know. Ed loves that house too. You've made it your own together.'

'Yeah. It's probably a bit big for what we need now but obviously we didn't know that at the time.'

There wasn't anything to say. Anything I could say. Abby knew I understood. As a teenager, she'd had a bad fall from a horse during a gymkhana and smashed her pelvis. Ed and I had been there watching. What nobody realised at the time was that the internal damage had resulted in an inability to have children. After three miscarriages, a tonne of medical investigations and a lot of heartache, they'd realised that that dream was not to be. Fostering and adoption were considered and looked into but somehow neither had felt right for them. It was a big commitment that you needed to be 100 per cent sure was the right choice, and they weren't.

'Did I tell you Ed wants to rescue some donkeys?' she said, her tears now ones of laughter.

'Donkeys?'

'I know. The paddock out the back is perfect, he says, and he sent me an email with a drawing of a fancy hen coop he's planning too.'

'Excellent. I expect free eggs, of course.'

Abby laughed. 'Honestly, you should see the size of this thing. I think we'll have enough to feed the entire village.'

'What with that and the rescue dogs you've been looking at, you've got a lot lined up.'

'Yeah. I know.' She put her hands to her cheeks as if trying to, unsuccessfully, contain her grin. 'I can't wait!'

'Me neither. You two are still the cutest couple. I can't wait to meet the menagerie!'

'So, in the meantime, what do we need to do to bring you the perfect man?'

'Well, I've started on my vision board. Being specific is super important. Kind of hard to make a mood board of a person, though, so it's a little bare at the moment.' I pulled a face.

'You could pin up pics of things you like to do, though. How you see your life with the right person. Like a beautiful garden, a cosy room with a snuggly sofa and maybe an open fire.'

'Ha! Definitely not Dr Grumpy then. Ooh! I could take a picture of The Vicarage and put it in there. Can you imagine? Opening those doors in the morning and wandering around that beautiful garden with a cup of tea?' My mind drifted. In my daydream, I could see myself laughing with a man, the right man, but his face was indistinct. Like he was just out of reach.

'Exactly!' Abby brought me back. 'Hang on, let me get a pen and we can make a list.'

By the time I was walking home from Abby's later that evening, Spud trotting happily beside me off his lead, we'd compiled a list of qualities and a bunch of ideas of things for me to find pictures of to put on my vision board. This time I was going to do it properly and it was going to work!

As I pondered on what else to add to my shopping list of manly attributes, my neighbour drove slowly past me and pulled in to the kerb in front of the house. He sat in the car for a few minutes as I approached home. Wait... was he avoiding me? I flicked my hair from the back of my neck as it caught and pulled on one of the crystal necklaces I'd layered on. Well, that saved me from having to pretend to be pleased to see him. Which I wasn't. Obviously. Oh damn, he was getting out of the car. Hang on, he was on the phone. Excellent. Always a good excuse not to talk to someone.

I raised my hand in a brief gesture before dropping my gaze to check Spud was turning in at the gate. But he was nowhere to be seen.

'Spud!' I called, panic lacing through my words even though, rationally, I knew he couldn't be far. He was just there a moment ago.

'I've got to go.' The deep tones drifted on the peaceful, still air of early evening. 'Speak to you later.'

'Spud!' I called again, a little more frantic.

'He's here.'

I whirled around to where Henry was still standing beside his car. 'Where?'

His eyes connected with mine. Not smiling. The gaze then lowered and I hurried around the car to see my dog sitting on his foot. Properly on it, not just near it. He had, for all intents and purposes, pinned our new neighbour to the tarmac.

'Oh, Spud!' I cried, half laughing, half exasperated as the panic receded. 'What are you doing?'

'I was wondering that myself.' Henry was standing there, rigid.

'Sorry,' I said, a little stiffly. 'He obviously likes you.' *No idea why!* 'He's very friendly. You can just ask him to move.'

Then I giggled. My hand shot to my mouth as the dark brow furrowed even more. 'Sorry. It's just…'

Dr Darcy was a good six foot four, I guessed. Maybe even a little taller, and solidly built with what my nan would have called 'strong rugby shoulders'. And there he stood, pinned to the floor by a small dog a fraction of his weight who was currently looking up at him adoringly. I glanced again but there wasn't even a hint of humour in those green eyes.

'Would you mind moving him?'

'Oh, yes, of course. Sorry. I didn't realise you were actually scared of dogs. I just thought you—'

'I'm not. I just don't have time to stand around all evening.'

'Then why don't you just move,' I snapped. 'It's not like he's heavy!' I bent and scooped Spud up, cuddling him close to me and kissing the top of his head. 'Come on, Spuddy, let's get you some dinner.' I turned my back and began a quick walk to my front gate, determined not to look up as I turned to close it.

'I…'

I turned, my eyes meeting his. I waited for a moment, but when nothing else came forth I raised my brows.

He was closer, a battered brown leather doctor's bag in one hand, his keys in the other.

'I'm not really a dog person.'

'Yes, you said. I'm sorry he bothered you.' I made to turn but a large hand rested momentarily on my arm, stopping me, the cool touch of the metal key in it causing the hair on my arms to tingle.

'That's not what I meant. I just... I'm not... I didn't want to hurt him. By moving my foot. I didn't...' He heaved in a deep breath and let it out in a sigh. 'Stupid as I'm sure it sounds, I didn't know what to do.' His gaze met mine, steady, vivid, challenging me to laugh at him.

But I had no intention of laughing. In fact, quite the opposite. For the first time, I smiled at my neighbour, properly and genuinely.

'Oh. I see. Then that was very kind of you. Thank you. And I am sorry. He really does only do that to people he's taken a shine to.'

'I've barely met you, let alone your dog.'

'Dogs can be far wiser than humans,' I said, shrugging my shoulders. 'Perhaps you're more of a dog person than you think you are.'

He gave a short, humourless laugh. 'I don't think so.'

I studied him for a moment. If there was ever a person in need of a dog, it was this man.

'They're very good for stress.'

'Causing it or easing it? Because your face when you thought he'd run off suggested more the former.'

'That's true. But I can say, hand on heart, Spud is the best thing to have ever happened to me.'

'And yet you still chose to name him after a vegetable.'

'Yes!' I replied, laughing. I wasn't sure if he was trying to be funny or not, but he was. 'As a puppy, he had a remarkable resemblance to one.'

Both of us looked down at the dog now snuggled contentedly in my arms, his eyes half closed in the early-evening sunshine. I looked back up. Perhaps I should try a little harder to be civil with my new neighbour. We'd certainly not got off on the right foot, but perhaps we could be polite to each other after all.

There were shadows under his eyes, I noted, and the strong shoulders had a slight sag to them, as though a weight rested there.

'Have a good evening.' He spoke before I gathered myself enough to ask how his day had been. He turned and pushed through his own gate, his eyes lowered as he closed it then focused on his keys as he covered the path to the door in a few long strides, before disappearing behind the newly black-painted front door.

'And you,' I said quietly, and sighed. 'Right, Mr Spud.' I looked down to see a sleepy face peer up at me, before he issued a satisfied yawn. 'Now that you've aged me at least five years with that hide-and-seek game, I think it's dinner time. Come on, pest.'

5

The noise-cancelling headphones were glued to my head for the next several weeks as I attempted to escape the din next door that started hideously early each and every day. Spud and I had even camped over at Abby's a couple of nights, just to get a decent night's sleep. But today had dawned bright and warm with the surety that spring had most definitely arrived. Spud was curled up in his bed between mine and the window and, most importantly for the colder months, next to the radiator. I pushed back the duvet, smiling as I did so. Yesterday had been fresh sheets night – and as everyone knows, that's the best night – and I'd put my new favourite duvet cover on. It was pure white with tiny deep pink rosebuds embroidered all over it. I let the bed air for a few minutes, slid into my slippers and padded over to the window. Spud raised a sleepy head and I crouched to give him his morning kiss and cuddle.

'Hello, my darling. And how are you?'

His fluffy little tail thumped against the soft padding of his bed in delight as he snuggled his head against mine. Standing, I pulled back the curtains that matched the duvet as Spud got to his feet and did a downward dog stretch any yogi would be proud of.

I opened the window and leant on my elbows, breathing in the pure, fresh morning air as I looked out over my garden and the paddock, an early mist hovering just above the ground, lending a mystical quality to the bucolic scene. How did I ever think that London could compare, let alone beat, this? This stillness, this calm, this... wait? It was quiet. For the first time since Dr Grumpy had moved in, the air wasn't filled with banging, hammering and machines whining away. Even weekends had been full of noise. God knows what he was paying them to work such long hours, although I understood his wish to get it over and done with. Today, thankfully, it appeared life was back to normal. My gaze slid over to the neighbouring garden. Was it finally finished? I mean, I guessed it was. Personally it looked far too sparse and spare to me, but I'd already learned my neighbour and I had very different viewpoints on style. Well, on most things, it would seem from the few interactions we'd had.

Over the weeks, I'd seen the skip outside filling up with dated bathrooms and kitchen, carpets, lino and everything else. The house must have been stripped to its very bones. I thought back to the previous evening. Of course! The skip outside had gone. Perhaps things would finally settle back into a rhythm here again.

'Come on, Spuddy. Let's get some breakfast.' Never needing to be asked twice, the dog scooted around the bed and was already waiting by the latch hook door, ready to scuttle down the steep stairs and into the kitchen.

Ten minutes later, Spud was happily demolishing his breakfast and I'd brewed a fresh mint tea, which I sipped as I walked to the bench at the bottom of the garden. The rays of the rising sun reached over the house now and were spreading their warming tendrils through the grass at the end of the garden and across the paddock. Over the other side I could see the horse and two rescue donkeys who called the place home munching the damp, dewy grass. As if sensing my interest, one of the donkeys, Pepper, lifted his head and looked over before letting out a loud bray. He then began a fast trot towards me, braying happily all the way.

'Hello, boy!' The smile was wide on my face as I leant on the wooden three-bar fence that separated us. His fur was bristly as he pressed against it, and I stroked his nose while he attempted to snuffle out the carrot I had in my dressing gown pocket.

'Wait a minute!' I said, laughing.

Spud had finished his morning circuits and barrelled down the garden to join us, as had the donkey's field mates. My dog was currently busy saying hello to his friend Olive, the horse.

'Here.' I laid my hand flat and offered one of the big carrots I'd bought in the village greengrocers yesterday for exactly this purpose.

Pepper crunched and munched and I'd have sworn he was smiling. Salt moseyed over more sedately and rested her nose on the top bar, big brown eyes looking dolefully up at me.

'Hello, girl,' I said, stroking her muzzle. 'Do you want one too?' I lifted another treat from my pocket and held it out. She took it gently and chomped as I stroked her flank.

By this point, Olive and Spud had finished their morning greeting and the horse was now nudging me with her smooth chestnut-coloured nose.

'Patience is a virtue!' I told her as I once again laid my hand flat and she took the third and final treat.

Pepper let out another bray and looked at me expectantly.

'That's all there is. Polly will be along to sort you out in a bit, and we don't want you filling up on snacks, do we?' I said, scratching his snout again. His bray this time was softer, although I wasn't sure if it was a murmur of agreement or not.

'Do they have to make that noise?' A sharp, deep, well-spoken voice popped the bubble of morning bliss. I closed my eyes then opened them slowly as I turned my head to see my neighbour standing at the bottom of his garden, dressed in an expensive-looking white T-shirt and deep indigo-blue jeans.

'Good morning.'

He blinked. 'Oh. Right. Yes. Good morning.'

'These are our neighbours. That's Olive,' I said, pointing at the horse. 'And these are Salt and Pepper.'

He rolled his eyes.

'What?'

'Nothing.'

'I assume you don't go around randomly rolling your eyes, which leads me to understand that there's a reason you did it.'

'Fine. I suppose I just thought that those are odd names for animals.'

Rather like 'Spud'?

'What would you call them?'

'I wouldn't,' he replied.

'What?'

'I wouldn't have animals therefore I'd have no need to name them.'

Now it was my turn to roll my eyes. 'Pretend that you did.'

'It's entirely unlikely.'

'Humour me!' My words, however, contained barely any of said humour by this point.

'Fine. I... I don't know.'

I fixed my eyes on him, waiting. His brow wrinkled even deeper. 'Richard and John.'

'Salt is a girl.' I pointed at the donkey who had wandered across to peer over the fence into next door.

Henry took a step back.

'She doesn't bite.'

'She could, and horse bites can be serious. They can exert a huge amount of force, causing skin necrosis.'

'I'm sure. Why don't you say hello?'

He looked at the donkey, then back at me. 'I'd rather not.'

'Well, that's just rude. So, what would you call her?'

'What?' he said, his eyes moving to where Pepper had joined his friend and both were sniffing the scent of my neighbour on the air.

'Her name. If it wasn't Salt, and it can't be John.'

'Joan,' he replied, his gaze swinging back to me. 'Happy now?'

I gave a shrug. 'It was just a question.'

'Do they do this every morning?'

'What?'

'Make that infernal noise!'

I really was trying to be pleasant, I promise. Desperately trying to let everything wash over me and put our previous disagreements behind us, but this man would try the patience of a saint!

'He was saying hello.'

'To whom?'

'To me.'

'Why?'

'Because that's what he does. Because I give them a carrot each morning, because it's what I do. And before you question that too, yes, I do have the permission of the owner.'

'Do you have to do it so bloody early?'

OK, I tried. I really, really tried.

'Yes. I do. And if I feel like it, I'll do it even earlier. In fact, I'll do it any bloody time I like! I live here and they live here and this is what we do. Besides, who the hell are you to make such a bloody song and dance about noise when your builders have been starting at the crack of dawn every single day, with no let-up, for weeks! But did I say anything? No.'

'I apologised for that!' he said, his feet planted squarely apart and surprisingly muscular arms crossed tensely over his broad chest.

'Once, you apologised. Once!'

'Oh, I'm sorry. Was I supposed to pop round every single day and offer my heartfelt regret that the work to make this place actually liveable would once again be disturbing you?'

'Of course not. That would be the last thing I'd expect from you. To do that would necessitate the owning of an actual heart, which from what I've seen so far is something you most certainly don't possess!'

With that, I turned and marched up the garden, back into the house, Spud at my heels, and gave the kitchen door a satisfying slam.

Well, that's how it was supposed to happen. Except as I'd turned, the front of my slider caught under one of the stepping stones laid in a meandering fashion down my garden, resulting in my stomp-off beginning with me tripping flat on my face, landing with a dull thud on the grass.

'Oh, God, are you all right?' Surprisingly, he did actually sound concerned.

'Perfectly all right, thank you,' I replied shortly, as I scrambled back to my feet as elegantly as I could, although I was pretty sure that ship had well and truly sailed and was now halfway across the sodding ocean. I took off the stupid bloody shoes and began my haughty march up the garden again, slamming the door as planned, but the impact just wasn't the same. I flung the sliders into a corner, grabbed a towel from the drawer to wipe my damp feet and plopped down on a kitchen chair to do so, the calm peaceful start to my day having now been drop-kicked out of sight.

Bloody Darcy! If I really had manifested my grouchy, cold neighbour, was it possible to 'unmanifest' him? Did the universe have a warranty period? *Sorry, this manifestation is most unsuitable for my needs, and I'd like a refund.* I had a horrible feeling the answer was no. Which meant, for any new manifestations, I had to be super specific and cognisant of exactly what I wanted. At least now I knew what I definitely didn't want. Flinging the towel into the washing machine, I peered out of the door. Dr Grumpy was still standing at the bottom of the garden, staring out over the paddock, alone. The animals had long since given up on him and, frankly, who could blame them?

After breakfast and a long walk with Spud that took in part of the South West Coast path, the sea lazing in the sunshine, its glinting waters reflecting the blue of the sky above, we ambled back home and made our way upstairs.

Opening the door to my workroom, Spud scooted beside me into one of his many beds, curled up and within three minutes was snoring softly. I sat down at my desk, popped on my glasses and peered at my current patient. Bob was a teddy from the early 1970s who'd been quickly diagnosed as 'loved to bits'. He was thinning in places, as males have a tendency to do, but that wasn't why he'd been admitted. His injuries included a missing ear and a large rip in one side that had been roughly mended some time ago, but the thread had begun to break down and, everywhere he went, poor Bob left a trail of stuffing behind him. Consequently his weight was now a worry. He wasn't a Steiff or a Merrythought, although I had several of those in the ward, but he was still special. He was someone's childhood friend. The one who'd listened to all her sorrows, shared in her joys and comforted her in the dark and through difficult times. And soon he would again. I pulled over the Jiffy bag that had arrived yesterday and removed the fur inside, holding it up to Bob.

'Perfect match!' I said, smiling.

Spud opened one eye, deemed my exclamation had nothing to do with either food or walkies, and went back to sleep.

'Right, Bob. Now let's take a look at your good ear.'

Studying my patient alongside a couple of photos of him in his prime, I'd soon made a paper pattern and laid it over the new fur to be cut. Next I slid my trusty hand-cranked Singer sewing machine across the desk and, as always, breathed in the evocative scent of wood and oil. The fur was tucked under the foot and, moments later, sewn ready to be turned, stuffed and attached. Bob's recovery was coming along nicely.

6

My tummy made its third loud rumble, determined this time to not be ignored.

'I'm going, I'm going,' I said, removing my glasses as I stood up from the chair and had a good stretch. Spud, sensing food, did the same thing, his own stretch accompanied by a squeaky yawn, before we both padded down the steep wooden stairs.

I switched on the grill and walked out into the back garden, heading for my herbal tea bed. From the corner of my eye, I saw my neighbour sitting on his new patio, but I wasn't in the mood to pretend everything was fine between us. I didn't like him, he didn't like me and that was that. I felt a little awkward knowing he could see me pottering about my garden. The low fence between the main part of the two gardens hadn't been a problem before, when my neighbours and I were friends, but now I rather wished that when Edie had had it replaced a few years ago after a particularly violent storm she'd gone for a six-foot one – at least! Still, I was sure Henry Darcy had no great desire to see me or my garden either, so it wouldn't surprise me if I was to look out one day and see my wish had been granted. In the meantime, I kept my eyes on my lemon verbena plant, picking leaves and popping them into the tiny trug I'd grabbed on the way out. When I had enough, I turned back, looking at this plant, touching the leaves of that one – everything and anything to keep my mind and eyes busy so that they didn't drift over to next door. Once back in the kitchen, I switched the kettle on to boil and popped some bread under the grill. I rinsed the fresh leaves before popping them into a glass teapot, then poured over the hot water and replaced the teapot's lid with its built-in diffuser. A few minutes later, I pulled the toast out from under the grill at the perfect moment.

Taking my toast, now smothered with homemade houmous, and my tea I headed out onto my own patio which, unlike next door's, was crammed with pots of spring bulbs. To one side was the white collection and to the other, the purple. And right here, a riotous, clashing burst of vibrant colour for all the bulbs that didn't fit a scheme but I hadn't been able to resist buying. The tulips were beginning to open, their heads nodding and swaying in the gentle breeze that rustled the leaves of the nearby trees lining the edge of the paddock and millpond. A few blossom petals from my cherry tree fluttered to the ground like confetti. I smiled, surrounded by nature, the scent of hyacinths filling the air, sipping on tea I'd grown in my own garden, and closed my eyes for a moment to savour the warm rays of the spring sunshine on my face.

Crunch, crunch, crunch! Bloody hell. Why does toast have to be so noisy? Was it always this noisy or was I just more aware of trying to eat quietly, knowing that Dr Grumpy was just the other side of that fence panel?

Crunch!

Oh, God. Was it me? Was I a really noisy eater? I put the toast back on the plate and glared at it for a moment. Then I glared at the fence, wiling him to go back inside so that I could munch as loudly as I liked in peace. But no, he was definitely there. Every so often I heard the turn of a page.

Oh, this is ridiculous. Willow, just eat your damn food, my stomach ordered before issuing another loud growl as if to back up its demand. I shook my head. I was in my own garden and I shouldn't feel like I couldn't do what I wanted.

I bit purposefully into the second bit of toast and promptly bit my tongue. Muffling a choice word or two, I finished the rest a little more carefully, enjoyed my tea and concentrated on the sounds of nature around me in an attempt to recentre myself before returning to work.

Upstairs, Bob was now back on the ward, having spent the afternoon in recovery, and was doing great. His hearing was now 100 per cent, ready and willing, once again, to be the listening ear for his owner that he'd been for so many years. I'd emailed over a clinic letter to his home and advised that he could be discharged Monday, if that suited.

As I finished filling in his medical records, the phone rang.

'Hello. Willow's Teddy Bear Hospital.'

'Oh, hi. It's Simon Bennet. You just emailed about Bob.'

'Oh, yes, hi! How are you?'

'Fine, thanks. So Bob's OK?'

'He's great. Looking forward to going home, though, I think.'

I could hear the smile in the man's voice as he replied. 'We're looking forward to having him home. So when can I come and get him? I don't suppose you work Sundays, do you?'

'No, I'm afraid I don't.'

'That's fine.' His tone told me the smile had faded. 'I'm away on business for the next few weeks, so it might have to wait until I'm home again. Is that a problem?'

'Can I ask something?'

A pause. 'OK.'

'Is Bob your bear?'

Another pause.

'I just had your wife's name down here, so I automatically assumed it was hers.'

'Umm.'

'There's nothing to be embarrassed about. Personally I think everyone should have a bear. It makes one far more well-adjusted.'

Simon laughed and I knew I'd had a breakthrough.

'So, I'm wondering if Bob normally accompanies you on your trips?'

There was silence on the other end of the line.

'I have a special bear that goes everywhere with me. Honestly, I don't know what I'd do if something happened to him.'

'But it's a bit different for blokes, isn't it?' His voice had lowered.

'Yes, I suppose it is. But it shouldn't be, and if knowing Bob is in your carry-on makes you less anxious, then we'll make sure you have him. What time can you get here tomorrow?'

'Are you sure?' A ripple of hope laced his words.

'Absolutely.'

'That's brilliant. Thanks so much. I'll put the payment across now. What time suits you best?'

* * *

The next morning, I discharged Bob.

'Thanks so much for putting yourself out like this,' Simon's wife said, giving her husband a smile as he took Bob carefully from me, looking him over, his face beaming.

'No trouble at all. It's always lovely to see a bear go back to such a loving home. He's obviously very special.'

'He certainly is. He was even at our wedding, would you believe?'

Simon's cheeks were beginning to flush. 'I'm sure Willow isn't interested in all that.'

'Oh, no,' I replied, giving Bob a little fuss. 'I really am.'

'His mum, bless her, had visions of carrying this chic little clutch but instead had to take this big old bag so that Bob could be in the vicinity.'

'That's so sweet. It's lovely that she, and you, appreciated how much he means. A wedding's a big day with lots of nerves about, so anything that can help sounds like a great idea to me. Especially if it involves bears!'

'I think the fact that Simon promised to buy her whatever bag she wanted, and the one she chose was Hermès, went some way to getting her on board.'

'I bet!' I said, laughing. 'Only the best for Bob! I'm glad to hear he travelled in style.'

'Well, we won't take up any more of your Sunday. Thanks ever so much for all your help.'

'And your amazing skills,' Simon added, turning his bear over again as he checked out my work. 'He looks great!'

The warmth flooded through me. 'Thank you. I'm so happy you're pleased, and I hope you and Bob have a safe and successful business trip.'

Bob waved through the window with the help of Simon's wife as they drove away. Another happy customer, I thought to myself as I turned to go back into the house, stopping to lift the nodding bloom of an early-flowering rose, the scent subtle but delicious.

I closed my eyes, taking in the dusky perfume and the velvety feel of the petals against my fingers. When I opened them again, I found myself looking directly into a pair of vivid green eyes.

'Are you all right?' Darcy's brow was its usual crumpled self as he looked down at me, a quizzical expression in the gaze.

'Perfectly!' I said, straightening suddenly.

'Oh. Right. You just... well, you had a rather odd look on your face.'

'I was taking a moment to smell the roses. Literally. Don't you ever do that?' Automatically both of us glanced towards his front garden, where no sign of natural life dared to exist. 'No, I don't suppose you do.'

There was a pause. 'No, not really.' The briefest hint of a shadow flitted across his face as he spoke, and the smart-arse quip I'd thought about making shrivelled inside me. Nothing else took its place and an awkward silence settled around us. Finding something to say to people – to strangers, to anyone – wasn't normally a problem but with this man, my mind was literally empty. There was absolutely nothing to say and clearly he felt the same. The only time we ever seemed to be able to converse freely was when we were disagreeing about something.

'Right. Well,' he said, eventually.

I waited for more, but that seemed the extent of his sentence. 'Yes. Right. Bye then,' I replied.

His eyes lingered on me for a moment, the frown remaining, dark brows shadowing the green, before he gave a short nod, turned and headed away towards the river and woods. His strides were long and purposeful and... oh! Well, that was unexpected. The good doctor had a really nice bum!

7

'Oh, no. Oh dear. Oh, that's not good.'

I stared at the pool of blood as it seeped into the pale carpet. Admittedly it wasn't a large pool of blood. Really quite small, in fact. But that wasn't the point. It was my blood, and it wasn't inside my body where it should be.

The room went soft at the edges and I gripped the back of my desk chair for support. The chair spun, causing me to stumble towards the door and perfectly collide with the architrave.

'Oh, for...' I paused, catching sight of all the innocent little bear and dolly faces peering back at me. 'Flippin' heck's sake.'

Sliding my hand down the banister, I managed to descend the stairs of my cottage without further incident. I paused to see if I'd managed to conquer my phobia of blood between the two floors. I took a tentative look, saw the scrap of fabric I'd grabbed had turned a deep crimson and felt myself turn even more green. So that was a no, then. Only such a dire situation as this would have forced me to do what I was about to.

'Bloody hell! Give me a minute!' The deep – and deeply grumpy – voice penetrated the solid oak front door before it was wrenched open. The owner of the voice appeared about to grouch out another sentence but changed his mind as I met his eyes.

'Oh, great,' he said as my world went entirely fuzzy and then faded to black.

* * *

I sat bolt upright and scared the poop out of my neighbour.

'Holy shit!' He jumped before regaining his composure and continued with the task of cleaning my cut with some gauze. 'You're awake then.'

I glanced and saw that the fabric was rather pink and suddenly took an interest in the muted colours of a modern art piece on the wall.

'Not great with blood, I take it.'

I shook my head.

'Keep still for a minute.'

'Sorry.'

'Not a problem, but you've got a nasty bump on your forehead. Probably best to keep your head still for the moment, for your own comfort. I'd like to check it once I've done this.'

'Sorry to interrupt your day.'

'No need to apologise.'

Spud gave a whine and I stretched my good hand out to reassure him. 'I'm fine, boy. Don't worry.'

'He's very attached to you.'

'It's mutual,' I replied as I collided with that mesmerising gaze. 'But... I don't remember Spud being with me when I left... I don't remember much, actually. Oh, God, there's blood on my carpet. That's going to be a bugger to get out.' I put my hand up to my mouth. 'Sorry.'

Dr Darcy was concentrating on my hand and I was concentrating on not concentrating on it, but I'm pretty sure I saw what might actually have been a smile. It was difficult to tell from that angle.

'My mum makes her own cleaning concoction. Works every time and I have some here. You can use that.'

'Oh. Thank you, that's really kind of you.'

'You're welcome.'

'Did she have a lot of cause to use it? I mean, if she went to the effort of making something up?'

'My brother and I both played rugby and went mountain biking. That, together with the fact that we were boys and would happily attack each other from time to time, was probably enough reason.'

I liked listening to him talk. There was a smooth timbre to his voice when he wasn't using it to snap or yell at me. It was deep and velvety, like warm melting choco—

'Willow?'

'Sorry, miles away.' Sort of.

'That's OK. I said I've put a couple of butterfly stitches on it. It's not as bad as it looks, just in an awkward place so that should give it a leg up in healing.'

I nodded, looking straight ahead. 'Thank you.'

Was that one of those elusive smiles, or at least a hint of one?

'You can look now. I've covered it with gauze to keep it clean.'

I did as he said. I still had all five digits and was no longer leaking blood. Result. Spud was sitting next to Henry, who was crouched on the floor watching me. My dog gave a polite woof, which I felt was him adding his thanks. I'd brought him up with manners. My mind whizzed back. 'Did Spud run out? Oh, God, I didn't even think about him!' I felt my insides tighten and tears suddenly filled my eyes. 'Spud, I'm so sorry.' I gave his head a scratch and then put my hand to my own and winced. 'I'm a horrible doggy mum!'

Henry covered my hand with his and gently moved it away from the wound. 'I still need to clean that. You've broken the skin. And no, you're not. You were clearly distressed and the whack on your head was enough to disorientate anyone.'

I gave a sniff and made an effort to pull myself together. I wasn't even entirely sure why I'd suddenly gone all weepy. Given the choice, Dr Darcy was the last person I'd have shown any vulnerabilities to, but today I was clearly going all out and laying them on display for him.

He was still holding my hand when he spoke. 'Anyone who has ever seen you with him can see that you are quite the opposite of that. Even me. And as we both know, I'm not a dog person. He clearly landed on his feet when you chose him.'

I gave another sniff but this time it was accompanied by a smile. 'Thank you. Was he out loose?'

'No. The gate closed behind you, but he was barking his head off once I took you inside. I nipped back out and closed your front door. Your keys were on the side, so I grabbed them in case your back door was locked. They're over there on the table. The dog just stuck beside me. It seemed he knew I'd take him to you.'

'Thank you. And his name is Spud.'

'Yes, of course.'

'Thank you for bringing him in here. He doesn't shed and is completely toilet trained.'

'Don't worry, I'm not as uptight as it might appear. Besides, he's been glued to that spot ever since he came in. Now, do you mind if I have a look at this bump on your head?'

When I'd got up that morning, the last thing I thought I'd be doing later that afternoon was staring into my nemesis neighbour's eyes as he asked me to look one way then the other and follow his finger as it moved back and forth. Even more astonishing was that it struck me those eyes were incredibly sexy. I put it down to the bump on the head. It was the only possible explanation.

'I don't think you've done any lasting damage, just given it a good whack, but do ring immediately if you start experiencing dizziness or nausea or double vision.'

'Umm... freaking me out a bit here!'

'Sorry. I don't mean to but it's important. OK?'

'OK.'

'What did you do?' he asked, his hands moving gently on my head as he cleaned up the cut and dressed it with a small square of gauze.

'Leant on my office chair trying to get to the door after I'd cut myself. It spun round. Not the best choice of support now I look back on it.'

'What did you hit?'

'The door-frame.'

'Sounds like you didn't miss your target by much. At least it wasn't anything dirty.'

'Nothing in my house is dirty!' I said, sitting a little straighter. As someone who prided myself on taking care of my cottage, the comment rankled.

He sat back and rolled his shoulders, as though to release tension. 'It wasn't my intention to suggest that it is. I just meant as opposed to something in the garden.'

'No. I'm sure. God, I'm sorry. Thank you for all this.' I watched the long, dextrous fingers as they tidied away his supplies.

He gave the merest hint of a nod. 'Try and keep the hand wound dry. I know it's a pain, but a plastic bag or similar in the shower will help protect it and speed up healing. It shouldn't cause you any problems. The stitches may well come off on their own but I'll check again in a week to ten days.'

'I've taken up too much of your time already. I'll make an appointment at the doctor's for that.' I caught the briefest of frowns. 'What was that look for?'

'What look?'

'The look you just gave, and don't tell me nothing.'

His gaze raised itself from the doctor's bag and hooked onto mine. 'Fine. But you did ask. I think it's a waste of a doctor's appointment when I've already said I can do it.'

My cheeks burned with embarrassment. 'I'm not in the habit of wasting anyone's time, let alone a doctor. And that includes you.'

'It's not wasting my time and I'd prefer to see first-hand how it's healed. No pun intended.'

I made to get to my feet but Henry put a large but gentle hand on my shoulder. 'Just sit there for a bit. You've had a shock and a fair bump on the head. It's probably best you don't rush off just yet. Can I get you a drink? Coffee, tea?'

'I've interrupted your day enough.'

'Please. I'd rather you stayed.'

The air crackled between us. I looked down at my feet, took a deep breath and let it out before meeting the striking green eyes once more. 'I bet that's a sentence you never thought you'd say,' I said, chuckling, waving a verbal olive branch – at least for the moment.

The dark brows shrugged in an expression that could have meant anything.

'Then tea would be lovely, thank you. Weak, no sugar, thanks.'

A few minutes later, he placed a plain white bone china mug down on the thick mango-wood coffee table next to me, then took a seat in the armchair adjacent to it. Silence descended. I sipped my drink. Suddenly he sat up straight.

'Should I get a drink for the…' He cleared his throat. 'Umm, Spud? He was quite distressed and barking. Might that have made him thirsty?'

'That would be so lovely, thank you.'

'I don't have a dog bowl. I'll see what I can find.' He strode across the open space to the kitchen and ducked down behind the island and began rummaging in a cupboard. Moments later, he returned with a small china bowl full of cold water.

'Is that all right?' he asked, putting it down near me. Barely had he asked the question when Spud was lapping enthusiastically. 'I assume that's a yes. Looks like he was thirsty.'

'Is that Spode china?' I asked, nervously.

'Err, yes. It seemed the best size for him. Is it OK? I don't have a lot of choice. I've not got around to restocking all my kitchen stuff yet.'

'It's perfect. I'm just terrified it might get broken if he knocks it over. He's very bright but antiques have never been his thing.'

'Don't worry. It was my nan's—'

'Oh, God!'

A laugh rumbled out as he touched my arm. 'No, I meant she'd love that it was being used for this. She adored dogs. Had them all her life.'

'Thank you.'

He smiled then focused back on the dog, who'd by now nearly finished the bowl. 'He really was thirsty! Can I take the bowl to put some more in it?'

'Yep. He's brilliant with his food and toys. He won't startle.'

Henry crouched and took the bowl. Spud looked up at him, confused. 'I'm going to get you some more,' he continued as he pointed at the tap. There was a momentary pause before he looked back at me. 'I'm talking to a dog.'

'I do it all the time. I'd rather talk to animals than people most of the time,' I replied with a shrug.

Henry straightened, crossed the room to the sink and refilled the bowl, Spud at his heels the whole time. Both returned, and he placed the bowl back down.

'Poor Spuddy.' I ran my hand along his back as he continued drinking.

Henry retook his seat and sipped at his own black coffee, and I surreptitiously pushed myself back up the slippy leather sofa for the third time. After a promising start, it was fair to say that the conversation wasn't exactly flowing.

'So,' I began, and he looked up, his expression expectant. I hadn't really thought past that, but just sitting in silence was beyond awkward. 'Are you settling in more now? Everyone is raving about you at the clinic.'

His brow rose. 'Always good to know that one is a subject of gossip.'

I wrinkled my nose. 'I wouldn't exactly say that people singing your praises counts as gossip.'

He cleared his throat. 'No. Perhaps not. It is at least good to know that patients are happy and not yet preparing to run me out of town.'

'I know we're more rural than London, but we're not quite the Wild West!'

A flash of a smile. A really rather lovely smile, in fact... 'Just a turn of phrase. How are you feeling?'

Oh, God, I'd outstayed my welcome. He was probably desperate to get his house back to himself. 'Much better, thanks,' I replied, replacing my mug carefully on the coaster and standing up.

Henry stood quickly and took a step closer.

'I'm fine, really. Sorry for being such a drama llama.'

'Drama llama?' There was that flicker of amusement again. It was so elusive and rare I was pretty sure it must have been on the endangered species list.

'You know. About the blood and stuff. Honestly, I'm pretty mortified I fainted, especially in front of you, of all people.'

Bugger.

'Me, of all people?'

Think! 'You know, being a doctor and stuff.' *Oh, God.*

'Surely, then, I'm the ideal person?'

Definitely not. Pretty to look at and clearly skilled but conversation skills need work. B minus. 'Just a turn of phrase,' I said, parroting his earlier words.

Henry looked down at me as I stopped by his front door, Spud at my feet. 'You really don't need to rush off. I'd rather you stayed until you felt entirely yourself.'

'Oh, I do!' I smiled brightly in the hope of emphasising that point.

He folded his arms across his chest, looking down out me, disbelief clear on his face. 'Don't hesitate to call me if you feel at all unwell. Even if it's nothing, it's best to check.'

'I will. But I'm fine, really.'

'OK. Here.' He turned and picked up a brown glass spray bottle from the side and handed it to me. 'Spray that on the stain, let it soak for a couple of minutes then blot it off with a white cloth. Will you be all right with that?'

I bristled. 'I think I've got it, thanks.'

He shook his head. 'No, I mean, it will loosen the stain and show red on the cloth.'

'Oh, yes, I see what you mean. Yes, I'll be fine now blood's not actually leaking out of me. Thank you.'

'I could do it for you if it's going to be difficult.'

'Thank you. That's very kind of you, but I'm sure I'll manage.'

'You know where I am.'

I suddenly had a vision of Henry on his hands and knees wearing a pinny and Marigolds and swallowed down a giggle, turning to the door to hide it. He reached over to open it for me, a fairly easy task for someone of his height. Especially when I wasn't wearing heels. I looked down. Oh, God! I wasn't just not wearing heels. I wasn't wearing shoes at all!

I spun round and waited for a moment until my eyes caught up with my brain. A strong hand on my upper arm steadied me.

'I really think you should stay a little longer.'

'No, honestly, I'm fine. Thank you. But just so you know, I don't make a habit of running around barefoot. I know you probably think I dance around a fairy ring at midnight but...' I lifted my chin to meet his gaze and found his own fixed on mine, intense, studying me. My sentence drifted off. He really was exceptionally good-looking. And it appeared he had a kind streak. It was just a shame that we had absolutely nothing in common and he had a finely honed skill of finding my very last nerve.

'But?' Was that amusement in those eyes? If it had been anyone else, I'd have sworn that was the flicker of a smile, but I knew better – those seemed in limited supply.

'I... well, nothing, really. I just wanted to explain.'

His hand was still resting on the latch of the door, his body close in the small entranceway. I could smell the faint hint of aftershave and the clean laundry smell that I'd always found so comforting. 'Willow, I know we don't always see eye to eye—'

'I don't think we've ever seen eye to eye,' I replied, honestly.

'I was trying to be diplomatic.'

There it was again – that shimmering amusement in the captivating eyes.

'Despite what you may think, I do not believe that you spend your evenings dancing around bonfires, dropping newts' eyes and frogs' toes into a cauldron.'

'Good to know.'

'What I'm trying to say is that, although we have different lifestyles and outlooks, I don't mean to judge you for that.' He cleared his throat. 'And if it has seemed like that so far, then I'm sorry.' His eyes drifted down to my feet. Thankfully, the previous night I'd treated myself to a little home spa session, so my toes were looking very respectable and a pleasing – to me, at least – shade of bright pink.

'I'm very glad you didn't delay coming round by worrying about appropriate footwear.'

'Thank you.' I met his eyes again. 'For this—' I raised my poorly hand and pointed to my head wound '—for looking after Spud and for all you just said.'

He nodded.

'I'm sure moving here hasn't exactly been what you expected. They say travelling to different countries can be a culture shock, but I'm sure it works on a smaller scale too.'

'You're right. I thought moving here would be a quiet life, but it seems the social calendar is pretty packed.'

'Don't forget it's up to you how much or how little you take part.'

He thought about that for a moment. 'It's certainly easier to be anonymous in the city.'

'Do you want to be anonymous?' I asked.

For a moment, the hard planes of his face softened, the guard dropped. I automatically held my breath so as not to make a move, almost as if he was a nervous animal and I didn't want to spook him. Outside, Pepper brayed loudly and the moment was broken. Shutters crashed back down into place and the serious expression once again took up residence.

'Do you have your phone?'

'No. It's next door somewhere.'

He frowned. 'Somewhere?'

'Yes. Why?'

'I'm just a little surprised. Most people seem to have their phone almost surgically attached to them these days.'

'I know. But it's not my thing. I wouldn't be without it, don't get me wrong, but it's so easy to get caught up in scrolling and then look up to find a couple of hours have gone by.'

'Agreed. It's hard not to start doomscrolling in the middle of the night when you can't sleep.'

I'd noticed the dark shadows under his eyes but didn't know him well enough to tell whether that was just part of his colouring. His accidental revelation confirmed to me that it wasn't.

'Perhaps you could put your phone in another room, switched off, if you have a tendency to reach for it and do that? Put a book by your bedside instead.'

'Switch it off?'

'Yes.'

He looked positively horrified. 'I can't do that.'

'Why not?'

'What if I'm needed?'

'Are you on call for the clinic here? Sorry, I didn't realise that.'

'I'm not, but still...'

'You have family you like to be available for?'

'That too.'

'I assume you were on call a lot in your previous job.'

'Yes, I was. And I didn't mind. I'd rather they called me, even if it turned out that I wasn't needed, than risk a patient.'

'You enjoyed it, then?'

There was a pause. 'Yes, I suppose I did.'

'So what made you move here? It's quite a change.'

He issued a small laugh and I couldn't help the corners of my mouth lifting in reply, but the brief shadow of a smile had already faded by the time he turned back to me. 'That's an understatement.' I waited for him to elaborate but the silence settled around us once more and I realised nothing more was going to be forthcoming.

'Well, I'd better take Spud home. I'm really sorry to disturb you.'

Henry looked up, almost startled. 'Sorry. I was miles away.'

I smiled gently. 'That's OK.' I had the feeling that whatever it was that had brought him here was perhaps something even he was still trying to figure out.

'You were right to come over,' he said, his hand still resting lazily on the latch of the front door.

'I know I'm the last person you'd want to find banging on your front door,' I replied, laughing. 'We both know that. But I'm not really the best with blood and I panicked.'

'Then, like I said, you did the right thing. Keep it dry and clean and I'll check on it in a few days.'

I didn't speak but clearly my face continued the conversation without my consent.

'Really, it's nothing,' he repeated. 'It's honestly a relief not to be dealing with stabbings and gunshots and RTAs.'

The haunted look in those striking green eyes suddenly made a little more sense.

'That must have been a lot to deal with every day.'

'I chose to be a trauma doctor,' he said, shrugging his broad shoulders. 'I knew what I was letting myself in for.'

'Still,' I countered. 'You're only human.' I studied him for a moment. 'I think.'

Wait a minute. Was I teasing my grumpy neighbour? Was I... flirting?

Henry stared at me for a moment and I felt a flush begin to creep up my chest. And then it happened. His eyes crinkled at the edges, the just-generous-enough mouth tilted up at the corners and a deep, throaty and disturbingly sexy laugh rumbled out.

'That's probably one of the nicest ways I've had that particular accusation made.'

I smiled back at him. He had a really good smile, great teeth, and there was no question about it – he was hot! Had I read him wrong? Had we read each other wrong?

'I'm sorry I had a go at you about ripping out the garden. You were right. It's your property and none of my business.'

'Perhaps I should have come round and introduced myself, explained what was going to happen. I'm sure it was a shock to you, especially if you were close to the previous neighbour, which I understand you were.'

'And how would you know that?' I asked, squinting my eyes, a half-smile on my lips. 'Have you been talking about me?'

Oh my God! I *was* flirting!

He shook his head. 'Not intentionally. People are just a little more open and chatty here, it would seem.' He paused. 'And surprisingly well informed.'

'The village grapevine is pretty much set at hyperdrive.'

'So I'm discovering. Admittedly, that's going to take some getting used to.'

'Try not to worry about it too much. People generally don't mean any harm. It's just how it is.'

'No. Everyone seems pleasant so far.'

'Apart from your neighbour.'

'We all have misunderstandings from time to time.' His hand dropped from the latch. 'Shall we call a truce?' he said, his gaze focused directly on mine.

'A truce? I think I probably owe you more than that, as you've just stitched me back together.'

'You don't owe me anything, Willow. I'd hardly hold a medical emergency over your head, let alone anything else.' I could practically see the shutters that had temporarily raised once more coming down over his eyes and, despite everything, suddenly I wanted to prevent that more than anything.

'No, I didn't mean that,' I said. Without thinking, I laid my hand on his forearm. The dark hairs there tickled my palm, his warm skin contrasting with my cool hand. 'I just meant... well, could I cook you dinner? As a thank you for this?'

'You don't need to thank me.' The shutters stilled.

'I know I don't have to. But I'd like to. And... perhaps we could try starting again?'

'Starting again?'

'Yes.'

Henry considered this for what felt like an age. If I was brutally honest, I'd have hoped for a swifter response, but I bit my tongue.

'On one condition.'

'Uh oh.' The words slipped out before I thought about them but, to my surprise, Henry just chuckled.

'We get a takeaway. I'm inclined to warn you away from sharp objects just at the moment.'

'That's a good plan. The only thing is there's not a lot of choice here for takeaway, unlike London.'

'Let me take care of that. When would suit you?'

'How about tonight?'

His smile was so unexpected that I couldn't help but return it.

'You're not a woman who hangs around, are you?'

'Life's too short.'

'That's certainly the truth.'

'Only if that suits you, of course. If you already have plans, that's absolutely fine. Just choose a day.'

'This evening sounds good to me. I'll get it arranged. What time?'

'What time do you like to eat?'

'I'm yet to build in a schedule. Years of shift work have taken their toll on things like that. What would you suggest?'

'How about coming round for half six, to eat at seven?'

'Sounds perfect.'

'Great!' I grinned. 'It's a date!' I slapped my hand to my mouth as if to try to catch the words and shove them back in but too late. They were out and streaking free. 'I didn't mean it like a "date" date. Obviously!'

'Obviously.'

I risked a glance up but his expression gave nothing away. I guess that kind of came in handy with his line of work. Everyone always said my face spoke most of the words for me. That was the good thing about being a teddy bear doctor. Teddies were far easier to manage than people.

'I'll leave you to get back to... whatever it was you were doing.'

He gave a nod but didn't fill in any blanks, merely twisted the latch and opened the door.

'Thanks again,' I said, as I stepped out into the warm sunshine of the late afternoon.

'You're welcome. I'll see you at half six.'

8

First off, clean-up time. Heading to the cupboard that had once been the old larder, I grabbed the plastic trug I kept my cleaning supplies in, took the spray bottle that Henry had given me with his mum's magic recipe in and went upstairs to my workroom to assess the damage.

Half an hour later, I'd cleared up the mess – I didn't know what was in that bottle, but it was nothing short of miraculous. I'd also removed the smear of blood from the architrave where my forehead had connected with it. I checked the clock in the shape of a teddy on my desk. There was still time to get a bit more work in before I needed to head downstairs and tidy up a little. Thankfully I'd cleaned the day before, so nothing too drastic was required. Sitting back at my desk, I picked up my patient.

'I'm sorry about that delay. Back on track now.' I leant over and pulled the cutting mat towards me, now also cleaned of blood. The rotary cutter was back in the drawer and I'd returned once more to my trusty scissors to cut the fabric needed to patch his paw. Once that was done, I set a timer on my phone to give me plenty of time to shower – with a plastic bag I'd dug out to go over my hand.

'Ooh, have you shaved your legs?' Abby asked when I called her later as I was getting ready.

'Not since yesterday. Why?'

She waggled her eyebrows.

'Oh, for goodness' sake,' I said, laughing. 'It's most definitely not like that.'

'It could be. You've called a truce. You're starting again. This really could be *it*.'

'I'm pretty sure it's not.'

'You said you flirted.'

'Accidentally. And he most certainly didn't flirt back. I think he just wants to have a neighbour with whom he's not at logger-heads and, honestly, that's pretty appealing to me too. Besides, we're far too different.'

'Opposites attract and all that.'

'Not in this case.' I checked the time. 'I'd better go. Talk to you later.'

'I want all the details!'

I shook my head. 'There won't be any details.'

'I heard there's a full moon tonight. That's supposed to be influential in stuff, isn't it?' Abby asked. 'So who knows?'

'*I* know. See you later.'

She waved and hung up.

Despite the odd flutter earlier, which I put down to blood loss – all several teaspoons' worth – I was honest with Abby. I did know. For a start, there's no way I could live in a house like his. Minimalist was most definitely not my style. There was barely a speck of colour anywhere apart from one painting. Everything had seemed black, white or grey, and from what I'd seen of the garden, that wasn't much of an improvement, the only colour coming from the plastic grass. And, just as his style wasn't mine, my aesthetic was probably just as much anathema to him. Still, if we could at least be friends, that would be a big improvement.

I was just giving another cushion a plump and chop when the doorbell rang. The clock on the mantelpiece above the log burner told me it was half past six on the dot. Henry's punctuality somehow didn't surprise me, and I pulled open the door.

'Hi.'

'Hi.'

My stomach fluttered and I gave it a mental telling off. Although I could see its point. In a white shirt and fitted khaki chinos, Henry Darcy was textbook bloody gorgeous.

'Come in.' I stood back from the door as he entered and suddenly the little entrance hall seemed snug with his bulk filling it.

'Thanks. I wasn't sure if you preferred red or white wine. But then I thought you might not drink at all, so I brought a non-alcoholic choice too.' His brow was furrowed as he studied the bottle, something that I'd noticed was an almost permanent state for his features.

'Henry, that's so kind of you. You didn't need to bring anything. You're already arranging the food, which, by the way, we are going halves on.'

He shook his head. 'Already paid for. And before you argue – as you clearly want to – it's done. Take it as payment for ripping out the plants next door.'

'I've already told you I was overreacting.'

'For a reason. I didn't realise at the time that you'd been such good friends with the previous owners, and I know now that you spent a lot of time together in each other's gardens. I can see now how having it all ripped out in front of you must have been difficult.'

I shook my head. 'It's silly really.'

'No.' His hand rested momentarily on my arm. 'It's not at all.'

'Edie and Ted were lovely and helped me so much when I moved back here. They'd been good friends with my nan. I barely knew one end of a plant from another, but they were really patient. They showed me how to plant up properly, and propagate, and shared a lot of their own plants with me, too, which has saved me a fortune over the years.'

'I'm sure they felt just as lucky to have you as a neighbour.'

'I hope so.'

'The word on the village grapevine tells me it's true.'

'I knew it wouldn't take you long to get hooked into that,' I said, laughing as I led him through into the kitchen.

'Is there a choice?'

'Good point. It can be useful, though, especially with some of our older neighbours. People here notice if they haven't seen anyone for a few days, or if someone strange has been seen hanging around.'

'Like me.'

'Hardly. I know Steve has been desperate for someone to join the clinic for ages, but he's got high standards. Some of the younger doctors aren't interested in working in what they consider the back of beyond.'

'I appreciate the intimation that my standards are thought high enough, but not so much the fact I'm clearly not considered young.'

His voice was serious and, when I turned from putting the white wine and cordial in the fridge, his face matched.

'With age comes wisdom.'

'You know that's not helping, don't you?'

I pulled a slight grimace. 'We're not exactly getting off to the best start here, are we? Feel free to leave if you want. I totally understand. I probably would, had you said the same.'

He shook his head. 'Not a chance. I've ordered some excellent food from a restaurant in the next town.'

'Where?'

'Sorrento's.'

'That place is good. I didn't know they did delivery, though.'

'They don't usually. But the owner's kid tried eating a piece of Lego when I was in there for lunch just after I moved here.'

'And you came to the rescue?'

'Hardly. The kid was fine. I assessed him and he was breathing normally and then started crying even harder because he'd swallowed it.'

'Oh! So then what happened?'

'I advised that nature would take its course, but that he might not want to play with that bit again.'

My laughter burst out and a smile etched itself briefly onto my neighbour's face, transforming the granite-edged planes into something much softer. 'Was that your professional opinion?'

'Yep. Took seven plus years of training to make decisions like that.'

'I'm sure it must have been awful for the parents, though, before they knew he was OK.'

'Yeah. That's sometimes the hardest bit for everyone. The not knowing. It's not fair to reassure people if you really don't know.'

'I can imagine.' There was a momentary lull between us. 'Actually, no, I can't. Not at all, and I don't think I'd want to.'

'You get used to it.'

'Do you, though?'

He'd been looking out on the garden but his gaze dropped to me. 'You can do. But I didn't want to. I wanted to get out while I still felt something. Once you're entirely numb against people's pain, you're lost.'

For a moment, we both just stood there.

'Sorry,' Henry said, turning away but not before I saw the hints of colour on his cheeks.

'Why are you sorry?' I asked, placing my hand on his arm. 'I'm interested.'

'Why?' He turned suddenly but the question seemed genuine. Confusion showed in his eyes along with, if I wasn't mistaken, suspicion.

'Because if we're going to be friends, it's good to know about each other.'

He opened his mouth to say something then closed it again.

'What?'

'Nothing.'

'It's obviously something.'

He shook his head. 'I have a habit of saying the wrong thing.'

'I imagine spending all day trying to say the right thing must burn through your resources somewhat. Now, whatever it is, just say it.'

His Adam's apple bobbed as he swallowed. 'I hadn't anticipated telling you any of that. I don't want it being the next bit of gossip on the grapevine.' He lifted his chin as if to absorb the verbal blow he clearly expected.

I understood and wasn't offended. 'It won't be.'

'Thank you.'

'Now, which of those lovely offerings you brought would you like to drink?'

He flashed a smile. 'Actually, I'm kind of wishing I'd brought a beer now.'

'Like this?' I grabbed one of a few I had left in the fridge from the last time Abby and Ed were round.

'Lifesaver.' This time the smile stayed longer and I found myself wishing it were there a lot more.

Dinner arrived shortly after and we sat at my small dining table, the French doors open and hooked back in honour of the warm spring evening. Peaceful sounds of the countryside drifted in: birds twittering, the fountain in my nature pond bubbling softly and, in the distance, sheep baaing and the low of a cow or two. Occasionally a donkey bray would be added in for effect.

'He does that a lot,' Henry said, looking past me down the garden to where the donkeys had wandered up to my fence.

'Oh, just ignore it. I'll take some carrots down in a bit.'

'He's kind of hard to ignore.'

'You'll get used to it.'

Henry cut his eyes to me, disbelief writ large on his face.

'I promise. Anyway, you have to be nice to him. He's had a hard life.'

'Yeah, munching in a field all day with you at his beck and call feeding him carrots.'

'It wasn't always like that. He was rescued in a right old state. His poor hooves had never been trimmed, so they were all curled up and he could barely walk, and you could count every rib on his body. You wouldn't think it to look at him today, but he would just lie down initially. It was like he had no will to live. It was so heartbreaking. Thankfully he grew to trust his new owner and other villagers who pass the field on the other side. Gradually things got a little better every day. And, of course, he has friends now too.'

Henry was silent for a few moments. 'OK, now I feel really shitty for being cross with him.'

'Don't worry. I'll give you a carrot to feed him in a bit and he'll love you forever.'

'That's probably asking a bit much, even of a donkey.'

I looked round at him but he'd already turned his eyes back to the animals. This man clearly had a story, but whether he'd ever share it with me was hard to say. What was certain was that there was more to Henry Darcy than I'd initially thought.

After a scrumptious dinner which, as he had intimated earlier, Henry refused to take any money for, I delved into the salad box in my fridge and pulled out a handful of carrots, passing a couple to Henry. He looked down at them.

'I didn't realise you were actually serious.'

'You want to make friends, don't you?'

He didn't reply, which wasn't exactly the enthusiasm I was hoping for.

'Horse bites really can be nasty.'

'Yes. So you said. But I don't plan to get bitten, and having lived here for some time, alongside these three, I haven't yet.'

'First time for everything.'

I went to take the vegetables back but he moved his hand away. 'I didn't say I didn't want to. I was just...'

'Finding the downside of every situation?'

He looked at his feet for a second. 'Sorry.'

There was a flash of something so raw there, so painful, that I immediately felt bad for having said anything at all. It had been in jest, but Henry had clearly taken it seriously.

'There's nothing to apologise for, Henry. I was joking.' I touched his bare forearm briefly, my words soft.

'Many a true word spoken in jest.'

'Maybe, but not in this case. Come on,' I said, taking his free hand and pulling him towards the patio doors.

'I don't have my shoes on,' he said, halting for a second, which meant I also came to a sudden stop and pinged backwards, stumbling against a solid chest.

'Oops! Come on,' I said, pulling him along again, which

taking into account the difference in our size he was clearly allowing me to do. 'You don't need shoes. Just take off your socks. The grass is dry. Feel the earth beneath your feet. It'll do you good.'

When he made no reply, I turned and looked up at him.

'What?'

He shook his head. 'Nothing. Although I have to say this is the first time I've ever been asked to remove my socks at a dinner party.'

'"Dinner party" is a very grand title for a takeaway between friends. And anyway, first time for everything,' I said, parroting his phrase back at him, with a grin.

'Smart arse.'

'Charming,' I replied, mock offended. 'I invite you to dinner and that's the thanks I get.'

'I did insist it wasn't necessary.' A glimmer of amusement danced in his eyes and, for whatever reason, I was desperate to keep it there.

'That's true, but I get the feeling you were secretly pleased,' I teased.

'And what makes you think that?' Henry asked, looking up at me from where he was now sitting on the ledge of my patio doors, pulling off his socks while I held the treats. Spud had already headed down to say hello ahead of us.

'Just a feeling,' I said with a shrug.

Henry looked down at his bare feet, then up at me, shook his head and stood up.

'Here.' I gave him half the veggies and led the way down the garden.

'You've crammed a lot in here,' he said, looking from one side to the other as we wound our way along the meandering path.

'I know. I'm not very good at saying no.'

I felt his eyes on me, and the blush on my cheeks. 'To plants, I mean.' I opted to avoid compounding my embarrassment by not looking at him and continuing on my way.

'Weirdly, it looks bigger than my garden even though it's stuffed full.'

'Planting can do that. There's so much for your eye to fall on, it somehow tricks your brain, perhaps exactly because there is so much to look at.' I gave a shrug. 'I don't know how it works. You're the doctor.'

'But not a psychologist.'

'I suppose. I'm not sure whether your comment was a compliment or criticism. Our styles are definitely opposite ends of the spectrum!'

'True. And yes, it was a compliment. It really is quite beautiful. I can understand now why you were so upset about what I've done next door.'

'Even though it's none of my business.'

'Even though it's none of your business.'

I tilted my head up to look at him as we came to the fence, and found his eyes on me.

'You must have been regretting moving here when I had a go at you.'

'Not really,' he replied simply. 'I've lived in London my whole life. It's just natural to whizz about in your own little bubble and ignore everyone else.'

'And that bubble has travelled down here with you?'

'Like I said, it's been forty-odd years. Not an easy thing to just drop.'

'Or pop?' I asked, casting my gaze across the paddock.

An unexpected chuckle made me look back up and he met my eyes. 'Indeed. Or pop.'

'How do you feel about that bubble now? Are you still as attached to it?'

'I think the walls of it may be getting thinner.'

'Then there's hope for you yet.'

He raised an eyebrow. 'I didn't know I was in need of hope.'

'Oh, yes,' I said, turning back to the field. 'You can't operate like that down here. I mean, what's the point of getting away from it all if you're still just shut up inside your own head?'

'Looks like we found the psychologist after all.'

'Pfft,' I said, dismissing the comment. 'It's just common sense.' Then I raised my fingers to my mouth and let out a two-tone whistle.

'Impressive.'

'Charlie Carter taught me that at primary school when we were nine,' I replied, waving my carrots at the three animals doing a fast trot towards us. Well, Salt and Olive were. Pepper was charging across in a full-on canter.

'I didn't really have you pegged as a tomboy.'

'I wasn't. But I wanted to know how to whistle like that. He said he wouldn't teach me.'

'But you clearly persuaded him.'

'I ignored him for two days and on the third one he said he'd teach me.'

'Interesting tactic. Could have backfired.'

'Nah, I knew he had a crush on me.'

'At nine?'

'Yeah,' I said, laughing as Pepper made satisfied noises while I scratched his nose. 'Boys aren't really the most subtle creatures at that age.'

'Or any age.'

'I don't know. Some people can be pretty hard to read.'

'I'm assuming that's a reference to me.'

'If the scrubs fit...'

There was a murmur of amusement.

Olive was dipping her head over the fence, sniffing out the carrots Henry held, and he took a step back.

'Here,' I said, lifting his hand with mine. 'Now, hold it flat on your palm. She's a gentle thing. I promise she won't bite you.'

He sent me a brief side-eye. 'Can I have that in writing? With witnesses.'

Olive, as promised, took the carrot carefully and crunched it happily before sniffing out some more.

'Olive, those were supposed to be for the donkeys, you greedy thing.' The horse gave a shake of her head and nuzzled Henry's shoulder.

'She likes you.'

'Great.' His voice, like his body, was rigid.

'Try and relax.'

'Easy for you to say. Have you seen the size of those teeth? Horses can have a bite force of 500 pounds per square inch.'

'Really? What's mine?'

'What?'

'Bite force.'

'About 200.'

'Interesting.'

'Why? Are you planning on biting somebody?'

'No. I was never really a biter. Were you?'

'I went to a very strict boys' boarding school. That wasn't really an option.'

'That explains some things.'

'Does it?' he asked, turning towards me now that the animals had realised they'd plundered our entire supply of carrots and wandered a little way along to graze lazily at some grass, sticking together in their little huddle.

'Mmm. So do you remember anyone you had a crush on at nine years old?'

'There wasn't really the opportunity for meeting girls for me at the time, being a boarder at a boys' school.'

'Shame.'

'I don't think it was a great loss. I can't whistle like that anyway.'

The laughter bubbled out of me and Henry smiled then turned back and leant on the top bar of the fence, his shoulders a little more relaxed now that the animals had moved further along.

'It really is quite beautiful. I can't remember the last time I saw a proper sunset before I moved here.'

'London still has sky,' I teased.

He sent me another of those sidelong looks, but I could see amusement in his eyes.

'Perhaps I should have expressed myself better. More that I hadn't really taken the time to notice it for some time.'

'And how long did it take for you to notice it after you'd moved in?'

Henry turned a little more. 'A few weeks.'

'I know how much I missed things like that when I lived up there. Everything is at such a pace that the simpler things get left behind in the dust. It's only when you get off the crazy round-about you realise all the things you were missing.'

'I assumed you'd always lived here, for some reason.'

'Why?'

He paused. 'You're... um... very...' He made a couple of vague gestures with his hands.

I tilted my head in query.

'You know...'

'No. I don't.'

'Earthy.' He cleared his throat.

'Not something I've been called before.'

'Perhaps that's not a good word. I mean that you seem very... in touch with nature. Is that better?'

'I do appreciate nature. I've found it very healing. Hopefully you will too.' I smiled at him before my gaze drifted over his shoulder to his sterile garden.

Henry shook his head and the smile I'd seen flashes of earlier stayed a little longer. 'Some people may indeed be hard to read, but you're definitely not one of them. You really do wear your heart on your sleeve, don't you?'

I chewed the inside of my cheek.

'It's fine. You're right about that.' He gave a tilt of his head back towards his own garden. 'But I've got this.' He spread his hands out to indicate the vista in front of us, the paddock with the animals contentedly munching, and the woods beyond with their brand-new leaves unfurled in various hues of fresh green. 'It's a start.'

'A very good start,' I agreed. 'Like I said before, perhaps there is hope for you yet. Now, would you like a herbal tea? I grow quite a few of the ingredients myself, so there's nothing nasty in them.'

'I don't really do herbal tea, but I'd go for a coffee if you have any?'

'I have some for visitors, yes.'

'Great.'

'It's decaf.'

'Fantastic.' The tone of his voice suggested it was anything but.

'I suspect over the years you've probably drunk enough caffeine to last a lifetime.'

'Likely true. But that doesn't mean I don't still like it. And coffee isn't all bad for you, you know.'

'No, I know.' I looked up at him. 'I'll get some in for you next time. How's that?'

'You planning on slicing more appendages?'

I laughed. 'Hopefully not. I was hoping we could build on a friendship that didn't involve any more drama.'

'Sounds like a plan. In fact, I'll bring the coffee myself. Deal?'

'Deal.'

9

'It's a gorgeous evening.'

The sun was beginning to think of setting as we stood at the threshold of my back door, looking out in companionable silence. Sliding a glance at the handsome profile of my neighbour, I could see there was still tension in his broad shoulders, but I was beginning to realise that this appeared to be a permanent thing and not just when I was in the vicinity. I'd seen him leaving for and coming back from work when I was out in the garden or in the front rooms and he had the same stance then. Another change I had made when I moved back to the countryside was taking up what I liked to call Piloga. Henry had laughed at my terminology when I'd mentioned it. Initially I'd done classes in both Pilates and yoga but gradually had begun to develop my own style that combined aspects of both and suited me well enough.

As Henry stretched his neck from side to side, it made a crack.

'Have you ever thought about yoga?'

He looked round. 'Yes. I've dealt with a few exercise-related incidents in my time. I'm sure some of them were probably yoga related.'

'I was more thinking about you taking it up. You're clearly carrying a lot of tension in your neck, back and shoulders. A friend of mine is a sports massage therapist. He might be able to loosen some of those knots.'

Henry turned his focus back to the setting sun. 'Thanks for the offer but I don't think I'm cut out for downward dog and tree pose.'

'But you know the terminology? Interesting.'

'My ex was very much into all that. It was hard not to pick up some of the lingo.'

'Right.'

There was a pause.

'But you never felt inclined to take it up, especially as you clearly had someone who could help or instruct you?'

'No.'

There was a finality to the word that suggested the discussion was most definitely closed.

'OK. It was just a thought. I'll give you the name of my friend's website, in case you want to think about that.'

'Thanks.'

Silence settled around us once again and this time there was a ripple of tension. Part of me wished I'd kept quiet, but I also knew what it was like to feel like your shoulders were glued to your ears all day and night, and I wanted to help.

More for something to do than anything else, I leant over and flipped a switch. Instantly the garden was lit by twists and twirls of fairy lights around tree trunks, over arches, through shrubs and around the small shed I grandly referred to as a summer house.

'Wow!' Henry said.

I gave a chuckle. 'I know it's a lot but...' I spread my hands. 'I love it.'

'I can see why. It's very you.' He looked round at me. 'From the little I know of you, anyway.'

'I'm not sure if it's a compliment or not but I'm going to take it as one.'

He gave one of those brief, enigmatic smiles and didn't elaborate.

'Well, I'd better be heading back. Leave you in peace.'

'Don't feel you have to.'

He stopped, and for a moment his expression wasn't serious or enigmatic. It was a proper, pure smile. 'I don't. Thank you. You have a very welcoming home.'

'Thanks. I'm glad we've managed to overcome our differences.'

There was something intent about the way he looked at me. 'Yes. So am I.'

I leant against the banister while he put his shoes on, and absentmindedly picked my phone off the tiny console table when it let out a ping.

'Oh, shit.'

Henry was upright and on alert in an instant. 'What's the matter?'

'Nothing. I just forgot I had a tonne of soil being delivered Friday morning for the new raised beds.'

'Right.' He paused. 'I'm failing to see the problem. Just get them to put the bags around the back. I don't profess to know much about gardening but the planting can wait a couple of weeks, can't it?'

'It's not that. It doesn't come in bags. When I say a tonne, I literally mean a tonne. I barrow it from the front to the back when it's delivered, otherwise it's just on the road. I should have told you, sorry. They're usually pretty good about dumping in front of my house. I'll be out there supervising the delivery and I'll make sure it doesn't go anywhere near your car.'

'Thanks. I can move the car a bit further up anyway. But you do know you can't be pushing a wheelbarrow with that hand injury, don't you? Can you not put it off?'

'Not now, no. Don't worry. I'll sort something out,' I said, looking back down at my phone.

'I'll move it for you.'

My head snapped up. 'What?'

'I'll move it for you.'

'No! I mean, thank you, but you can't.'

'Why not?'

'Because it will take ages and I barely know you!' I said, laughing.

'Is there a specific length of time one has to be acquainted before being allowed to help out with garden chores? I've never had a garden, so I'm not au fait with the etiquette.'

I grinned up at him. When he wasn't being all moody and serious, he was actually pretty funny. And sooooo good-looking...

'It's not that, it's just... Well, it doesn't seem right.'

'That's your best argument?'

'For the moment, yes. Give me a minute, though.'

'Denied. What time is it coming?'

'No, wait!' I said, catching his hand. 'I've got it. It's coming Friday. You'll be at work then anyway.'

'Good try, but I've got a day off.'

'Really?' The astonishment in my voice was hard to disguise.

'You seem surprised.'

'Honestly? I am. You just don't seem the type to take days off.'

'Acutely observed. I'm not. At least I wasn't, but that was another change that needed to happen when I moved here. So

Friday is my first proper day off in...' He looked up towards the ceiling as he thought.

'The fact that you even have to think about it shows it's far too long.'

'You're probably right.'

'Which means I am even more adamant about you not wasting it shovelling muck!'

'It will be good for me. Physical work and all that.'

'Henry.'

'Willow.'

I heaved out a deep sigh.

'If that's the extent of your argument, then I win. I'll call my brother. He's at home this week and can come down and help me.'

'Oh, God, then there will be two of you to rue the day you met me.'

'Hardly. Now, stop stressing. Go and do some Piloga or something.'

'Oh, ha ha. Very funny.'

He flashed that smile again and I felt a little flutter in my tummy. I made a point of ignoring it. This evening was progress, but Henry Darcy was most definitely not The One. There was too much we differed on. I couldn't live in a place like his and, although he was complimentary about my welcoming home, was obvious from the way he'd looked around that it was vastly different to his own idea of the perfect interior. But friends was good.

'Keep that dressing dry and be careful. Give it time to heal.'

'Yes, Doctor.'

The smile was softer this time. 'Goodnight, Willow.'

'Night, Henry.'

Spud stood at his ankles looking up, waiting. Henry paused.

'Is he seeing me off the premises?'

'Not at all. He's waiting for you to say goodbye to him too.'

Henry shot me a look.

'Go on.'

He cleared his throat. 'Umm. Goodbye, Spud.'

The little dog's tail wagged even faster.

'See?'

Henry shook his head and, to my surprise, bent and gave Spud a quick pat before quickly straightening. It was as though he'd momentarily let himself relax but then snapped back into his usual, tightly wound self. With that he opened the door and strode down my path. I waved as he turned into his own gate and then closed the door.

'Well,' I said, bending down and scooping Spud into my arms. 'That didn't go so badly, did it?' Spud wagged his tail and snuggled into my neck. 'Perhaps we can all be friends after all.'

* * *

'Sounds like you had quite the cosy evening together.' Abby was grinning mischievously over the top of her latte.

'It wasn't like that.'

'Really? Not even a little bit?'

'Not even a little bit,' I reaffirmed. 'It was pleasant, but that was it.'

'Oh. I was wondering whether we might have got the whole accidentally-manifesting-the-perfect-neighbour thing right after all.'

'Nope. Although it's most certainly not to my taste, at least Edie's house is no longer sitting there looking sad and empty.'

'Dr Darcy's house.'

'Huh?'

'It's Henry's house now, not Edie's.'

'Oh. Yes, of course. I think it will probably take a little while to get used to thinking of it like that.'

'Perhaps a few more dinners together would help?'

I shot her a look.

'What? It's not like he's hard on the eye. Things could be far worse.'

'If I'm going to the effort of another long-term relationship, I'm not going to settle for someone because "things could be worse".'

'No. Obviously not. I just meant maybe he's not as bad as you first thought.'

'No, he probably isn't, but he's not The One.'

'How do you know?'

'Because I'd know.'

Abby shrugged. 'If you say so.'

'I do. I'd have thought you of all people would know. You and Ed are still gooey together. You knew he was The One.'

'Yeah, I guess you've got a point.'

'I have,' I replied as I checked my watch. I was one of the few women I knew that still wore one, or at least one that did nothing more than tell the time, but it saved me checking my phone and accidentally getting drawn into either mindless scrolling or doomscrolling, or mindless doomscrolling. 'I'd better get back to work.'

'How's business?'

'Crazy busy at the moment. Ever since that article in the local paper got picked up by the nationals, it's gone mad. Which is good, obviously, but the waiting list is getting longer, which isn't ideal.'

'Have you thought about employing someone?'

'I go back and forth on it. I don't want to take someone on and then things taper off for whatever reason. Plus there's sick pay and pension contributions and everything else to consider. It's not like there's a massive profit margin to be playing with, so I need to sit down and really work out whether it's worth it, and whether I can afford it.'

'Maybe someone part time or ad hoc?'

'That's a possibility. Space is another issue, though. The room isn't huge, so having two of us in there could be a bit snug.'

'You need one of those studios in the garden.'

I plopped my chin on my hands. 'Oh, that would be heaven, although I'm not sure exactly where I'd put it. I've planted up most of the space.'

'Perhaps Dr Dishy would let you rent some space in his.'

'Ha! We might have got past the initial hiccups, but I don't think we're at that stage yet. Or any time soon. Plus I think looking out at that sterile landscape every time I raised my head would do my noggin in. Right. Back to reality.' I stood and dropped a kiss on my friend's cheek as I hugged her. 'See you later.'

'OK. Love you.'

'Love you back.'

* * *

Thursday rolled around and I was all prepped for the next day's earth delivery. As I pottered about in the front garden deadheading, an unfamiliar car trundled down the road and came to a halt outside Henry's house. Obviously I was dying to have a nose, but I maintained a pretty good air of nonchalance as the stranger emerged from the vehicle.

'Hi,' he called as he pushed the door shut and beeped it

locked. An overnight bag was slung across his shoulder and the resemblance to Henry was unmistakeable.

'Hello,' I replied with a smile.

'How are you?' he asked, slowing and resting on the separating wall of our front gardens.

'Fine, thanks. How are you?'

'Ready and willing to shovel—'

'George!' Henry's door opened and the rare smile lit up his face at the sight of his brother.

'There he is!' The two men embraced, the affection obvious, their smiles infectious. 'I don't see him for ages and then when he invites me down, it's for manual labour.'

The smile slid off my face. 'I'm afraid that's my fault.'

'No, it's not,' Henry replied, quickly. 'Willow's injured her hand but the delivery for her garden was already organised, so I offered our services.'

'I don't mind, really. At least it's a chance to see my big brother. And frankly it's good to hear that he's not working all the hours God sends, now he's moved here.'

'That was rather the idea.'

'I know,' George countered, 'but it was entirely possible, knowing you, that it could have been a case of same life, different surroundings.'

'Well, it's not,' Henry replied, a slightly prickly edge to his voice. 'Now, are you coming in or staying out here to bother the neighbours?'

George made a show of thinking about the question. Henry sent me a glance. 'He thinks he's hilarious. Always has done. Come on. I'm sure Willow has better things to do with her time than be bothered by you.'

'Hardly. I'm very grateful to both of you. It's very kind.'

'See?' George said in a mock sniffy manner. 'She wants to chat.'

Henry shook his head but the amusement and love in his eyes was still clear. 'Get inside, pipsqueak.'

'He loves me really.' George grinned and picked up his bag, which Henry immediately took from him. 'See you later.'

'Bye. Nice to meet you.'

10

As darkness fell, I set out on my nightly slug hunt. Armed with my bucket, I began collecting them and their pestilent shelled cousins to add to the compost. There was plenty in there they could munch to their hearts' content without causing me to curse their very existence.

I kept the main patio lights off and moved diligently around with my little pen torch, carefully spotting the slimy offenders and flicking them off my gloves into the bucket. From next door I could hear the crackling of the fire pit and the deep voices of the two men chatting easily, laughter drifting on the still air of the evening. I was pleased that Henry's brother was someone he could clearly truly relax with. Continuing with my task, I tuned out of their conversation and was just yanking a particularly clingy snail off one of my newest hostas when my attention was caught by a change of topic.

'So when were you going to tell us your neighbour was hot?'

There was a pause followed by the sound of a bottle being placed on the table. 'I wasn't.'

'Any reason why?'

'You know why.'

Ooh... intrigue...

And yes, I know I shouldn't have been listening, but it's not as easy as that, is it? Anyway, it wasn't on purpose. I was doing what I always did at that time of night, and if they chose to sit outside, I couldn't help it if I overheard the conversation, could I?

Henry continued. 'Don't forget, you're here to help me out. Nothing else.'

'Yeah, yeah. I know.' Although there had clearly been a warning note to the older brother's tone, George's reply sounded good-natured. Even from the brief meeting I'd had the two brothers, although clearly close, seemed very different in their character. George had all the laid-back ease while Henry was serious, strait-laced and focused. There had been flashes of humour when he'd come round for dinner, but he was certainly the more buttoned-up of the two.

'I'm just extra muscle to help move the earth. Fair enough. And I'd certainly be more than happy to make the earth move for her.'

'Don't speak about her like that.' Henry's voice was unexpectedly sharp.

'Bloody hell. It was just a joke. What's the problem, anyway?' In my mind's eye, I could almost see him shrugging before he continued. 'You're clearly not interested in her and she seems nice.'

'That's because you've never seen her angry,' his brother countered and, to be fair, he probably had a point.

'Perhaps if you were a bit less anti ever having a relationship again, you might be less inclined to wind up every woman that you meet.'

'I don't wind every woman up. Besides, I was just minding my own business this time but it seemed whatever I did was wrong.'

'If you say so.'

'I do. And I never said I'm against meeting someone.'

George gave a snort. 'When was the last time you went on a proper date? And no, the odd drink doesn't count. I mean actually getting to know someone.'

'Yeah, because that worked out so well last time.' Henry's voice was tight and sharp. His brother had hit a nerve. The bottle was put down more heavily on the metal table this time. When he spoke again, the words were still sarcastic and icy cold. 'In fact, it turned out I didn't know her at all!'

I winced in empathy. Was that why Henry had left London? If so, who could blame him? I made a move to head back inside. Eavesdropping hadn't been my intention, and now that the conversation had turned personal it didn't feel right to continue. As quietly as I could, I put the lid on the bucket to keep the munching devils contained. The compost heap was further down the garden, and I didn't want to alert the brothers to the fact I'd overheard part of their conversation by tramping down there. As I took off my gloves and set my tools aside, the conversation next door continued.

'Agreed, that was shit,' George replied. 'But it doesn't mean that was your one and only chance at finding someone and being happy.'

There was a sound from Henry which could have been agreement or disagreement, it was hard to tell. It could just as likely have been indigestion.

My neighbour's brother, however, was proving to be a stubborn soul.

'Maybe someone like Willow is exactly what you need?'

Wait, what?

'Is that so?' Henry replied, sarcasm as thick as treacle laced through his words. 'You seem to know a lot about her from a few minutes' conversation.'

'I don't know anything much other than what you've said and what I gathered earlier, which is that she seems nice, she's bright and, as I mentioned before, kind of hot.'

The conversation lulled. Clearly Henry was in no hurry to back those assumptions up. And yes, I know I said I was going inside, and I was. Just quite slowly.

'OK, the natural, softer side of life clearly appeals to her more than you, but she's also single.'

'How do you know that?'

'Because when you told me off just now, you never mentioned how her boyfriend or husband would be interested to hear my comments.'

'OK, genius.'

'So?'

'So what?'

'So, what about it? You said you had dinner together.'

'There was nothing in that.'

'Still. It gave you a chance to spend time with her.'

'George, just stop, OK? She's my neighbour and nothing else. I was just trying to stem the attrition of neighbourly warring. Willow is most certainly not my type.'

'Exactly. That's rather my point.'

Henry gave a groan. 'Just because I'm not looking for someone whose main goal in life is to smash through the glass ceiling at any cost, neither am I looking to go out with someone whose grip on reality can sometimes be described as tenuous at best.'

Excuse me?

'All right, she's a bit different, but that's not necessarily a bad thing.'

'No. Just no. Honestly, did you know she's thought of as a witch in these parts? Although apparently the good kind, so I suppose that's something.' Sarcasm dripped from the words. 'She said she doesn't dance naked around bonfires, but I wouldn't put it past her.'

'Still not seeing the problem. Actually that sounds like a bonus, if anything.'

'Can you imagine me turning up to a function with woo-woo Willow? I'd be a laughing stock, and quite frankly I've had enough of that to last a lifetime.'

Tears burned in my eyes and my throat stung raw. There was a reason people told you not to listen at keyholes, or on adjoining patios. You ran the risk of hearing something unpleasant. I closed the door quietly behind me, turned the key and pulled down the blinds. Spud padded up to me and, in that magical way dogs often do, immediately sensed something was wrong. He gave a small whine and I crouched down to give him a rub and kiss his fuzzy head.

'Who cares what a stupid man thinks anyway, eh, boy?' I said, although the tear running down my cheek somewhat took the edge off the attempt at bravado. The dog looked up at me as if to say, 'You, apparently.' And OK, yes, he was right. In that moment Henry Darcy's words were hurtful, especially as I'd thought the couple of hours we had spent together for dinner had meant something. Not in a romantic way, but in a way that suggested that actually, yes, we could be friends. That we might not agree on décor or garden design, but we had enough respect for each other to accept those differences. I let out a humourless laugh.

'How wrong could I be?'

Switching off the lights, I told Spud to get Colin the Cabbage, which he dutifully did, and we plodded up the creaky wooden stairs to bed. Tomorrow was going to be a busy day and I needed rest.

* * *

'What the hell are you doing?'

I was on my third wheelbarrow load when the front door to my neighbour's house was yanked open and Henry, looking almost unrecognisable in T-shirt and battered Levi's, was striding down the path with a face like thunder.

'I would have thought that was perfectly obvious. What does it look like I'm doing?' I said, casting barely a glance at him before continuing with my task.

'It looks like you're completely disobeying your doctor's orders!' he said, practically ripping the gate from its hinges to meet me on the pavement next to the pile of soil that had been delivered early that morning. 'You're going to open the wound up again and make it worse, not to mention risking sepsis!' He went to take the spade from me, but I snatched it away and glared up at him before shovelling another load into the barrow. Shoving the tool into the heap, I bent my knees and lifted the handles of the barrow, preparing to wheel it through to the back garden. Henry placed himself square in front of it.

'Excuse me.'

He folded his arms across his chest. 'No.'

I tried pushing it to the side, but he merely took a step in the same direction, blocking my path. Already pink-cheeked from the effort, I could feel my face beginning to burn with annoyance, frustration and remembered hurt. A fleeting thought of just ramming his damn shins with the barrow darted through my head as our eyes, fury showing in both, locked.

'Try it,' he said, his bare feet planted solidly apart in front of me.

I never was good at hiding my emotions.

'Believe me, I'm thinking about it!'

'I don't doubt that, but before you do perhaps you could explain what the hell you're doing when we already arranged that George and I would do this today?' He flicked a hand angrily at the task before us.

Behind him, his brother wandered out of the house, coffee mug in hand.

'Hi, Willow.'

I gave him a brief smile. This was between me and Henry and I didn't want George getting caught in the crossfire.

'Oh, right, so he gets civility?' Henry snapped.

I glared at him before making another attempt at getting my load through to the back garden. Henry stepped forward, his shins now dangerously close to the metal edge of the barrow.

'Argh!' I yelled in frustration and slammed it down, some of the earth spilling over onto his feet as I did so. Still he refused to move.

'Are you going to answer my question?'

'I changed my mind.'

'Too bad,' he said, stepping towards me. 'I'm medically over-ruling you. And clearly that's not the only reason as it doesn't explain why you're smiling at my brother and looking at me like I'm the devil incarnate.'

'Just leave me alone!'

'No. Not until you tell me what's going on.'

'Morning!' Jerry accompanied his greeting with a wave. 'Couple of letters there for you, Doc. Nothing for you today, Willow.'

'Thanks, Jerry. Have a good weekend.'

Great. Jerry was a love but I knew this little tableau would be being recounted all over the village by the end of the day. Not that I gave a monkey's brass one about that. But I knew someone who would. Henry, as expected, was looking momentarily less sure of himself.

'You'd better go back inside. I wouldn't want to cause you further embarrassment by being seen associating with "woo-woo Willow".'

It took a moment and then realisation dawned across his face, the colour draining from it. 'You weren't supposed to hear that.'

'No, I imagine I wasn't, but I'm glad I did. At least now I know what you actually think despite my attempt at building bridges.'

His jaw tightened. 'It's not polite to listen in on people's private conversations, you know!'

Behind him, George gave a slow shake of his head and threw me an apologetic look.

'That's your answer? Unbelievable. Believe me, it wasn't intentional,' I snapped back at Henry. 'I was actually out slug hunting.'

'In the dark?' Scepticism laced his words.

'Yes, obviously. They come out at night.'

He was staring at me. I turned away from the laser glare and yanked up the barrow again.

'You're going to open the wound.' His voice was raised.

'Then I'll stick a bloody plaster on it, won't I?'

'For God's sake. You have stitches! I wouldn't have stitched it if a sodding plaster would have sufficed, would I?'

'As much as I hate to ever agree with my big brother if I can help it—' George's languid tones contrasted with our furious ones '—he's probably right. I mean, don't get me wrong, he has a lot of faults—'

'Is this actually going somewhere, George?' Henry snapped.

George gave him an unbothered look. 'The point is, he's a brilliant doctor, so what he's saying is probably right.'

I stood there steaming for a couple more moments then plonked the barrow back down.

'Thank you,' said Henry. 'Now, I think it would be a good idea to check the wound and make sure it hasn't opened or got dirt in it.'

'It's fine.'

Henry pinched the bridge of his nose. 'Look. I'd prefer it if I could check it.'

'Well, I'd prefer it if people didn't say nasty things behind my back, but I guess neither of us are going to get what we want, are we?'

'Do you think we might move past that? I did apologise.'

'No. You didn't!'

He sucked in a deep breath and then let it out, the unexpectedly fit body tightening the fabric of the black T-shirt as he did so. 'I'm sure I did.'

'She's right, mate. You didn't. You just accused Willow of eavesdropping. That was it.'

Henry shot his brother a dark look. 'Thank you, George, for that clarification.'

'You're welcome.' His brother raised his coffee mug in reply.

'Willow, I'm sorry you overheard me speaking about you like that.'

George shook his head again, let out a sigh and took another slurp of coffee while I grabbed the wheelbarrow with renewed gusto and struggled to restrain myself from driving it straight into Henry's shins.

'Can you just bloody move?'

'What?' Henry threw up his hands.

'You're unbelievable.'

'I apologised! Now what's wrong?'

'You didn't bloody apologise!' I replied, slamming the barrow down with such force that it overturned entirely. 'Shit! Now look what's happened. As for you supposedly apologising, you didn't at all. This time you said you were sorry I overheard you, which is entirely different!'

'For God's sake, that's just semantics. You know what I meant.'

'For an intelligent man, it would seem you can be extremely dim at times! It's not semantics. It's rude and hurtful, two-faced and judgemental.'

Silence wrapped around us, thick and suffocating.

George burst the toxic bubble with his laughter as he put his mug down on the wall. We both spun to face him.

'She is absolutely the perfect neighbour for you!' he said with a grin, ambling down the path and out through the gate. He took the handles of the barrow I'd relinquished after righting and refilling it as I'd yelled at his brother. The truth was it really was bloody hurting my hand, but I wasn't about to show any weakness to Henry Darcy. 'Apparently he's supposed to be good-looking. Never seen it myself, but still. And of course, once they find out he's a consultant, well! It's really been quite sickening to watch women fawn over him. This, however, is perfect!'

Henry switched his glare to his sibling, his brow deeply furrowed as though etched in stone.

'I can assure you,' I said, addressing George, 'that there is absolutely zero chance of that happening here.'

'Good to hear!' he replied, laughing. 'Now, where's this lot going?'

'Through there.' I pointed to the side path. 'You'll see a couple of new raised beds part way down.'

'Right. Now, Willow, firstly you need to let Henry check your hand. And Henry, you need to apologise. Properly this time.' He gave him a meaningful look, then wheeled the barrow off, leaving us both standing there.

Henry cleared his throat.

I waited.

'I really am sorry that I said what I said. I didn't mean it how it sounded.'

'I don't see too many other ways of interpreting it.'

Henry looked down at his bare feet then back up at me.

'You're right. There is no excuse. It was rude and unkind and I don't have any defence for what I said, but I am, truly, sorry.'

His eyes remained on mine until I let out a sigh. 'Thank you.'

He gave a small shake of his head and the apology, now he'd calmed down, appeared genuine.

'Now, please would you let me check your wound?'

'Honestly, it's fine.' I reached for the spade and grimaced as I felt the wooden handle whack into my injury. Automatically releasing it with the pain, I felt myself overbalancing. Two muscled arms wrapped quickly around me and stopped me falling onto my backside on the pavement. Embarrassed, I wriggled out of them.

'Willow, please. You've got an open wound and have been digging about in soil. The last thing I want is for you to risk sepsis just because I was an unthinking arse!' His features were serious and the striking eyes were focused on me, concern writ large across his face.

'I've got gloves on,' I said, lifting my hands to show him, although my bravado was waning a little in the face of his worry. Didn't they say you should only worry if the doctor's worried? His mouth became a grim line as he looked down and I followed his eyeline. The plastic glove on my injured hand had a large split in it and the dressing he'd put on it was decidedly grubby. 'Oh.'

'Let me check it.' He looked down at me. 'Please?' he added.

I swallowed hard. I'd seen a programme about sepsis and how easily it could be missed and with what dire consequences. 'OK.' My voice felt small and suddenly my actions in the face of wounded pride seemed petty.

'I'm sure it's fine.' His voice was softer this time.

I looked up and he smiled. I could see just how good a bedside manner he must have.

'Honestly. It's just for peace of mind. But that dressing needs changing anyway.'

'I didn't think...'

'I know. And as I said, I'm sure everything is perfectly all right. You just need a clean dressing and to rest it again now, just until it heals.'

Henry gestured for me to go ahead of him into his house. I stopped and took off my trainers while he grabbed a towel and wiped his feet from where the soil had tipped out of the barrow onto them.

'Sorry about that.' I pulled a face.

'Don't worry. Probably the least I deserved. I know you were dying to ram that barrow into my shins and I wasn't entirely convinced you wouldn't.'

'Neither was I.' I sent a brief grin as I straightened, and he returned it.

'At least you're honest.'

I gave a shrug and, following his direction, headed into the kitchen.

'Just take a seat there and we'll give it a check.' He took my other hand, which was clenched in a fist. 'Try to relax.'

I flicked a glance at him before dropping it down to my lap again. The large, warm hand covered mine.

'I'm sorry I shouted at you and obviously frightened you. That wasn't good practice.'

I looked up at him from under my lashes. 'We don't really seem to bring out the best in each other, do we?'

'Maybe we could start again?'

'We tried that once. It doesn't appear to have worked.'

'Yes, well, that's my fault. Would you allow me another attempt? Third time lucky?'

I nodded.

'Thank you. Now let's have a look at this.'

11

His touch was gentle and I turned my head to look out of his bifold doors, which were open to the warmth of the spring morning.

'What are you planning to grow in all this soil then?'

'Um, I was planning on making them cut flower beds.'

'That sounds good. I can imagine you're a fan of having vases full of fresh flowers, and they're pretty expensive to buy. Much nicer to get them from your own garden, I'm sure.'

I could feel his fingers working gently, removing the dressing, cleaning the wound once more, all while he chatted away about something he knew I was interested in. A classic distraction technique, and I appreciated it more than he knew.

'Right, all done. Everything looks good. I've given it all a bit of a clean-up but the wound itself looked OK. But – and this is important – if you feel unwell at any time, anything that doesn't feel right, you call me, OK? It doesn't matter what time it is.'

I nodded and he covered my small hands with his.

'I mean it.'

I looked up to meet his intense gaze.

'I'm serious. Anything. OK? You have to promise.'

There was something in the way he said it. Almost a desperation that made me do just that.

'Thank you,' he replied. 'Now, did you have breakfast before you set out on your task this morning, or were you fuelled entirely by fury?'

'Fury alone, I'm afraid.'

'That's what I thought.' He glanced at the clock. Half past eight. 'And there was me thinking moving to the country meant a lie-in.'

I screwed up my nose. 'Sorry.'

The deep laugh was as smooth as melting chocolate. 'Not at all. There's something wonderful about sitting outside early here and just *being*.'

'Hmm, you'd better be careful with talk like that. People will think you've been spending too much time with me.'

He gave me a look. 'I'm not going to live that down, am I?'

'Ooh, not for a while yet.' The truth was, although I appreciated his apology and had no doubt that he genuinely meant it, parts of what I'd overheard still stung. I gave him a smile but he didn't return it. 'I'd better go and see how your brother's getting on. Has he eaten?'

Henry took a glance around. 'There's no bombsite in here, which means no.'

'You're quite different from each other, aren't you?'

'Only in the ways that don't matter. But truth be told, I wish I were more like him.' He'd stepped to the edge of the kitchen and was watching his brother empty another load of soil into the raised bed next door. 'I'd better get some food inside him.' He went to walk down his garden but I put a hand on his arm to stop him. He looked down at me and I raised a brow.

'Be my guest,' Henry said, reading the unspoken question.

I raised my fingers, let out a shrill two-tone whistle and George looked up and round.

'Breakfast!' Henry called.

George gave him a thumbs up, leapt the small fence between us and trudged up the garden, kicking off his trainers at the threshold.

'All good?' he asked, nodding at my hand as he washed his own.

'Yes, thanks.'

'When d'you learn how to whistle like that?' he asked, looking at Henry as he dried his hands.

Henry pointed to me.

'Really?'

I did a mini curtsey.

'A woman of constant surprises. That garden over there is amazing, by the way,' he said, taking a seat at the kitchen table. 'Really beautiful.'

'It's taken years but I enjoy doing it. But it's not for everyone. It takes almost constant work and not everybody has the time or inclination for that.'

George looked from me to Henry. 'You realise she's actually sticking up for you and your plastic monstrosity, don't you?'

Henry looked over at him from where he was cooking a delicious-smelling breakfast at the hob on the island.

'Yes, I got that, thank you.'

George grinned as he turned back to face me. 'Super bright in some areas but less so in others, so I find it best to check.'

Behind him, Henry was shaking his head, concentrating on his task, but his amusement and affection were impossible to hide.

'I'll leave you to your breakfast. Thank you both for what

you're doing today. And thank you for this.' I held up my hand as Henry looked up.

'Aren't you staying? There's more than enough for three.'

'Oh, no, I'm taking up way too much of your time today already.'

'Nonsense. Please?' Henry indicated the seat I'd just vacated.

I hesitated.

'Come on.' George gave a gentle tug on my good hand. 'He's got loads of making up to do after last night. Take advantage of it! He's actually not a bad cook, which is amazing considering he ate crap for decades.'

'Thank you for that,' his brother replied.

'Am I wrong?' George asked.

'No, but that's not the point.'

'It's exactly the point. Now, Willow, please stay, otherwise I'm stuck alone with his conversation.'

'Are you sure?' I asked Henry.

'Very,' he replied. His eyes crinkled at the corners just enough and I retook my seat.

*　*　*

By the end of the morning, the earth was all in its rightful place. George had collected an extra wheelbarrow from the brothers' parents on his way down and, once we'd all eaten, Henry had heaved that out of the car and the two had set to work. Although they'd flipped a coin for who got to use the family one and who continued using my bright pink version. Henry lost – or, as I chose to think, won – and had spent the next couple of hours filling and wheeling the Barbie-pink barrow to and from my back garden.

'Here, I can do that,' he said, holding out his hand as I walked to the patch of dirt where the earth had been piled first thing that morning, broom in hand.

'You've done more than enough.'

'I'm already sweaty. No point both of us getting that way.'

'Oh, I don't know,' George chuckled, coming up behind him, waggling his eyebrows.

'Grow up, muppet,' his brother replied, but it was obvious the chide was good-natured. Henry wrapped his hand around the broom handle but I held on.

'God, you really are stubborn,' he said, his words coming out on a laugh.

I let go. My neighbour was undoubtedly good-looking, but when he laughed it increased tenfold. I'd never been one for the mean and moody type. I was pretty patient, but I couldn't be arsed with all that. If you were mean and moody, I didn't have the energy for your drama, and if you were just pretending to be that way, that was even worse. But something about Henry Darcy intrigued me. I wasn't interested in him romantically, which was probably a relief on both sides, but there were clearly more layers to him than I'd first thought.

'Thank you,' he said, and began sweeping the remaining debris into a neat pile, which I then scooped up into a dustpan and tipped onto one of the front garden borders.

'I really must thank you both in some way for all your hard work.'

'There's no need,' Henry replied.

'Hang on,' George chimed in. 'Let's see what the offer is first.'

'I'm beginning to think perhaps doing this on my own might have been easier,' Henry said, sighing at his brother.

'But without George's peacekeeping duties, we might well still be stood here glaring at each other.'

Henry appeared to consider this for a moment. 'That is true.

OK, fair enough,' he said, half turning towards his brother. 'I'm glad you came.'

'Wow. I'm so overcome with emotion,' George said, his tone flat. 'I may have to sit down.'

'Can I take you both out to dinner?'

'That's not necessary.'

'I know, but still.'

'Perhaps another time. We've arranged to meet up with our parents on George's way home.'

'Willow could always come!' George put in.

'Oh, no! Thank you, but I've intruded enough on your family. As you say, perhaps another time.'

* * *

'So there's really no chance of getting together with him?' Abby asked as I propped up my phone on my dressing table and finished rubbing in my face moisturiser.

'No, I told you. We're far too different, but it's fine. Being neighbours that don't hate each other is good. It's great, actually, and definitely a vast improvement. I already feel less stressed about it all.'

'OK. But what about the brother? You said he seemed far more chilled than Dr Dishy.'

'Definitely, and he was nice-looking. They've obviously got good genes – but I didn't get any flutters.'

'So what now?' Abby asked as I screwed the lid back on my pot and placed it neatly on the silver fretwork tray that sat on my dressing table, corralling my skincare and perfume.

'I focus. I finished the vision board last night so that's now up on the wall in my office, and I'm popping over to the beach to drop into "Crystal Clear" this week, when I get a chance, to pick up a few extra crystals that are particularly powerful for romance. I'll see if there's anything else that might be useful while I'm there.'

'In for a penny, in for a pound, eh?'

I picked up the phone as I walked into my work room and shrugged at my bestie. 'I'm thirty-nine years old, Abs. I've had a failed marriage and I've tried all the conventional ways of meeting someone and I'm still single.'

She pulled a face. 'I know, and I have no idea why. I'd marry you.'

'Aww, thanks, lovey. Clearly not everyone has such good taste as you.'

'Clearly not.'

'I've got my home, a successful business and darling Spud. I know I should be grateful,' I said, plopping down in the comfy armchair next to the window, knowing my first task was some hand sewing on a teddy's muzzle. 'And I am. I don't need a man, I know that. But the truth is I want someone special. Someone to share my life with.'

'You deserve the best. Never settle for anything less, will you?'

'Nope. Been there, done that. Not doing it again. Oh, did I tell you the final stages of the divorce are in hand too? Mark decided he didn't fancy a trip to the country after all – a stag do to Ibiza took precedence – so we're going to do it over the phone this week.'

'Huh, shocker. Mark wanting to party rather than take time out for you.'

'It really doesn't matter. I knew he'd be bored down here within an hour, so it would have been a waste of both our time, really.'

'I suppose that's true. I'm just glad it's finally getting sorted now. Make sure it does!'

'I will. I didn't think it mattered that much, but maybe you were right. Maybe the universe thought I was still holding out for him, to revive my marriage.'

'It's definitely got the message now.'

'Let's hope so!'

'Good. Right, I can see you've got a lot of patients there, so I'll let you get on. Speak to you later.'

I hung up the phone, put it on the desk and picked up my first patient of the day. He'd recently had a muzzle reconstruction and was now well enough to regain his smile. Unwinding the black embroidery thread, I separated some strands and picked out a needle from the pincushion, held it up to the window for the best light and pushed the thread through the eye.

'Right, Charlie. Let's get you ready to go home with a big smile on your face.'

* * *

I stretched my back and made my way downstairs after making sure my last patient of the day was comfortable and headed into the kitchen to make a cup of tea. Spooning the dried Darjeeling leaves into the teapot, I poured on the water and watched through the glass walls of the pot as they drifted around while it brewed. A few minutes later, I was out in my garden, feeling the cool grass beneath my feet, tickling my toes, and sipping tea as I mooched. The late sun was warm and I wandered up the side to check on the progress of my front rose border. I'd treated myself to a couple of classic David Austin roses last year and they'd bloomed wonderfully, enabling me to save enough petals to add to soaps and lotions, and make some wonderfully fragrant rose water that reminded me of my nan, as well as drying some for tea. I'd been so eager for them to bloom again this year, remembering their scent greeting me each time I approached my house, drifting up in the day while I worked and at night on still, balmy air through the open windows.

I heard a car and looked up to see Henry slowing to pull up in front of the house. I moved to lean on the wall and waved as he got out.

'Evening,' he said, straightening from the car and closing the door with a solid thud, the lights flashing once as he locked it.

'Hello. Good day?'

'Not bad, thanks. You?'

'Busy. I've just finished and thought I'd bring my tea out here to unwind and check on my roses.'

'They're pretty spectacular.'

'Aren't they? I think I might cut a few to take inside. Would you like some?' I tilted my head. 'Or is that a bit too girly for you?'

'It's a generous offer, thank you, but I feel they'd be fighting rather a losing battle in bringing some sort of softness to my hard-edged aesthetic.'

I lifted a shell pink, velvety bloom to my nose and inhaled its musky scent. 'Let me know if you change your mind.'

'Thanks. I will. What are you up to tonight then? Feet up?' he asked.

'Yeah. I've been trying to start a new book I got weeks ago but haven't had a chance. It's such a nice evening. I think I'll take my dinner outside and start it with that.'

'Sounds like a good plan.'

'You?'

'I've got some paperwork to look through, and George has told me about some documentary on Netflix he recommends, so I might take a look at that.' He paused. 'Although I—'

Music blaring through the open windows of a car pulling up in front of my house drew the attention of both of us. The engine was turned off and the sound cut abruptly. Henry looked over at me. I shrugged. The door to the car opened and out stepped a man, a wide grin on his face as he caught sight of me.

'Hi, honey, I'm home!'

'Mark?' I said, staring at him in shock. 'What are you doing here?'

Mark glanced over at Henry, then back at me. 'Willow, darling. Is that any way to greet your husband?'

'Ex-husband,' I reminded him as I opened the gate.

Mark looked at me. 'Not yet.' He gave Henry another glance. 'Aren't you going to introduce us?'

'Mark, this is Henry Darcy, my neighbour. He's a consultant up at the clinic. Henry, this is my soon-to-be ex-husband, Mark Haines.'

'Nice to meet you.' Mark put out his hand and Henry took it.

'And you,' Henry replied, although the tension that had drifted back into his face suggested otherwise. I imagined Mark with his blaring music was exactly what he didn't need, having moved here for peace and quiet.

'I guess I could be seeing more of you soon.'

Henry and I both frowned. 'Sorry?' he asked.

Mark turned towards me. 'You know, the whole divorce thing?'

'Yeeeeees?' I replied, wary now.

'Well, I was thinking, what if we don't?'

From the corner of my eye, I caught Henry's head turn sharply.

'Don't what, exactly, Mark?'

'Get divorced.'

I stared at him before being jolted back to the moment by a throat-clear.

'It was nice to see you, Willow.' Henry's eyes met mine then he turned and began striding up his front path.

My mouth opened and closed but no sound came out, the shock of Mark's words still bouncing around my brain. By the time I was able to form words, Henry's door was already closing. I turned back to face my husband.

'You'd better come in.'

12

_____

'So, I was thinking how about we just stay married and give it another go?'

We were sitting at my kitchen table, eating fish and chips from the paper while Mark told me his plan.

'What do you think?'

'I think the answer is no.'

He dropped the chip he'd been holding. 'Really?'

It was hard not to laugh. 'Yes. Really.'

'Why?'

'Because we've been there and done that, Mark. You've only been here a couple of hours and have already asked me twice how I can bear it being so quiet.'

'It's just a question.'

I laid my hand on his arm as he picked the chip back up and popped it in his mouth. 'I know. But the fact that you've asked it twice not only shows you don't know me any more, but also that you could never be happy here. The quiet is what fuels me. What fills me with joy every day.'

'You sure that's the only thing?' he asked.

I picked up another perfect chip. Fluffy on the inside, crunchy on the outside with just the right amount of salt and vinegar. It was ages since I'd been to the chippy and I'd forgotten how perfect they were. 'What's that supposed to mean?'

'Nothing to do with your neighbour?'

I chewed the chip and made shooshing motions with my hands, pointing at the open French doors. I had no idea whether Henry was on his patio, but even with the doors open which, bearing in mind the warmth, was likely, it was easy for voices to travel.

Mark shrugged.

'No, definitely not,' I replied back in a whisper.

'Seemed pretty friendly when I was driving up.'

'And that's all it is. Believe me, it's amazing we're even that. Henry and I have got even less in common than you and me!'

Mark went back to his dinner.

'What's brought all this on, anyway? It's been eight years.'

'I miss you.'

'Do you, though?'

He looked round. 'Yes.'

'But not as a wife.'

Mark let out a sigh then took a swig of the beer he'd picked up in the off licence next to the chippy while I was waiting. 'Everyone's married or with someone, settled down.'

'And?'

'I don't know. I guess I started thinking if I should be too.'

I leant my head on his shoulder and he touched his head to mine. 'Not really the best reason to get back together, though, is it?'

'I suppose not.' He lifted his head and I looked across at him. 'I do miss you, though.'

'I know. I miss you too. You're always welcome here, you

know. I haven't invited you because I had a feeling you'd be bored within half an hour.'

'There's not a lot to do here, is there?'

'There is, but that depends on what you're looking for.'

'Silence?' He jumped back in his seat as a bumblebee lazily buzzed through the open doors, had a nose around and then flew back out again. 'Correction. Silence and mutant bees!'

'It wasn't mutant,' I said, laughing and pulling him gently back towards the table.

'Did you see it? It was massive! I'm sure it had engines. Probably on its way to Heathrow!'

Mark downed the rest of the beer then looked around, his eyes taking in the cottagecore vibe of the place, the full borders in the garden spilling over onto the lawn, Spud curled up on the floor, snoring softly as he sunbathed. His gaze landed back on me, my face bare of make-up as it usually was, unlike when I'd lived in London, my feet also bare, resting on the chair next to me.

'It suits you here. You've built yourself a good life.'

'Thanks. I'm trying.'

'Are you happy?'

'Yes.' It was the truth. I was happy. Even if it still felt like there was something missing, I knew, as much as I cared for him, that it wasn't the man sitting in front of me. 'I want you to be happy too but I'm not the answer.'

'No. I suppose not.' He took my hand and kissed it. 'Shame, though.'

'Yeah.' I curled my fingers around his. 'But you'll find the right answer soon.'

'You think?'

'I do. Maybe you just need to take some time and decide exactly what it is you want.'

'I was thinking of taking a sabbatical from work. Finally getting to New Zealand.'

'You should! You've wanted to go there as long as I've known you.'

'Yeah.' He looked up. 'You know what, I think I will.'

'You do know New Zealand is famed for its landscape, not its nightclubs, though, right?'

'Ha ha.'

I'd only been half joking.

'I suppose you'd like me to sign those papers then.'

'You have them with you?'

'They've been in my car boot for about the last two years.'

'Why?'

'I was decluttering some paperwork from the flat.'

'You do know decluttering doesn't just mean moving it from your house to the car, don't you?'

He made a gentle flapping motion with his hands. 'Baby steps, baby steps!'

I dropped my feet to the ground and pushed my chair back. 'You go and get the papers. I'll get the champagne.'

'Champagne?' He put a hand to his chest. 'I'm hurt.'

Laughing, I wrapped him in a hug, his arms automatically folding around me. 'No, you're not.' I leant back a little so I could see his face. 'I reckon this is exactly what we both need. Cut those final threads that are holding us together.'

'Let's be better friends than we were husband and wife. Deal?'

'Deal.'

Half an hour later the papers were signed and ready to be returned to the solicitor. The pop of the champagne cork resonated in the evening air as the sun set, its colours smudged across the sky, violet, red and orange mixing together as the fiery ball balanced on the horizon.

'To us!' Mark toasted.

'To us and new starts!'

Bubbles tickled my nose and fizzed on my tongue as I took a sip. I tilted my head back and looked up, way up, then closed my eyes.

I've done it. The last thread has been cut. I'm free now, universe. Open and free to love…

* * *

Despite my plan to get to the beach and gather additional manifesting supplies, now that I was truly ready and raring to go, the next few weeks passed in a blur of work. I'd managed a glance at my relationship vision board each morning but that was about the extent of it. I'd been working longer hours than I had originally envisioned, but the waiting list for patients never seemed to wane.

I was, of course, thankful for the work but I hated to keep people waiting. Many of my patients were special friends, comfort in good times and bad. Others were a connection to a person who might no longer be around, and those were just as important. I was starting earlier and working later just to try to keep up. Despite planning to pop down to the coast as I'd said, it had been over a month since my conversation with Abby and I still hadn't been. In fact, I'd barely left the house apart from a quick slug hunt at night and the odd carrot feeding to the animals at the bottom of the garden. The cut flower beds sat untouched and each time I saw them, I felt a mix of emotions including guilt for the effort that Henry and his brother had put in to get them ready for me.

That night, looking down at them once more from where I

was yanking slugs off my hostas, I let out a sigh and sank down on one of the bistro chairs on my patio.

'That sounded like a heartfelt sigh.' The deep voice drifted on the still evening air from the other side of the fence.

'Oh.' I gave an embarrassed laugh. 'Sorry. I didn't know you were out there.'

'Not a problem. Is everything all right?'

'Yes, sorry.'

'Stop apologising.'

I heard a chair scrape and moments later a serious-looking face peered over the top of the fence. 'Am I interrupting?' The strong features were lit by the bright moon hanging languidly in the clear sky above us.

I flipped a snail I'd missed initially into the bucket and put the lid on it. 'No, not at all. I think that's the last one.'

'Many tonight?'

'No, not really,' I replied as I pulled off my gloves. 'The frogs, newts and birds are doing their job, plus the hedgehogs are out of hibernation so I could really just leave it to nature. Sometimes I think I use it as an excuse to come out here and say hello to the garden.'

'Do you need an excuse?' He tilted his head a little and the moonbeams contoured the sharp cheekbones better than any Kardashian ever could.

I plopped my chin onto my hands and rested my elbows on the bistro table. 'No, not really. I've just been pretty busy lately and I suppose I feel a bit guilty when I'm out here instead of inside working.'

'I haven't seen you lately. I did wonder if it was something I'd said or done, as we both know that's entirely possible.'

The laughter was a release, and I felt the tension in my shoulders lessen just that little bit.

'You're right, it is entirely possible, but not this time.'

He mock wiped his brow and I giggled again.

'How are things at the clinic?'

'Good, thanks. I'm really enjoying it. I love—' He stopped suddenly and I straightened. 'Look, would you like to come round for a glass of wine? Or hot chocolate? Or... something? Standing here peering over the fence into the dark seems a little... awkward.'

'I didn't mean to interrupt your peace.'

'You didn't. In fact, I've been wondering about knocking on the door for the past week or so as I hadn't seen you in the garden or around in the village and was beginning to worry.'

'Worry?'

'Yes.'

'Oh.'

'So, want to pop round? But only if you're not too tired. I certainly don't want to compound things with my attempt at being neighbourly.'

'That would be lovely. Thank you.' I stood up. 'I'll just go and get some shoes and come round the front, shall I?'

Henry shook his head then disappeared. Moments later, he reappeared two panels down, where the fence dropped to waist height.

'Just hop over here.'

'What?' I said, laughing as I moved closer to him. In all the time I'd spent next door before Edie finally left, I'd never once not gone via the front door, nor had it occurred to me not to.

'Come on. There's a bottle of very good white getting warm over here.'

'What about Spud?' I asked, looking down at where he was standing, next to the three-bar fence with its stock wire lining to stop him getting out.

Henry leant over the fence, scooped up my dog and lifted him up and over, Spud delightedly wriggling in his arms and snuggling into his collarbone. 'Yes, yes, you're very welcome too.' He looked back over at me. 'Friendly.'

'Very,' I said as he put Spud back down, the dog immediately shooting off to hurtle around the new space and see what sniffs he could find.

'Right then,' I said, hoiking a chunk of the fabric of my long skirt into the elastic of my knickers so I could see my feet better. I placed my left foot on the bottom bar, my hands gripping the top one.

'Here,' Henry said, holding out his hand.

I took it and felt its strength as I took another step up and wobbled a little. My other hand gripped his arm. 'I'm a little out of practice in clambering over fences!'

'May I?'

I met his eyes, not quite understanding until he leant a little closer and moved his hands to my waist. With minimal effort, I was lifted over the fence and placed gently down onto the plastic grass that butted up against the fence on my neighbour's side.

I looked up at Henry and he gave a shrug. 'Quickest route.'

'Apparently so,' I replied, grinning as I pulled my skirt out of my pants. The smile turned to horror as I caught sight of Spud watering a corner of the garden. 'Spud!' I called, running over.

He gave me a quick look over his shoulder and finished his task.

'Naughty boy!' I used my best 'I'm cross with you' voice and stayed strong, ignoring the big brown puppy eyes he looked up at me with as his head sank low into his shoulders. I scooped him up and carried him back to where Henry was watching us from under a darkly rumpled brow. 'I'm so sorry,' I called over. 'I should have checked whether he needed one before we came over.'

'Right.'

'I can't think what he was scenting as it's not like there can be much nature in here.'

Henry tilted his head a little.

'Sorry. I'm making it worse, aren't I? Look, do you have a watering can? No, of course you don't. I'll nip back and get one and wash the grass—'

Henry laid his hands on my shoulders. 'In my professional capacity as a doctor, I'd first advise you to take a breath.'

I did as he said. And then took another. 'You're right. That does help.'

'It usually does.'

'I'll go and get...'

He shook his head. 'You're absolutely right. Not having one single living thing in this garden, the need for a watering can is pretty minimal. I do, however, have a jug that I can put water in, which I'm guessing will do much the same task.'

'Oh. Right. Yes, of course. But I'll do it.'

'No.' He shook his head. 'You won't. You're a guest.'

'But it was my dog.'

'I may not be a dog person...'

Taking advantage of the pause, I covered Spud's ears and received that quizzical look once more.

'You'll hurt his feelings,' I whispered.

'Obviously I wouldn't want to do that.'

I searched his face for the sarcasm. A glint of a smile hovered around his lips but the initial impatient look I'd experienced so often in the early days of him moving to the village was no longer there.

'What I was going to say was that although—' he mouthed 'dogs' '—are not my thing, I know they have a predilection to scent mark as he's just done. And,' he continued as I made to reply, 'I also know he's exceedingly well behaved. I've lived here long enough now to suss out whether I'm living next door to a menace or not.'

'Are you still talking about Spud?'

'That I will leave up to you to decide.'

'Very funny.'

'Not my forte but I'm trying.'

'You do better than you think.'

He tilted his head towards me in a tiny bow. 'That's very kind of you to say, but I know where my skills lie.'

'And that is?'

'My work.' He held out his hand and indicated for us to walk up the garden towards the house.

'But you must have something outside of work? Something you do to relax?'

Henry appeared to be thinking.

'Golf?' I suggested.

He pulled a face. 'Never once seen the point of hitting a small ball with a stick and following it round for miles.'

'But have you tried it?' I asked, laughing at his description.

'Yes. Once. And, believe me, once was enough.' He stopped suddenly and turned to me. 'Don't tell me, you're an expert golfer and I've now managed to insult you on yet another level.'

'Nope, not me. Finally we agree on something. Not my thing either. My ex liked to play so I did try it once, like you, but I was bored rigid. The only good thing I could see about it was the buggies, but I got banned from the course for taking one for a drive.'

Henry let out a short bark of laughter and both Spud and I

looked up at him. He was handsome when serious, but when he smiled? Well, hello, Major Hot!

'They banned you?'

'Yep. Excessive, right? Not that I had any inclination to go back anyway.'

'It does seem a bit much.'

'Yeah, apparently hooning up and down a fairway and racing the buggy along to get it to lift off the ground over humps is seriously frowned upon.'

He was really laughing now and I couldn't help but join him. 'That sounds like the best day out ever at a golf course to me.'

'See? I thought so too. Unfortunately they didn't agree and I got ejected. I'd had a lovely time but my husband was furious.'

'Is that why it's now ex-husband?'

'No, although I don't think he spoke to me for two whole days.'

'Seriously? Over a stupid golf club? Did he not know who you were when he married you?'

I turned and looked down the garden towards the paddock, where the moon lit the tops of the trees and glittered on the surface of the millpond. 'I guess not. To be honest, I'm not sure I knew who I was when I married him.'

'So, you are actually divorced now? I wasn't sure after—' As soon as he'd spoken, he held up his hands. 'Sorry, that's none of my business.'

'It's fine. And yes, we are. Or at least we've signed the papers. Finally, after eight years of dallying.'

He'd taken a step towards the house but at this he stopped and turned.

'You were unsure, too, then?'

'No. We both knew it was the right decision really. Mark was just having a moment when he came down here. He's taken a break from work and is about to go off travelling in New Zealand. I think that's what he needed. Not me. We'd just never got round to the filing, but I suppose neither of us had a reason and things weren't acrimonious, so it just drifted on. But it's done now.'

'Any particular reason you wanted to get it done now after all this time?'

'Yes, actually. I'm manifesting a new, successful relationship. At least that's the plan. Work has taken over a bit the last few weeks.'

Henry appeared to ponder this for a beat then headed inside, only to appear moments later with a large jug of water. I reached to take the jug and he lifted it up to a point where I couldn't reach it.

'That's cheating.'

With a flick of his eyebrows, he wandered down to where my dog had watered his fake grass. He emptied the jug and walked back up.

'I'll reimburse you if it dies, obviously,' I said as he approached the patio.

'I should hope so. It takes me hours to get it looking like this every day. Now, please, take a seat and stop fretting about it. So, what can I get you? I've got some wine and whiskey. And obviously tea and coffee. Ahh...' He slapped a hand to his head. 'But not herbal tea. Damn. Sorry.'

'That's OK. I do drink other things. And actually a whiskey sounds great.'

'Coming up.' He turned momentarily. 'I have to say, I definitely didn't have you down as a whiskey girl.'

'Ah, well, it's nice to not be predictable all of the time.'

'Predictable is definitely not something I'd had you down as either.'

He crossed the threshold, through the open bifold doors, into the light, bright kitchen. I got up and followed him in, stepping onto the cool limestone tiles and walking across to the one piece of art in the kitchen, the splash of paint providing the only colour amongst the sleek grey cabinets and stainless-steel worktops.

'You hate it, don't you?'

'What?'

He pointed with his glass towards the painting as he handed me the other with its golden liquid colouring the bottom of the crystal, ice cubes clanking against the sides.

'Not at all. *Sláinte*,' I said, tapping his glass with mine.

'Ah, and now perhaps there's a clue where the whiskey lover comes from.'

'Maybe indeed.'

'So, I'm guessing you want the full tour?'

'It'd be rude not to, now you've offered.'

'Of course it would,' he replied, looking down at me with a patient expression and a smile in his eyes.

'You like cooking then, with all this cheffy stainless steel? Your breakfast was certainly yummy.' I rested my hand on the cold counter and quickly removed it.

'Yeah, I do enjoy it but don't get a lot of time to do it. At least I didn't before I moved here.'

'But you do now?'

'Yes. It's taking a while to get used to that, though. Old habits can be hard to break.'

'I'm sure. I can see how that could be difficult after years of not being able to.'

'Try decades.'

'At least it's all here when you're ready.'

'That's true. Do you want to see upstairs?'

'Obviously.'

Henry led the way.

13

'It's lovely,' I said tactfully when the tour ended and we stepped back out onto the patio and took our seats at the table that Spud was still snoozing contentedly underneath.

Henry topped up our drinks then placed the bottle back on the table. It was an expensive Irish brand, so smooth I could imagine it would be far too easy to drink too much of it. 'You really are an awful liar. Has anyone ever told you that?'

'Thank you. Yes, several times. But more tactfully. But then you're probably one of the bluntest people I've met.'

'It's hard to change who you are.'

'But is that really you?'

'It would appear so,' Henry replied.

'I'm not so sure.'

He pulled his gaze back from the garden to meet mine, then slowly took another sip of whiskey. 'Oh, this is going to be interesting.'

I took up the challenge. 'As you said,' I began, 'it's not so easy to change who you are and, from what I've heard and my own experience, when you're "on duty", you're patient and kind and emit an aura of peace that gives your patients utter confidence in you.'

'I wasn't aware I had an aura.'

'Everyone has an aura.' I motioned with my glass. 'But that's not the point. My point is that you can't put on an entirely separate personality each time you put on your doctor's coat.'

'I don't have a doctor's coat.'

I put my glass down. 'Henry. You're focusing on all the wrong things here.'

'I don't know what you mean.' He took another sip, the green eyes flickering with amusement over the rim of his glass.

I crossed my arms.

Henry put his own glass down. 'So you're saying I might actually be a nice guy?'

'I wouldn't go that far.' I was desperately trying to hold on to the snooty look but failing miserably.

There was that smile. Wow. It was lucky I'd already built up an immunity to Dr Darcy because, otherwise, this could have been a very different situation.

'Like I said, you're a terrible liar.'

I shrugged. 'There are worse things to be bad at.'

'Very true. In fact, it's one of the qualities I admire about you.'

'It is?'

'It is.'

I waited for him to say something else.

'So what's going on with you that you've barely been seen in the village, causing me to wonder if you were flat out on the kitchen floor being eaten by your dog?'

'Such a charmer.'

'I try.'

'Ha. I don't think you do, but still. It's just work. I've got more than I can handle at the moment, but I can't really say no.'

'Of course you can. It's a short word.'

'Says the overworked surgeon.'

'Aha! No longer. And I'm not the one who's struggling to keep her eyes open.'

'I'm not!' Not exactly, anyway, although my bed was definitely calling.

'Near enough. Besides, we're not talking about me.'

'No, I noticed that. Nice deflection.'

'It's not a deflection. I'm interested. What is it that you do anyway?'

'I run a hospital.'

He sat up a little more. 'You do? Which one? Would I know it?'

'Unlikely. I run it from my home.'

The dark brows knitted so deeply they were practically a monobrow.

'Do you have your phone?' I held out my hand.

Henry removed his phone from a back pocket, unlocked it and handed it over. Interestingly, all without question, which wasn't what I was expecting. This man had more layers than a Spanish onion.

I opened the Internet, typed in my website address and waited for it to load before handing the device back to him.

'"Willow's Hospital for Teddy Bears and Poorly Dollies",' he read out, then looked back at me. 'This is it?

'Yes. That's it,' I replied, doing my best not to bristle. Apparently unsuccessfully.

'Sorry, I didn't mean it like that. I'm just...' He ran a hand through his hair and gave a couple of quick scratches. 'I'm just surprised that it can keep you that busy.'

'It does.'

'I'm not doubting it. It was obvious from the moment I saw

you this evening.'

'Meaning?'

'Willow.' He let out a huff of air through his nose that was almost, but not quite, a laugh. 'You look exhausted. I asked you over because I was worried you were going to start working on something that you don't have the energy for.'

'Ah, I knew there must be a reason.'

'Also, believe it or not, I'm attempting to be neighbourly. And desperately trying not to cock it up this time.'

'You have been neighbourly. You and George shifted all the earth for me. I just feel guilty I haven't had a chance to plant it up yet.'

'Is it too late?'

'Now?'

'No!' The laugh this time was relaxed and hearty. 'Now is definitely too late. I meant in the year.'

'Oh. No. I just planned to be a bit more ahead of where I am at the moment.'

'Man, or woman, plans, God laughs. Isn't that what they say?'

'They do and they're right.'

'I'm sure you'll get there. And, if there's anything I can do, just shout.'

'Thanks.'

'As you can see,' he said, indicating his garden with a grand sweep of his arm, 'I am a gardener extraordinaire. There is nothing I don't know about planting and maintaining... stuff.'

'Thanks,' I replied through my laughter. 'I'll bear that in mind.'

'Tell me about this hospital, then. How did you get into that? I have to admit I didn't even know it was a thing.'

'It all came about by accident really. Before Abby's cake business took off, she was a primary school teacher and there was an incident with a bear. My nan taught me to sew when I was little, and the child's mum couldn't, so I said I'd have a look. I managed to put him back together again and word spread through the village.'

'I've noticed that happens a lot around here.'

I laughed. 'It does. But this time it was a good thing. It turned out there were a lot of teddies and dolls waiting patiently for a bit of love and attention. Or rather just the attention. The most usual case I see is that the toy has been loved to bits.'

'That's your official diagnosis?'

'It is. I have patient records, so I could show you, but they are confidential. However, being a doctor, I think you could be trusted.'

'I appreciate the compliment but I'm happy to take your word for it. Do you really have patient records?'

'Yep. Treating each toy as you would a living creature is important to me. It takes a lot to hand over something that precious to a stranger. I do everything I can to reassure them that their furry friend is in good hands and will be well cared for.'

Henry smiled at me. 'I'm pretty sure the moment they start talking to you, they'll know that. It comes across in how you talk about it all.'

'Thank you. That's lovely to hear.'

'What sort of things do you do? Is it sewing heads back on and so on?'

'Sometimes, and limb reattachments, but there's also restuffing if someone has been well loved and gone a bit flat. Older bears can need restringing, and occasionally there's the need for fur or skin grafts.'

'George had one that was almost completely bald. What would you have done with that?'

'It depends. I can try and match fur, but if it's a case of

entirely recovering something, it can feel like it isn't the same toy any more, so I'll discuss it with the owner and go from there. A good bath and plumping up can do wonders.'

'Do they just go in the washing machine?'

I gave a gasp and Henry laughed.

'I'm assuming that's a no.'

'No. Even if a toy says machine washable, it's not ideal. The filling can clump together and go lumpy. It's best to wash them gently by hand if possible. If it's a newer bear, and he or she has come in for a restuff, I'll take out the stuffing and then give the outer a gentle hand wash and dry it naturally before refilling it with new stuffing to the desired level of the owner.'

'Meaning?'

'Some arrive more floppy than others, and depending on the owner, they may want their bears to stay that way while others may want them fed up a bit so they are more like when they were new.'

'I see.' Henry was leaning forward, one long leg crossed at right angles over the other, his elbow resting on his knee, chin resting on his hand. 'What about really old ones? Have you had any of those?'

'A few, yes. They're the ones that generally need restringing and they can't be washed in the same way, so I'll just surface clean those as well as possible.'

'And then you post them back?'

'Sometimes. Although it's always a tracked package. Some people won't post them at all and will come in person. I get that. Even tracked parcels can get lost. Quite a few have electronic tags in them so that the owner can track their progress regularly, and I'll return those with them so they can monitor their friend's return.'

'Their friend,' he repeated.

'Yes.' I waited for the comment, the slight dig. It wouldn't be the first time.

'That's a lovely way of putting it.'

I swallowed hard and smiled. 'It's the best word for them.'

He nodded. 'George lost his one day and was absolutely distraught. It was like he lost a friend.'

'Oh, no! What happened?'

Henry huffed out a laugh. 'I spent the next two days tracking back over the places we'd played and asking everyone I saw if they'd seen a ratty old Pooh Bear anywhere.'

'And?' I said, now perched on the edge of my seat.

'I finally found him wedged behind a bench near a sand dune that we'd been clambering over. He must have fallen out of the rucksack and then got stuck down the back of the seat. Probably just as well, really, because he was at least out of sight. He was in a bit of a state but at least I could take him home.' He paused and wrinkled his nose. 'I hate to say that Mum put him in the washing machine, though.'

'Don't worry,' I said, with a laugh. 'I'm not going to report her. That was lovely of you to put so much effort into finding your brother's bear. He's very lucky.'

'I couldn't stand looking at his miserable face any more, so probably not as altruistic as you think.'

I sat back and crossed my arms. 'I don't believe you. I think, under all that bluff, you're actually a bit of a softie. Just like George's Pooh Bear.'

Henry leant over and swiped my glass from in front of me. 'I think you've had plenty of that. You're beginning to talk nonsense.'

I swiped it back. 'Don't worry. I won't tell anyone.'

'Good.'

A couple more minutes of comfortable silence passed until I

leant on the table and rested my chin on my hands. 'Can I ask something?'

He acknowledged and assented with a slow blink.

'What's all this about? The garden, I mean.'

'The fake garden, you mean?'

'Yes. I get that you're not into gardening, but still.'

'Honestly?'

'Ideally.'

Henry sucked in a big breath and let it out slowly. 'Absolute, total overwhelm.'

'In what way?'

He blew out another breath. 'I had this romanticised idea of moving to the country, getting away from London, doing up a place and just having a better quality of life.'

'Sounds good so far.'

'Yeah, sounding good was the problem.'

'You hadn't counted on a nightmare neighbour whose grasp on reality was tenuous at best?'

Henry let out a groan. 'You're not going to let me forget that, are you?'

'Hmm. Depends on how nice you are to me.'

'Fair enough. But no, that wasn't a factor. At least not immediately.'

I suddenly felt guilty for the tease. I'd never meant to make him feel unwelcome.

'Honestly, if I'd have had your knowledge of plants and stuff, I'd love to have tamed what was there, but by that point the noise and upheaval of having the house redone was getting to me. I'd moved here for peace and quiet and I was living in a building site. In hindsight, I should have had it all done before I moved, but you know what it's like when you have momentum.'

'Yeah, I do. Was there nowhere you could have stayed? A hotel or a friend or relative?'

'Probably all of the above but all I wanted at the time was to decompress. I didn't want to interact with anyone, other than the least amount that I could get away with. Also I didn't actually mention the fact it was bothering me to my brother or parents.'

'Why not?'

'Because they would have been down here like a shot.'

I swallowed at the sudden lump in my throat. 'That sounds lovely.'

'It is, and I'm totally aware I sound like an ungrateful git, but... I don't know how to explain it well. I just needed to be by myself. Even though every last nerve I had was frayed and on edge.'

'I'm so sorry. I feel like a total shit now.'

'Don't be silly. I should have introduced myself when I got here. Told you what was happening and, of course, warned you about the noise. It was driving me round the bend, so I know it was as bad for you. Especially now I know you work from home so couldn't get away from it either.'

'It's done now.'

'Yes, thank God. But then, every time I looked out the window there was this absolute wilderness. I didn't have a clue where to start. I know I could have got in a landscaper, had it done properly, but by that point I was at my wits' end and I just wanted it all to stop. Stripping it out and putting the fake stuff down was the quickest option. I didn't even pause to consider that it was no good for nature or anything like that.'

'Sounds like you had enough going on up there to think about.' I tapped the side of my head.

'I guess.'

'So. Now that it's all done, are you finding the serenity you hoped for when you moved here?'

There was another sigh as he sat back in the chair, long legs stretching out in front of him. 'Slowly. I think I am, yeah.'

'That's wonderful.'

'And what about you?'

'What about me?'

'What are we going to do about getting you a better work–life balance?'

'We?'

'Oh, yeah. You're stuck with me now. Don't you know when someone's dog wees on your plastic grass, it bonds you for life?'

'For life?'

Henry let out another burst of laughter. 'Don't sound quite so horrified! It was just a joke.'

'I'm not,' I replied, joining him in his laughter.

'You could have fooled me. What are you doing tomorrow? And don't say work.'

'No, I was actually going to take a day off tomorrow.'

'First in how long?'

'Kind of a month.'

'Kind of?'

I met his eyes.

'That's what I thought. I'm going down to the beach to see if I can remember how to surf. Want to come?'

'Surfing? Thanks, but God, no. The water's far too cold.'

'Rubbish. It's positively balmy. But I meant perhaps you and Spud could have a walk on the beach and then you could show me around a bit. Only if you don't have plans, of course. Sorry, I should have led with that.'

'I don't have plans, no. And only if you're sure you don't mind driving?'

'Not at all. Saves lugging the surf gear about, and I'm going there anyway so...' He turned his palms up. 'Maybe some fresh sea air is just what you need?'

'I think you might be right. Do you have your own stuff or are you hiring from Vijay?'

'Yeah, I was going to hire a board from a place on the beach I looked up. Is that him? I sold mine ages ago as I never used it. Still got the wetsuit, though, luckily.'

Images of Henry in a wetsuit drifted unbidden into my mind. I quickly elbowed them out.

'It does sound wonderful. I can introduce you to Vijay properly too.'

'You know him?'

'Yes. We went to primary school together. He actually trained as a doctor but chucked it all in to run a surf business, much to his parents' disgust.'

'Is he happier doing that, though?'

'Oh, God, yes. The Beach Hut is just one aspect. There's an online shop and I think he's got other investments too. I think that's what pays the bills. He's chilled but sharp as a tack.'

'How do his parents feel about it all now?'

'Still not thrilled. As far as they can see, he spends his days lounging on the beach. But he has two luxury holidays a year and drives a latest-model Range Rover, so he's not doing too badly, and I think by this point it's more of a habit of giving him grief about it than any meaningful criticism. He's lovely, though. You'll like him.'

'So you're coming?'

'It sounds great, thanks. What do you think, Spuddy?' I asked, bending down. Spud opened one eye then closed it again. I sat back up. 'He'll definitely be more enthusiastic about it in the morning. My friend took him out for me today when he did his run, and although Spud thoroughly enjoyed it, he's a little pooped. But just wait until he gets there tomorrow. He does a little dance every time his paws touch the sand the first time. It's enormously cute.'

Henry gave an 'Oh, OK' kind of chin lift and I had to remember that he wasn't a dog person, so the cuteness was probably lost on him.

14

———————

'This is nice,' I said, looking around the patio he'd had built. 'The slabs are gorgeous.' I tapped one with my bare toes.

'They should be. Shipped from Italy. The latest thing, apparently.'

'Oh. I didn't have you pegged as a "latest thing" type.'

'I'm not really. The builders persuaded me and by that point I just wanted it all done and finished and peace restored. They could have sold me anything, to be honest. But I do like them.'

'Luckily.'

'Luckily,' he repeated with a faint smile. 'Even if I hadn't, I'd have kept them. I need to walk on them every day for the next twenty-five years to get my money's worth.'

I did a little sitting down run on the spot. 'There you go, a few more steps to add in.'

'Thanks.' The smile appeared to be showing a little easier now.

'So you're planning to stay for a while then?'

'I have to now I've had this lot laid!'

'True. And if you hadn't?'

Henry inhaled deeply and rested his head back on the chair. 'I can't say it's been the easiest transition, and I've certainly had some romantic notions about living in the country dispelled, but in answer to your question, yes. Even without the eye-wateringly expensive Italian stone apparently crafted by fairies, I'm pretty sure I would.' He leant forward and topped up my glass.

'Thanks.'

'What?' he asked, placing the bottle back on the table.

'What?'

'Willow, never play poker. Or at least don't bet anything of value. At a wild guess, I'm going to assume you didn't have me pegged as someone who'd have romantic notions about moving here?'

'Or anything, to be honest.'

'Ouch.'

'Sorry.' I pulled a face. 'I didn't mean that quite how it sounded.' I paused and made a winding motion beside my head with my finger. 'Now I hear it back it doesn't sound great.'

'It's fine.' He waved a hand. 'You're right, I'm not the romantic type so I can assure you I was just as surprised as you to find I had any such ideas. But as I say, they've pretty much had a baseball bat taken to them.'

'What were they?' I asked, filing away the fact he'd dismissed being the romantic type as another reason he definitely hadn't been conjured up by the universe for me.

He rubbed his jaw, darkened with a day's growth. 'OK, so firstly I didn't know I'd be living next door to a donkey who likes to make himself known at odd intervals during the day.'

'He's growing on you, I can tell.'

'Hmm, the jury's still out on that one.'

'What else?'

'That I'd have the same level of anonymity but just in a quieter setting.'

'Where on earth did you get that idea from?'

'No clue. My own head, I think. Having never lived anywhere where people know their neighbours or are remotely interested in them, I guess I superimposed that over a different location.'

'I can imagine that that's been a bit tricky to negotiate. But you're new to the village, a surgeon and apparently single so, sorry, but you're probably going to be of interest to the gossip mill for some time yet.'

'Excellent,' he replied, his voice monotone.

'Anything else?'

'Not that I can think of.'

'Is there anything you've been pleasantly surprised about?'

He took a sip as he pondered. 'Weirdly, the same things as above.'

'Really?'

'Yeah, I know. It's hard to explain. I mean, obviously I'd rather not be the focus of village gossip, but apart from that... It's actually nice that people ask how you're settling in, how things are going and so on, and seem to actually mean it.'

'They do mean it.'

'It's nice. Different, but good.'

'And Pepper?'

'He's growing on me.'

'I knew it!' I said, punching the air.

Henry let out a laugh. 'So,' he asked. 'You said you lived in London but you seem to know a lot of people from school here. What's the story with that?'

'I was brought up here by my nan. My mother had me really young, my father wasn't interested so he took off as soon as he found out she was pregnant. She wasn't really interested either.

She felt she had a life to live and then I arrived. Thankfully Nan took over and Mum never looked back.'

'You don't have any contact with her?'

'Nope. She could find me if she wanted to, as could my father. Clearly, they don't. I was lucky to have such an amazing nan. She was all the family I needed. But still, like most youngsters, I couldn't wait to get away from the village, thinking I was destined for a much bigger life than what this place could offer me. I found a job in London and didn't look back. At least not for a while. By the time my marriage was well and truly on the rocks, I didn't really know what I wanted. A friend of mine from primary school was getting married and I came back for that and that's when it hit me. This, here, this was what I wanted. What I needed. I felt completely different that weekend and it spurred me into doing something about it.'

'How long was it until you moved back?'

'Two months.'

'Wow. You don't hang about, do you?'

I grinned. 'Not really. Not this time, anyway. I couldn't afford to. I'd always loved these houses and this one was up for sale. Stanley had died—'

'Stanley?'

'The previous owner.'

'Did he die in it?'

'No. Why?'

'No reason.'

'I'm not carrying on until you tell me.'

'Nothing to tell,' Henry said, leaning back and sipping at his drink. 'But I'm happy to sit in silence if you want.'

I waited for all of thirty seconds. 'Ugh. You're annoying. You do know that, don't you?'

'She says to the kindly neighbour who's offered to take her to the beach tomorrow.'

'Only because you want a free tour guide.'

'Fair enough. And yes, I can be annoying. And stubborn. And vague and various other questionable attributes, I'm afraid.'

As he spoke, the light that had danced in his eyes earlier dimmed, shadowed by something else, but I already knew better than to question it.

'I'm only teasing,' I nudged him, desperate to bring the lightness back.

He gave me a brief smile but it didn't reach his eyes and I could have kicked myself.

'So anyway, it just seemed like a sign.'

'What did?'

'That it was up for sale.'

'So it was an actual sign. For Sale.' He made the shape with his hands.

'Oh, ha ha,' I grinned, happy to take the tease now that a glimmer of amusement was back in his expression. 'You know what I mean. Like, from the universe.'

'Not from the estate agent?'

'You're hilarious. You know what I mean.'

'I really don't, but carry on.'

'Well, I felt it was a sign, and when I got back to London a couple of days later I handed in my notice and told my ex I was moving out. I had some holiday saved, so I didn't have to do the full three months, and Stanley's executor wanted a quick sale, so it all went through pretty quickly.'

'Got a bargain?'

'Ha, no. It was still market price, unfortunately. He dropped a bit but as you already pointed out, poker face is not my forte. He knew I loved it, even though I tried my best to play it cool.'

'Yeah, I can see how that might have been tricky for you. But hiding your emotions isn't always all it's cracked up to be. Don't beat yourself up.'

I tilted my glass towards him at the understanding and kind words. 'Thanks.' He tilted his own back.

'So, did you feel you'd done the right thing?'

'Immediately. Even though the house was incredibly dated and I couldn't afford to do much in one go. It's amazing what a multitude of sins a few coats of paint will hide. The kitchen was bright orange. Walls, cupboards, everything.'

Henry screwed up his face. 'Seriously?'

'Yeah. How to guarantee a migraine to start your day! Luckily I was still looking for a job at the time so I had plenty of time to fill with painting.'

'You did the cupboards too?'

'Yep. By the time I was finished, it actually looked pretty good. It served me well for a few years until I could afford to have it ripped out and a fitted one more suited to my needs put in.'

'It didn't even occur to me to do anything like that.'

'Oh, no, if I'd had the chance to gut it in one go, believe me, I would have. I was really quite envious of you being able to do that.'

'Have you done everything you want to now?'

'Mostly. Ideally I'd have somewhere like your garden room as the hospital. I know people would still be coming to my address, but they wouldn't have to come into my actual house. And for me, there'd be some separation from work and home. As much as I love what I do, it would be nice.'

'I get that. That's why I put that in. I could have an office in a bedroom, but this provides that degree of separation. All the medical stuff is out there, all the home life is in there.' He thumbed behind him to the house.

'Sounds ideal.'

'You've got room. It's the same size garden as this.'

'Agreed, but rather fuller. I'm not sure I could find a spare bit big enough even if I could afford it.'

'I guess that's true. You have rather packed stuff in.'

'I rarely meet a plant I don't like. They say you're supposed to only buy them if you know where you're going to put them, but that doesn't work for me.'

'Who says you're supposed to do it like that anyway? I literally know nothing about gardening, but your garden looks pretty damn beautiful to me, so I'd say keep doing what you're doing.'

I tilted my head to the side. 'I think that's the nicest thing you've ever said to me. Thank you. I've worked hard on it.'

'It shows.'

'But I enjoy it, so it's not a chore. Plus it's good for the mind as well as the body.'

'That is true. I know a couple of GP friends of mine have encouraged some patients to take up gardening with good results.'

'Perhaps you should try it?'

Henry screwed up his nose. 'Not really for me.'

'Why not?'

'This is the first time I've had outside space with any home I've owned. Every houseplant I've ever been given has died. There's a reason why my grass is plastic.'

'Oh, well. Perhaps the idea will grow on you. No pun intended.'

'Perhaps,' he said in a tone that suggested the idea was unlikely. 'In the meantime, I'll just enjoy the view of yours and the low maintenance of mine. Best of both worlds.'

'Also cheating.'

He flashed a grin before looking up at the sky. 'I'm still getting used to the fact that you can see the stars here.'

'Beautiful, isn't it?'

'It really is.'

We sat in comfortable silence, gazing up at the sky, until Spud shuffled from under the table, stretched and let out a rather spectacular fart. He looked round, apparently surprised at the noise.

'Oh, God, I'm so sorry,' I said to Henry before addressing my dog. 'Spuddy, you're a guest. You can't just do things like that here. We're doing our best to convert Dr Darcy here to become a doggy person and that sort of behaviour isn't going to help.'

Spud looked up, his brown eyes studying us for a moment, then tilted his head to one side. My heart melted all over again. I glanced up at Henry with a smile. His face remained passive and expressionless. Looked like there was still a lot of work to do on that front.

'I think we'd better head home.'

'You still up for tomorrow?'

'Yes, if you're sure. But do you want me to drive? I'd hate to mess up your nice car.'

'I'll cope. Pick you up at eight, or is that too early?'

'Fine with us. We're usually up pretty early anyway. Thanks for this.' I waved at the table.

'Thanks for coming. Which way did you want to go home?'

'I'll use the door this time, if that's OK?' I replied, laughing.

'Your choice. Longer way round.'

'Also less chance of me landing flat on my face.'

'I wouldn't let you fall.'

I turned to look at him in the soft, ambient lighting he'd had installed over the patio, the warm glow casting sharp shadows on his cheekbones. His eyes met mine and, despite all our previous disagreements, I knew that he wouldn't.

'Thank you,' I returned quietly.

We trooped through the house and down the path, and I headed back to my own. I turned to wave just before I disappeared around the side and entered my home through the patio door I'd left open earlier.

As Spud noisily lapped up some water, I closed the door and locked up, turning off the lights once Spud was done, and threw the bolt on the wooden front door before heading upstairs.

Ten minutes later, my teeth were brushed, face washed and hair tied back.

'In your bed, Spuddy.'

The little dog hopped into his bed, scooted round three times and flopped down with a sigh, Colin the Cabbage acting as a pillow.

'Night, night, my darling.' I crouched down beside him and placed a kiss on the top of his head before clambering into my own bed.

I leant over and picked up my phone from the bedside to set an alarm and switch it to flight mode and noticed a message from Abby. Or, more accurately, several messages beginning with a casual hi, followed a short time later by a 'You busy?' followed by 'Are you OK?' and then three missed calls and an instruction to 'Call me!' I had never been one to be attached to my phone, but Abby and I messaged every day and I generally replied to her pretty quickly. Had it been in the day, I knew she wouldn't have been worried, but with no reply for several hours in the evening, I knew my friend's imagination would be running wild.

Hi!

Moments later, a return message pinged in.

Where have you been? Are you OK?

Fine. I was next door.

Next door?

I could practically hear my bestie thinking before another message bounced in.

With Dr Delicious???

With my neighbour, yes. Is there anything to report? No.

I chewed my lip for a second.

But before you hear it from any gossips, I am going to the beach with him tomorrow.

The phone rang almost immediately and I answered the video call.

'Tell me everything,' Abby said.

'There's nothing to tell, Abs. Honestly. He asked if I was free to show him around a bit tomorrow after he does some surfing.'

'God, I bet he looks gorgeous in a wetsuit,' she said in a dreamy tone. In the background, Ed, cleared his throat. Abby giggled, blew him a kiss and turned back to me. 'So what were you doing tonight?'

'Having a glass of whiskey in a neighbourly manner.'

'So, what, he just popped round and invited you?'

'No, we were both in the garden and he asked if I was free for a drink. And before you read anything into it, it was merely his way of attempting to bury the hatchet. Nothing more.'

'Are you sure?'

'Absolutely.'

'Still a shame you're not sharing a bed, I reckon.'

'He's obviously not The One, so it's fine. I know the universe has a plan.'

Behind her, Ed snorted.

'I heard that!' I called.

Abby turned the phone towards Ed, who waved, the cheeky grin exactly the same as it had been when we were kids.

'So tomorrow isn't anything?'

'I'm hoping it will be a pleasant morning out. But that's it. I'm going to walk Spuddy on the beach while Henry freezes his bum off in the sea.'

'Chantelle at the clinic said it's a nice bum, so that'd be a shame.'

'Still right here,' Ed put in.

Abby waved his comment away with a grin and I ignored it.

'And then just show him around a little bit.'

'I still think it's a shame it's not a romantic thing, but it'll do you good to get out. You've barely been out apart from to walk the dog for the last month.'

'I know. You're right, it will be good.'

'You are taking the whole weekend off?'

I paused before replying.

'Wils, you need to. You're going to run yourself into the ground. You have to look after yourself as well as your customers.'

'I know. I know. And OK, yes, I promise. I'll take this weekend off.'

'And by that I don't mean knocking your guts out in the garden!'

'There's a lot to do out there.'

'I don't care! You need some rest and recuperation.'

'I find gardening restful and restorative.'

'Ohmygod.' Abby rolled her eyes and turned to her husband. 'Can you talk any sense into her?'

Ed pushed himself up from the sofa, loped over to my friend and slung an arm around her shoulder as he kissed her cheek. 'Don't overdo it, Twig.'

I gave him a salute in reply, at which he nodded and turned back to the sofa.

'That's it?' Abby asked him, throwing up her hands.

'She knows what she's about. Stop fussing, woman.'

Abby let out a dramatic sigh. 'I don't know why I bother.'

'Because you love us,' I grinned. 'I promise, I will take it easy. It's not a hard ask, as I'm knackered anyway. I'm going to read for a bit now and then get some sleep.'

'I'll let you go, then. I look forward to hearing all about tomorrow, though!'

I laughed. 'There won't be much to tell.'

'Have you warned him that the village won't necessarily see it that way and may well fill in their own blanks?'

'Oh. No, I didn't. I'll ask tomorrow before we leave and he can always pull out if he wants.'

'What about you?'

'What?'

'Don't you mind being the focus of gossip about spending time with the new dishy doctor?'

'Nope. There's nothing in it, but people will always make up their own stories if the truth isn't interesting enough. Not a lot either of us can do about it.'

'That's true.'

'Night, Abs. Night, Ed.'

Ed raised a hand, his head turned towards something violent and noisy on the telly. Abby blew a kiss and I hung up.

Ten pages later, my eyelids were as droopy as a pair of old tights. Closing the book, I laid it on the bedside, turned my phone over so the display was hidden and switched off the light. I wriggled down under the duvet and was asleep within minutes.

15

At five to eight the next morning, Spud and I were fed, watered and waiting outside the front gate for Henry. I closed my eyes against the warm rays of the late spring sunshine as the dog sniffed up and down the walls and watered a couple of spots. I heard a door close behind me and, opening my eyes, turned around to see Henry walking down the path, a kitbag slung over one shoulder. He wore a white T-shirt and light tan cargo shorts and looked, objectively, bloody gorgeous.

'Good morning,' he called.

'Morning. How are you?'

'Well, thanks,' he said, pulling the gate closed behind him. 'How did you sleep?'

'Deeply! Think that whiskey sent me off.'

'So long as it was that and not the stimulating company.'

'Let's see how today goes and I'll tell you tomorrow.'

'Fair enough. You both ready to go?' Henry glanced down at Spud, who was sitting patiently at his feet, his tail wagging like an out-of-control metronome, his big, soft brown puppy eyes looking up at Henry expectantly. Spud gave a tiny whimper of excitement and did a bum shuffle closer to Henry so that he was practically sitting on his trainers.

'Is he all right?'

'Yes. He's saying hello.'

'Oh. Right. I see. Well, hello,' he said, looking down briefly and addressing my dog as if he were a colleague. I was half expecting him to stick out his hand and wait for it to be shaken. 'Ready?' he asked, looking back at me.

Definitely not a dog guy.

I scooped up my now-rather-bewildered dog. 'Yep.'

Henry opened the door for us, and I slid in, popped on the seatbelt and clipped Spud's belt to mine as Henry got in and closed the door, the scent of rich leather enveloping us.

'That's clever,' he said, noticing our now-conjoined harnesses.

'Safety first. It's actually illegal not to have a dog restrained during travel. It clips onto a rear seatbelt too.' I glanced round to the non-existent back seat. 'When other seats are available.'

'Is he all right on your lap?'

'Yeah. He's more than happy and so am I. We're OK, aren't we, Spuddy boy?'

Spud wagged his tail and then snuggled into my chest, and I laughed and fussed him for a moment. As I lifted my head, Henry was watching us but with an expression I couldn't quite make out. 'Everything OK?'

Henry started. 'Yes. Absolutely.'

'You looked like you were miles away.'

The engine gave a low throaty burble. 'Not at all.' We pulled away smoothly before Henry turned the car around and pointed us towards the beach.

The journey was pleasant and short, and Spud was trying to get out of the car before I'd even opened the door. The moment I did, he scooted off my lap, harness still on, and charged around the low wall and onto the pale golden freshly washed sand, his paws dancing as he felt the change in texture below them.

'You were right about him being a fan of the beach.'

'Can you tell?' I asked, laughing as the little dog charged full pelt down towards where the sea met the sand, and started playing chicken with it, darting in and back and letting out the occasional bark of delight. As the summer season was yet to kick in, the beach was still quiet, with just a few locals walking their own dogs or getting ready for the surf, just as Henry was planning to.

'Does it get rammed during the summer?'

'It can get busier but we're really lucky that the cove is still mostly off the main tourist track, so we've managed to keep it more of a secret, thank goodness. So far, at least.'

Henry scanned the horizon, one large hand shading his eyes from the strengthening sun. 'It's stunning. I can see why the locals would want to keep it to themselves.'

'Don't forget you're a local, too, now.' I nudged him with my arm.

'Huh. Yeah.' He turned to me. 'I guess I am.'

'Still getting used to that?'

'Definitely. I'm thinking it might take a while, but if this is one of the benefits, I reckon it could speed things up.'

'That's good to hear. Shall we head over to get your board?'

'Great. So you say you know this chap from school?'

'That's right. It was great getting invited to Vijay's house for tea. His mum's an amazing cook. Literally the best samosas and dahl outside of India.'

'Wilma!' Vijay yelled across the beach, his distinctive Devonian-with-a-twist-of-Indian tones full of laughter.

'Wilma?' Henry repeated, quietly.

'Vijay was a massive fan of *The Flintstones* at school.' I paused a moment. 'Probably still is.'

I waved back and called Spud, who came charging up the beach towards us, noticed Vijay crouching down with his arms out and took a sharp right towards him. My friend caught him and rolled onto his back, laughing as he covered his face and Spud tried to bury under his hands. After a few moments, he rolled over, caught the dog under his arm and stood up in one smooth movement.

'Wilma, you've come to ask me to run away with you at last?' he asked, pulling me in for a hug with his free arm.

'Maybe later,' I said, hugging him back, laughing at his teasing. Vijay was utterly dedicated to his wife and four children.

'Fair enough. I'll be here waiting. You here to surf?'

'Nope.' I shook my head as I turned to Henry. 'Last time I went out there with this hooligan I had bruises for weeks.'

'Surf was kind of rough but I knew she was up to it, and you got up on the board a couple of times.'

'And I fell off a whole lot more. I'll stick to the sand, I think. This is my neighbour, Henry Darcy. He's booked to hire some gear from you. Henry, this is Vijay. Vijay, Henry.'

'Nice to meet you, Henry. You're the new doc up at the clinic, right?'

Henry shook his hand. 'That's right.'

'You surfed before?'

'A bit, although not for some time.'

'You OK to go out on your own?'

'Absolutely.'

It was hard not to notice the prickle behind the one-word reply, but Vijay's easy-going personality meant it slid right off him.

'Fantastic,' my friend replied with his wide, easy smile. 'You want to come in and choose some kit?'

Henry nodded then turned to me. 'You OK?'

'Yep. Spud and I have a lovely long walk scheduled so you take as long as you like. See you both later. Come on, Spuddy. Want to go for a walk?'

Spud gave a quick, excited bark, scooted around my legs and hopped up briefly onto his back legs as he danced in delight.

'It's a real shame he doesn't like his walks, isn't it?' Vijay asked.

'Terrible. Come on, you. Have a good time, Henry. Be careful.'

'I'll keep an eye, don't worry, Wil.'

'I'll be fine,' Henry replied, still sounding tense. He'd seemed all right driving down and it was too gorgeous a day to worry about his pride. If he was still spiky when we met back up, the tour I had roughly planned out in my head might end up shorter than I'd envisioned.

'You got a suit, or you need to borrow one?'

Henry twisted slightly, enough to show Vijay the kitbag he had slung over his shoulder. 'Got one, thanks. Just the board.'

'Great! Come in and see what takes your fancy.'

I left them to it, stuck a ball in the lobber and laughed with joy as Spud took off after it as fast as his short legs would carry him. Getting a dog had done wonders for my mental health. Spud raring to go, whatever the forecast, had got me into a habit of daily walks and consequently I was now in better shape physically as well as mentally. As a bonus, I didn't worry too much about the odd slice of cake here and there. Company, laughter and cake allowance. Spud had brought all of this into my life.

But something was still missing. As much as I knew I didn't need a man – I was more of a dab hand with a power tool than my ex, who didn't know one end of a screwdriver from the other –

the truth was I wanted one. Or to be more specific I wanted The One. I wanted someone to build a life with. Someone who appreciated me and whom I could respect and appreciate. When I thought about it like that, it didn't seem such a lot to ask but, from experience, it clearly was. That was why I was bringing the universe in on it. It was time to get out the big guns. Today was the day. I knew it was going to work. It had to.

16

A couple of hours later, Spud and I returned to the shack. Vijay was sitting on his deck, his long skinny legs stretched out in front of him, soaking up the sun, eyes closed. Spud took a running leap and landed square in his lap, causing my friend to emit a heartfelt – or more likely *something-else*-felt, considering where the dog had landed – 'Oof'.

'Spud!' I said, crossly.

The dog turned his head and looked up at me.

It was all I could do not to forgive him immediately. I grasped onto my serious expression. 'That's bad manners and you know it.'

His little head drooped lower.

'Oh, I don't mind, do I, boy?' Vijay bent and touched his head to Spud's, ruffling his fur.

'You're not helping.'

'I know, sorry. But he's just so cute, aren't you?' he said, snuggling his face against the dog's. 'Do you want a treat?'

Spud's head shot up.

'You're incorrigible. Both of you!' I said, widening my eyes as

Spud gave me a brief glance, as if checking it was OK, and then he was off.

'So?' Vijay asked as he appeared a minute later, a packet of nuts under one arm and Spud under the other, munching noisily on a bit of watermelon. 'You and the doc a thing? You kept that quiet.'

I took a seat and toed off my trainers. 'Nope. Not a thing. Just neighbours.'

'Right.'

'It's true,' I said, turning to him and his dismissive-sounding reply.

'Why?'

'Why what?'

'Why is it true? It's about time you found someone.'

'You make it sound easy.'

'Yeah, well, it was for me. Mine and Sakshmi's parents decided. Luckily she's hot and kind, so it all worked out.'

'For you, anyway.'

My friend grinned. Everyone knew that they were one of the happiest families in the village, despite what had seemed to some a rather archaic way of meeting.

'How are you all, anyway? Sorry, I've been absolutely besieged by work lately. I've barely seen anyone.'

Vijay threw back his head, laughing.

'Why is that funny?'

'Barely…'

I looked at him blankly and he sat straighter. 'You're ruining the joke, you know that.'

'What exactly is the joke?'

'You run a teddy *bear* hospital. Barely seen anyone? Oh, never mind. You had to be there.'

I threw a cashew at him from the packet he'd put down on

the little table between us. He retaliated and I caught it in my mouth.

'Nicely done. You're forgiven.'

'Thanks.'

'We're all fine, anyway. Kids can't wait for the summer holidays, of course. Every day they ask how much longer. Thankfully it's a little while yet.'

'How's business?'

'Mad! Which is good. But *you* need to get some help in, by the sounds of it,' he said, munching on the nuts.

'I've thought about it, but I need to be sure this isn't just a blip. I'd hate to take someone on and then have to ask them to leave again.'

'Yeah, that'd be rubbish, but somehow I don't think that's a problem. You've been up to your ears in fuzzy bears ever since you started, and it's only getting busier by the sounds. Might be worth thinking about.'

'Yeah. I will.'

My friend looked over his glass at me.

'I will! I promise.'

'Good. Ah, here comes the hero of the hour.'

Henry strode up the beach, board tucked under his arm. His hair was slicked back from the water and the wetsuit was, well, let's go with flattering.

'You're drooling,' Vijay said without looking at me as he stood up to go and greet his client.

'I am not,' I said, subtly double-checking just in case. 'He's not my type.'

'Yeah, I can see there's plenty that could put you off.'

'Ha ha,' I replied, lowering my voice. 'He's not a dog person!'

My friend gave me a quick glance, brow furrowed, then shrugged and turned back. 'Fair enough. Anyone who knows you knows that's a deal breaker.' He raised his voice. 'How was it?'

For the first time since I'd met him, my neighbour looked truly relaxed. He was even smiling for more than two seconds. 'Fantastic. I forgot how good it could be.'

'Yeah, I'm sure Wilma feels the same.'

I stretched and gave my friend a kick, knowing exactly where he'd aimed that particular remark.

Henry gave a slightly puzzled look, the smile still in place.

'Ignore him. He still thinks we're in primary school. You had a good surf then?'

'I did.'

'You're a real local now, and Vijay's is the best place in town for hiring and buying gear and for lessons, if they're needed.'

'What my friend here omitted to say is that I'm also the *only* place in town. But she is right in that I'm also the best.' He took a mini bow.

Henry laughed. It sounded easy and relaxed. He definitely needed to do this more often if this was the result.

'Want a drink?' Vijay asked as Henry leant the surfboard up against the building.

'I don't want to put you to any trouble.'

'No trouble at all. Coffee? Tea? Herbal tea?' He added the last as he cast a look at me, and I raised my cup.

'Coffee would be great. The stronger the better.'

Vijay slapped him on the shoulder. 'Man after my own heart. Be back in a mo.' With that he disappeared into the back of the building and clattered around with the business of making drinks.

'It looks like that's done you the power of good,' I said, looking up at Henry from behind my sunnies.

'It really has,' he replied, unzipping the wetsuit as he turned his back and began trying to shrug off the shoulder. Unsuccessfully.

'Want a hand?'

'No, thanks. I've got it,' he said, intensifying his attempts to turn himself into a pretzel.

I stood up, grabbed the shoulder of the suit and eased it off. 'We'll be here until sunset the way you're going.'

He tossed a look over his shoulder. 'Funny. And thanks.'

'You're welcome.'

He managed the rest of the suit on his own and moments later was sitting in a third chair that Vijay had pointed to, damp, shirtless and looking like a surfing god. Thank God that a) I still had my sunglasses on and b) Vijay could talk for both Britain and India and was happily chatting away. I mean, I knew we had very little in common but that didn't mean I was unable to appreciate beautiful things and, right then, my neighbour looked like Adonis as he sat, finally relaxed, soaking up the fabulous landscape and warmth of the day, chatting with my friend.

'We'd better be getting on,' Henry said eventually and, it sounded, somewhat reluctantly.

'You can stay longer if you like. Spud and I are happy to catch the bus back. It's not a problem. You look pretty comfy there.' He'd been into the hut, showered and changed, and was now back to the T-shirt and shorts. Calling Vijay's place a hut made it sound far rougher than it actually was. Vijay had quite the swanky set-up but he loved the quirkiness of its title.

'Nope.' Henry stood, his shoulders still straight but with less tension in them than there had been previously. 'You don't get out of being the tour guide that easily.'

'It was worth a try,' I teased back.

Henry reached down and grabbed his bag, slinging it over

one shoulder. 'I'd be disappointed if you hadn't,' he said, catching my eye as he straightened.

Were we flirting? No! Of course we weren't.

Vijay cleared his throat and I looked round to find a ruddy great grin on his face. Oh, God. He definitely thought we were flirting. I stole a glance at Henry but his expression was just his normal stoic one. Definitely not flirty.

'Right. As you've now seen the beach, and met one of the local characters...'

Vijay held his side. 'There goes another rib.'

I stuck my tongue out with a grin and continued. 'Let's head to the harbour up the other end. Then we can work our way to the centre of the village.'

'Sounds great. Lead the way.'

I hugged Vijay and we both said our goodbyes before walking on down the beach towards the harbour.

'I'm so glad you enjoyed your surfing.'

'I really did. Like I said, I'd forgotten how much I loved it. It's been so long since I last went, it took a little while to get the feel for it again, and I was definitely in the water more than on it. I'm pretty sure there's several gallons less in the ocean.'

'But now you've done it once, do you think you'll try and make it more of a regular thing?'

'Without question.'

'That's good to hear. You certainly looked more relaxed after than you did before.'

'Is that so?'

'Yep.'

'I see. I know that I'm certainly more hungry than I was before. Is there anywhere to eat around here?'

'You must be a mind reader. I was just about to ask if you were hungry. There's a place just along the harbour wall called

The Grumpy Crab. The breakfasts will ruin you for anywhere else.'

'That's a heck of a claim, although I'm loving the name.'

'Great, isn't it?' I agreed, with a wide smile.

'It is. Do we need to book if it's that good?'

'We'll be fine. Come on, it's this way.'

* * *

'Willow, my love!' Penny-lope greeted us both with a wide smile. 'We haven't seen you in here for a while now. I was beginning to worry you'd found a better place!'

'Oh, Pen. You know there's no better place than this. Just work.'

'She's a hard worker, this one.' Penny turned to Henry. 'Done that place up all with her own fair hands, give or take.' I felt the blush beginning to rise. 'And you must be the dashing Dr Darcy everyone's been talking about.'

Now it was time for Henry's cheeks to colour.

'I thought it must be. Lovely to see you together,' she said, plucking a couple of menus out from the holder.

'Oh! We're not together, Pen.'

She turned back to us and frowned. 'Oh? Not a table for two then?'

'Well, yes. But I thought you meant...' I drifted off, well aware of Penny-lope and Henry both fixing their eyes on me. The blush was back with a vengeance. 'Never mind.' I flapped the air and emitted a little laugh that was supposed to be tinkly but instead sounded like I'd just choked. I half wished I had.

'Right then, table for two it is. This way.'

Penny marched off ahead and we hurried after her, Henry indicating with one arm for me to go first. I spent the short walk thinking of cold things to try to reduce the heat racing around my face. Of course she hadn't meant we were a couple. Why would she? God, what would Henry think? Oh, no! I hoped he didn't think I'd said anything to anyone about me wanting us to be together! I felt the blush deepen. Bugger. Ice cubes. Winter. Snow. The sea in December. The hottest my water ever got when I moved in... OK, my skin was feeling on the way back to normal and anything more I could blame on the weather.

'Here you go, my dears. Gorgeous view for you. You don't get that in London, do you?'

'You most certainly don't.' Henry gave the expected reply with a smile.

Penny bustled off. I made a point of looking out of the window and taking an intense interest in the fishing boats moored in the harbour, their hulls beginning to be washed with the incoming tide.

'Sorry. I should have considered that you might be subjected to some gossip for this.' Henry's deep voice was gentle and velvety soft as he spoke.

I turned back, my brows raised a little in surprise. 'No, really. It's me who should have been apologising. I'm not sure why I was so adamant about telling Penny that we aren't a thing. That this,' I gave a subtle bat of my hand back and forth, 'isn't a "thing". I'm sure that came across as rude. I mean, it's not like you're not good-looking. You are. Obviously. But I'm not looking for that. Well, it would be nice, of course. What I'm saying is...'

As I rambled on, part of me sat horrified in the corner of my brain, hands over her eyes, refusing to any longer be associated with the keeper of said brain. But for some reason, once I'd started, I couldn't stop.

'What I'm saying is that just because someone is nice-looking doesn't mean they're necessarily a nice person so it's not everything, is it? I'm not saying you're not a nice person. I mean, I know you are. I just mean—'

Henry laid his large, warm hands over mine, which were flapping around on the table like a couple of recently landed fish from the boats outside. They stilled beneath the subtle weight and my words followed suit.

'I know what you mean. I agree. And again, I'm sorry if any of this is going to be awkward for you.'

I shook my head, resolving this time to stay silent while I had a serious mental word with my tongue. Once I felt it was under control and had taken the message on board, I ventured to speak.

'It's not, really. Although you may get the odd tease any time you are seen with a woman. It's a small village. There's not always a lot to do.'

'I'm sure I'll cope. Plus I always have the serenity of my garden to return to.' His expression was deadly serious.

Mustn't laugh. Mustn't laugh.

'If you keep those giggles in any longer, you're going to rupture something that might be beyond my medical capabilities.'

A wide, relaxed smile followed the words and I let the giggles burst forth. Seriously, he really needed to go surfing more often if this was just a glimpse of the person he was beneath all that stress and three-piece suit.

'So, where did you learn to surf?' I asked, once Penny-lope had taken our orders. Henry had gone for the Force 12 breakfast, the whole works, while I had opted for the avocado on toast with tomato salsa, chia seeds and poached eggs.

'My brother moved to Australia for a while, years ago, with work and spent all his free time surfing. He made it sound so great that I ended up jacking in my job and going out to do the same.'

'Did you work out there too?'

'Yeah. Luckily I have a job that is needed pretty much everywhere, so I got a placement and basically just hung out with my brother surfing when I wasn't on duty.'

I lifted my glass and trapped the paper straw between my lips, the fresh lemon and cucumber water cooling my throat. 'You didn't fancy staying out there?'

'My brother was relocating back here. I enjoyed my life out there but somehow it had never quite seemed like home and I knew that, without George there, it wasn't going to be the same.'

'So you came back to London.'

'Yep,' he nodded and downed nearly a whole glass of water in one. 'Still trying to get the taste of salt out of my mouth,' he smiled, topping up both our glasses from the water jug.

'And then what?'

'Then what, what?'

'It sounds like you had a pretty good work–life balance out there. And then when you returned to London you didn't. What happened?'

'Honestly, I don't know. Things just edged more and more that way, I guess. I met someone, also a doctor, very ambitious, and the next thing I knew, years had gone by and, apart from my career, I had nothing to show for it. No holiday memories, no family memories.' His face was turned to the sea and I noticed that the tension had returned to his frame. 'Nothing,' he finished.

'So how did you discover our little corner of paradise?' I asked, desperate to bring that smile back to his face.

'Completely by accident.'

'Really?'

He nodded. 'I had a conference in Exeter and the bloody sat nav packed up. It was dark and none of the roads were lit, and very few signposted. I don't know what I did. Clearly took a few wrong turns but I ended up here, pretty certain it wasn't Exeter.'

'We're often mistaken for each other.'

'That's extremely understandable.' His mouth was serious but the smile was back in those vivid eyes. God, why couldn't he have been a dog lover?

'Anyway, I was absolutely ravenous, so I stopped and went into the first restaurant I found, had an amazing meal and decided to go for a walk before getting back into the car. I'd been working then driving and I really needed fresh air. The more I walked around, took in the sea air, even in the dark, the more I calmed. On a whim, I asked if the hotel had a room free, which they did, being off season, and I stayed in a cosy, homely inn instead of the beautiful but soulless hotel I had booked in the city. The next morning, I got up early and had a walk around in the daylight. I guess I fell in love, there and then. Not just with the place but with the feeling it brought. I'd known for ages that I needed a change. A big change. But until that moment, I didn't know what it was, or where it was. That night, thanks to a wonky sat nav, I found it.'

'Or fate.'

'Huh?'

'Maybe it was fate that brought you here. Showed you what you needed when you needed it.'

'I don't believe in fate.'

'That doesn't mean it's not true.'

He linked long fingers together and rested his chin on them, studying me. 'And let me guess, you do believe in fate.'

'I do.'

'Of course you do.'

'Don't you think it was convenient that you ended up here, of all places, when you were supposed to be in a city and were feeling lost, in more ways than one?'

'I'm not sure I'd have categorised myself as "lost", and yes, I agree it was convenient, but nothing more than that. Circumstances presented an opportunity and I took it. Nothing more woo-woo than that.'

'Sounds like the same thing to me.'

'It definitely isn't,' he said, sitting back. Glancing over my shoulder, his eyes locked on to what I imagined was our breakfast heading towards us.

Moments later, a young waitress placed them down. 'Morning, Dr Darcy. I'm guessing this is yours.' She gave him a smile and then plonked mine down with a little less elegance.

'Thanks.'

'Can I get you anything else?'

Henry glanced at me to check and I shook my head. 'No, I think we're fine, thanks.'

'Great. Well, just wave if you want anything.'

He smiled then focused back down on his breakfast and began tucking in.

* * *

'That was amazing,' Henry said, placing his cutlery together on the plate. 'You were right about this place. It gives me great confidence about the rest of the tour.'

'You do know how small the village is, don't you?' I replied, laughing. 'It's not going to be much of a tour.'

'It's not about size.'

Henry spoke just as the waitress moved to us from the table just behind him. A momentary flash of disappointment crossed her face before the smile returned.

Having assessed our only further need was for the bill, she made her way back to the till to prepare it. I'd been exceptionally controlled and was rather proud of myself. Henry had exhibited no flicker of amusement but I knew that, had I been with Abby or Vijay or any of the others, we'd have been purple in the face by then. However, my neighbour's humour was clearly rather less puerile than ours, so I was concentrating on keeping a straight face.

'That was rather perfect timing, wasn't it?' The green eyes crinkled at the edges and white teeth showed as he chuckled. So he did edge towards the puerile after all. There was hope for him yet.

'I'm afraid you may have just shattered the image she had of you.'

'I think that's probably a good thing. I was already halfway through med school before she was even born, by the looks of things.'

'Show me a man who doesn't feel flattered by a younger woman's attention.'

Henry pointed to himself.

I lifted a brow.

'It depends what you mean by younger. In such instances as that, nope. Not for me. Although, you're right, there are some men who feel it's a badge of honour. I prefer not to feel older than I am when a cultural reference goes sailing over their head.'

'I know what you mean. I said something to my hairdresser's assistant the other week and you could practically see the tumbleweed. I felt about a hundred years old!'

'Are you splitting the bill?' The waitress reappeared with the credit card machine. There was a hint of interest in her tone that she'd not yet learned to hide.

'No.'

'Yes.'

We stared at each other.

'No,' Henry repeated and held out his credit card to tap the machine, adding a generous tip on top, which brought the smile back to the waitress's face.

'You didn't need to do that,' I said as we got back outside.

'I know, but you're giving up your time to show me around and I wanted to show my appreciation.'

'Well, thank you. But I'm paying when we stop for coffee and cake at Bernito's.'

'You're expecting me to find room for cake after that massive breakfast?'

'I'm pretty sure you burned a tonne of calories this morning. It'll soon settle. That's not for a while yet anyway. In the meantime, we can continue the tour if you're up for it.'

'Definitely. Lead on.'

17

We walked along the harbour wall, watching the boats bobbing in the water. I pulled my floppy straw hat back out of my basket and put it on, feeling the shade on my shoulders and face as I did so.

'Good job hats suit you with that colouring.'

'Do you think?' I asked, turning to him. 'Sorry. That sounded like a real fish.'

'No, it didn't. And yes, they do. Even if they didn't, I'd want you to wear one. It's so difficult to get people to take note of how they can help keep the skin safe.'

'Yeah, I can only imagine it must be extra frustrating from a doctor's point of view.'

'Luckily I didn't have to deal with that too often in A&E, but a few GPs I know have times when they feel like they're banging their head against a wall.'

'Coco Chanel has a lot to answer for.'

'She does. Great style, though.'

I flashed a smile at him. 'I didn't have you down as a fashionista.'

'That's just as well then. But my mum is and clearly more than I realised has rubbed off on me.'

'Are you close with you parents?' I asked as we got to a part of the wall where you could get up on to a higher part, a miniature version of the Cobb further along the coast at Lyme Regis. Spud scrambled up the worn stone steps with a speed that defied his size.

'Here. Let me go first.' Henry made to go past. 'I can put out a hand then.'

I placed my foot on the bottom step. 'That's very gallant but I've been running up and down these steps since I was a kid.'

'That doesn't mean you couldn't slip now.' His dark brow rumpled and the hard planes of his face were set as stoically as the stone I was climbing on.

'True. But I don't plan to, and if you're behind me, then you can catch me. Deal?'

He gave me a hard stare.

'Excellent. Come on. Spud's miles in front of us.'

The ascent was made without incident and we strolled along the top, the soft, warm breeze that smelled and tasted of the sea teasing our hair as we walked. Spud was doing his usual trick of trying to make friends with the small gulls that pottered around the end of the rock, his furry little face disappointed when another flew off.

'Spuddy!' I crouched down, arms wide, and he came haring back to me. A quick cuddle, a tasty treat and he was happy again, padding alongside us.

'You'd think he hadn't seen you in years, the way he greets you.'

'Isn't it wonderful?' I said with a laugh. 'It's definitely one of the best things about having a dog. Everyone likes to feel wanted, right?'

Henry gave a shrug. 'I guess.'

I stopped. 'You guess?'

He turned. 'Yes. Some people find it, I suppose, over-whelming to be needed that much.'

'Are you one of those people?'

He kept his face turned towards the horizon. 'I didn't say that. I was just commenting that different people have different levels of need.'

'And what are your levels?'

Henry removed his sunglasses and turned his head towards me.

'You're not going to tell me, are you?' I answered for him. 'That's fair enough. We're probably not there yet, bearing in mind a short time ago we couldn't stand the sight of each other.'

'I never felt like that about you.'

'Oh!' I looked up at him. Even with my sunglasses on, the surprise on my face was evident.

'Clearly we didn't feel the same.' He slid the expensive avia-tors back on, but not before I'd caught a glimpse of amusement in the eyes they were shading. 'So where next?'

We walked back along the ridge and, for the sake of peace-keeping, I took his hand as I descended the stone steps back onto the harbour wall.

'There's a gorgeous little bookshop two doors up. I know you're a fan now I've seen your well-stocked shelves. Shall I meet you in there in a bit?'

'Where are you going?'

'In here.' I pointed to the shop doorway I was close to.

Henry took a step back to read the signage. '"Crystal Clear". Curious. What is this?' He peered in the window.

'I don't think it will interest you.'

'I don't know about that,' he said, ignoring the massive hint and proceeding to push the door open. 'After you.'

'Thanks,' I said, tension racing up my body. 'Look.' I turned to him as soon as the door had closed and whispered, 'Crystal is a friend of mine. I know you don't believe in any of this stuff but please don't say anything, or make a joke out of it in here, OK? She's really sweet.'

'I won't.'

I hesitated a moment. Henry's hands lifted to rest gently on my upper arms. 'I promise. Come on. Show me what this is all about.'

'You'll only laugh.'

'Not in here I won't. And it's educational, no matter what I believe.'

When I didn't move, he turned me around himself, gently but with purpose. 'Lead the way.'

* * *

'Hi, Crystal! How are you?'

'Willow, my love. How are you? I still can't get over what an amazing repair you did on Ethelred's teddy. Honestly,' she turned to Henry, 'you wouldn't have thought there was anything that could be done, and Ethelred, that's my grandson, well, he was absolutely beside himself! Oh, sorry, duck. I should have introduced myself. I'm Crystal. You must be the new doctor.'

'I am. It's a pleasure to meet you. Everyone is remarkably well informed around here.'

Crystal let out a raucous laugh that had never seemed to match her slender, pixie-like build. It was like she'd picked up the wrong one early on in life and just decided to go with it.

'Don't you worry about it. You'll get used to it in time, and nobody means anything by it, do they, Willow?'

'Nope. They'll get bored of you soon enough.'

Crystal gave another chuckle. 'No pushover, this one, and that's for sure.'

'No, I came to be aware of that very early in our acquaintance. So, may I ask what happened to the teddy in question?' Henry neatly, and thankfully, diverted the subject from its trajectory back to the bear.

'The lawnmower, dear!' She put a hand on his arm and gripped. 'Awful, it was! You never saw such a mess.'

Henry threw me a look over her head. I knew he'd seen a lot worse.

'Fluff and fur everywhere, there was!'

And then I saw it. The twitch in his jaw. He rolled his lips together, face locked in concentration ostensibly on Crystal's words, but the real reason was quite different. I shook my head minutely at him and he started chewing the inside of his cheek.

'Well, there's Ethelred bawling his head off and me trying to comfort him while his mum and dad go round the garden retrieving bits of teddy. It was a shock how far one bear could travel in opposite directions.'

Henry snorted and coughed. I leant over and gave him a hefty pat on the back. 'He was inhaling his food earlier over at The Grumpy Crab and something went down the wrong way,' I explained to my friend before turning back to Henry. 'I told you that'd come back to bite you, didn't I?'

'You should listen to her, you know,' Crystal backed me up. 'She's very wise. A green witch, you see. Anyway, you should know better than gobbling your food, being a doctor and all.'

Henry flashed me a look and cleared his throat. 'Yes, you're quite right. Both of you. Please go on.'

'Well, I rang Willow in a right pickle and, bless her heart, she said to bring Rufus, that's the bear, over right away. We all know that she's up to her eyeballs in work. You know there's a waiting list for her services?'

'I didn't, no.'

'There is. She's very in demand but she knew how attached my little grandson is to his teddy, so she took him in as an emergency and must have worked hours on him.'

'It wasn't a big deal.' I shifted, getting a little too warm under the limelight.

'Not a big deal? This thing was in pieces.'

Henry clenched his jaw again but thankfully remained composed.

'She's a miracle worker, that's all I can say. You wouldn't know anything had even happened to Rufus now, and that boy never leaves him anywhere. It's practically glued to his side.'

'Definitely not a miracle, but I'm glad Red is looking after his bear now.'

'Oh, it was a real lesson, that's for sure.'

'And how are you? Shop busy?'

'Can't complain. I tick over well enough.'

A couple of young women entered the shop as she spoke, the bell above the door tinkling as they did so. Truth was, my friend did very well. Ever since Glastonbury several years ago and a well-known model with millions of social media followers had done a vlog from the shop, Crystal Clear had been firmly on the alternative map.

'I'd better go and see if they need any help. Just shout if you want anything. It's lovely to meet you, Doctor.'

'Henry, please.'

'Oh, no, no,' she replied with an almost girlish laugh. 'I

couldn't not call you Doctor. No, no, no.' She flapped her hand and bustled off in a cloud of patchouli.

Henry met my eyes. 'I'm sorry. I don't know what came over me.'

'I think it's perfectly awful of you to laugh at such a catastrophe, but I will allow that Crystal's retelling of it does add a rather comedic effect, so I'm going to let you off. Just this once, mind!'

'Thank you.'

I turned away and moved to look at some crystals.

'Was it a real mess, then? The bear?' he asked.

'That's putting it mildly. As she said, fluff and fur everywhere.'

Henry looked at me, a warning in his eyes. 'Don't.'

I flashed a grin. 'But no, it really was. Even I was a bit worried but, when he wasn't leaving it on the grass to be mowed, Red was obsessed with it. He's had it since he was born.'

'How old is he now?'

'Thirty-two.'

Henry let out a bark of laughter that caused the others to turn. He held up a hand in apology and dipped his head. 'You are trouble,' he murmured.

'He's five.'

'But you saved the day?'

'I did my job. I put bears back together.' I looked up at him. 'Not people.'

'Doesn't make it any less valuable. What's this?' He'd been peering at the different crystals as we talked and had picked one up and was looking it over.

'Ooh, that's labradorite. I was looking for that.'

'Labradorite?'

'Yes. And don't start.'

'I didn't say anything.'

'You didn't have to. It was all right there in your tone, neatly encapsulated in that one word.'

'OK. So what does this do?' He wiggled the fingers of one hand in, I assume, what he thought was a spooky manner.

I took the crystal from him and continued looking along the display of stones laid out before us.

'So?'

'Hmm?' I asked, reading the card of a pale purple coloured crystal.

'What do they do?'

'Are you actually interested, or are you just going to make fun?' I asked, turning to him with the small stone in my hand.

'I'm interested. Just because I don't believe any of it doesn't mean I'm not interested in what you believe.'

I paused, studying him for a moment.

He held up his hands, palms towards me. 'Honest. I know I was an arse about it all before but I'm getting to know you now.'

'Hmm.'

'Come on, what's this one?'

His hand cupped mine, the lilac stone resting in my palm, the warmth of his skin against mine momentarily throwing me mentally off balance. But then I remembered who he was and how different we were.

'You OK?' His concentration switched from the stone to my face, dark brows drawing closer as he asked.

'Yep, absolutely. So this one is called kunzite. Isn't it beautiful?'

'It is, actually. From what I understand they're all supposed to have powers. What's this one's power?'

'Several things. They are all claimed to help alleviate different physical ailments, but I'm not even going to go there with a doctor. Even as I said that your face changed.'

'Rubbish. I have an excellent poker face. It's sometimes necessary in my line of work, unfortunately.'

'Yeah, I can imagine,' I replied, softening for a moment. 'I literally couldn't do what you do.'

'You kind of do.'

A wide smile slid over my face. 'That's a nice thing to say. Not everyone gets it.' Which was true. I'd come across more than one person in my time who dismissed my business. I shook my head. 'Anyway. So other aspects of kunzite's power include helping alleviate anxiety and nervousness. Spiritually it is supposed to help with opening you up to loving, compassionate thought. It's also supposed to assist in fostering greater tolerance.'

'Interesting. Perhaps we both should have got some of these when I moved in.'

'I'm not sure there are any big enough for what we needed back then.'

Henry flashed a grin. 'Possibly. But look at this, we managed to come to a level of tolerance even without magic woo-woo.'

'Oi.'

'Sorry.' He winced. 'I'm trying. Honestly.'

I gave him a patient look.

'You're just dying to say, "Extremely trying," aren't you?'

'I was thinking about *very*, but yours is better.'

'Come on, what else are you going to get?' Henry asked as he put the kunzite back in the correct tray. 'Why did you want the dog one?'

'What dog one?'

'The shih-tzu-ite.' He pointed to my hand.

'Oh, ha ha. It's labradorite, as I'm pretty sure you know. And actually I'm reckoning I might need some of that tolerance one after all.' I turned to move back to get it and Henry caught me.

'No,' he said, laughing as he gently moved me back around. 'I promise. No more mucking about.' He gave a salute. 'Cub's honour.'

'Isn't it supposed to be Scout's honour?'

'I didn't get as far as Scouts.'

'Why not?'

'Too disruptive, apparently.'

'Really?' This sounded like a story. 'Do tell.'

'Another time,' he chuckled. 'Come on, what's the stone for? At least, what are you looking to get from it?'

'It's supposed to be a strengthening crystal for manifestation.'

'Manifestation? Right. And that's something you're interested in doing?'

'It is,' I replied, tilting my chin up just that little bit more. I'd guessed his height at about six four, which meant he had nearly eleven inches height advantage on me, but I was very much not about to let that bother me.

'Even if I wanted to argue, that face and stance would have put me off.'

'Good. It worked, then.'

'It did. So what are you planning to manifest? Or is it a secret like when you blow out the candles on a birthday cake?'

I looked up sharply, but his expression was serious, that slight dip to his head I noticed he did when he was concentrating.

He met my eyes. 'I've heard of the process, but that's the full extent of my knowledge, I'm afraid. I didn't know if it's something that you're supposed to keep in your heart, you know, like wishes.'

'No, manifesting is more about acknowledging that wish, that dream. Seeing yourself in the place, the position you want to be in. Really believing in it and working towards it in any way you can.'

Henry took the blue-toned crystal from my hand and held it up to the light. 'It's actually quite beautiful, isn't it?'

'It is.'

'Am I allowed to ask what you're manifesting? Where you're seeing yourself?'

The intense eyes were on me, studying me, listening, waiting. And then he looked away, stepping back as though to put physical as well as mental distance between us.

'Sorry. I shouldn't have asked that. It's personal and absolutely none of my business. I think this place must be working a spell on me.' One side of his mouth tilted in a half-smile.

'Maybe.'

'Is there anything else you're looking for?'

'A couple of bits. Shall I meet you in the bookshop?'

'No. I mean... I'm happy to stay here if that's all right with you?'

'Of course. So I just want to get some...' I tapped my finger against my lip as my eyes scanned the colours in front of us. 'Ah, there it is. One of those, and one of...' I reached over. 'Those. Right, I think that's all I need there. I just want to look over here, if that's OK?'

'Of course. Take all the time you need. Do you want me to hold them?' Henry asked as I juggled the stones in one hand and attempted to pick up a book and nose inside it. 'Here,' he said, holding out his hand without waiting for an answer.

'Thanks.'

'What are these ones?' he asked as I read the back of the book and then flicked through a few pages.

'The more solid green one is emerald and the lighter one is green aventurine.'

'And they're all for the same purpose?'

'These two are, yes. Aspects of it, anyway.'

He gave a nod, closed a large, tanned hand around the stones and ran his eyes over the books, picking one up and turning it over to read the back. I leant over to see which it was. 'Ooh, that one's really interesting.'

'Yeah?' He flicked me a glance. 'You've read it?'

'I have.'

'Says he's a medical doctor.'

'That's right. I've got a copy if you want to borrow it.'

Henry shook his head. 'Thanks, that's OK.'

I waited for him to return the book but instead he tucked it under his arm. His face broke into a smile as he caught me watching. 'I'm not stealing it, don't worry.'

'I didn't think you were!'

'And thanks for the offer but I'll buy my own copy. That way I can annotate it and I also get to support a local business.'

'That's really kind, thanks.'

'You're looking at me funny.'

'Am I?' I asked.

'Yes. Like I'm a particularly problematic patient.'

'Yours or mine?'

'Either.'

'Honestly, I'm just surprised that you're open to reading it. Anything other than standard Western medicine, really.'

'I can see why you might think that and, granted, I do think a lot of it is...' He paused and I wondered what word he was going to substitute for the one I was pretty sure he was about to say. 'Unusual and not necessarily something I put a lot of stock in, but there's no doubt the mind is a powerful thing, so it will be interesting to read something on the subject written from a different perspective. And if I don't get anything else from it, at least I'll have more of an understanding of the things that interest you, which may make it a little less likely I put my size thirteen in the conversation somewhere further along the line.'

'Thank you.'

He shook his head. 'Thank you. The village might be small, but there's certainly a lot of potential for knowledge expansion.'

'And we're not done yet!'

I headed over to the till and we chatted to Crystal as she wrapped and we paid for our purchases before waving goodbye and stepping back out into the bright sunshine. Blinking like two moles bursting through the earth, we rammed our sunglasses back on our faces.

'Ready for a coffee yet?'

'Always ready for a coffee.'

'We're really going to have to get you drinking some herbal tea.'

'I've been in my first alternative therapy shop and bought a book on the subject. That's quite enough for one day, I think. Right now, I'd kill for a strong black coffee.'

'I suppose you're right. Rome wasn't built in a day and all that. And luckily I know just the place to get you an amazing coffee.'

'Lead on!'

18

'So how do you know the coffee is as good as you say?' Henry asked once we'd placed our order and found a comfy sofa to sit on. 'I thought you only ever drank herbal tea.'

'Not true. I do have normal tea too, just decaffeinated. But I, too, was once like you, living from coffee to coffee.'

He sat back in mock amazement. 'I don't believe it.'

'I know, right.' I grinned, joining him in the laughter. 'But true. Until I came back here for that wedding and realised what I'd been missing. What I needed. I'd already begun to make changes when I was in London, going out less, drinking less, all that, but it wasn't enough. My relationship was on the rocks because of the differences between us and I wasn't really sleeping. Now I think part of that was due to the amount of coffee I was chugging.'

'Sounds like it might have been a lot of things.'

'Yes, you're right. I think it was. It was only when I started growing my own herbs the following summer that I began to get interested in the subject and look into it more.'

'I can see how that would interest you. It's a very direct connection with nature. Even I didn't take long to realise that's something that's important to you.'

'And I feel so much better for that connection. It's got me through some pretty dark times.'

Henry looked down briefly at the table and then back at me and was about to speak.

'One Vietnamese rich roast, black, and one peppermint tea.' Lena smiled as she put them down. 'Doesn't take much to work out whose is whose on this order. I'm surprised Willow hasn't converted you to herbal tea yet, Doc. Although, and don't let the boss hear, these are nothing on her homegrown ones.'

'Thanks, Lena. I'm just showing Henry around the village. I've no influence over what he chooses.'

'Aah, I see. Shame. I thought you'd scooped her for a minute, there, Doc.'

'Nope. Just neighbours. Being neighbourly,' I reiterated for Lena, and the rest of the café, who were studiously pretending not to listen.

'Okeydokes. Nice to see you both.' And off she went.

'People aren't shy about coming forward here, are they?'

'Doesn't bother me.' I shrugged the comment off. 'I've lived here long enough to know what to expect. I probably should have warned you, though.'

'I've been called worse things than a potential suitor, so I'll cope.'

'A potential suitor? That's a very chivalrous term. I won't tell you what the text I got from one of the friends I waved to earlier said.'

'Well, now you have to.'

'Nooo!' I shook my head, laughing.

'Nope. Come on. If it concerns me, it's only fair I should know.'

'No! It's embarrassing!'

Henry folded his arms across his muscular chest, the T-shirt pulling enough to show anyone who might be interested just what they were missing. 'I'm going to sit here until you do.'

'Fine.' I concentrated on pouring my tea and smiled down at Spud as he lay on my toes and munched on the dog treat Lena had left for him.

'I meant to say I was thinking about getting the builders back in to do a bit of work on the garden. Apparently the thing to have is a hot tub with a bar. Then I could have some real garden parties.'

I met his eyes with a steely gaze. 'You wouldn't dare.'

'Do you really want to take that bet? I've already made what I know you consider to be some pretty hideous choices in my outdoor style. Maybe this might improve it? And I know some of my London friends would love a few parties over the summer...'

I narrowed my eyes and he met the glare head on. 'All you have to do is show me the text.'

I let out a laugh. 'Fine.' I pulled up the text. 'Although I don't know why it matters. It was just a comment in passing.'

'I'm interested,' he replied, focusing on the phone screen as I turned it round to face him. 'Ah. Shagfest. Yes, that is rather a different way of putting it.'

I gave him a tight smile and laid the phone face down on the table.

'I see you didn't reply.'

'He's coming over later in the week to prune a couple of my trees. I'll discuss the matter with him then by way of a clip round the ear.'

Henry huffed out a laugh as he lifted the cup to his lips. 'You have a lot of friends here.' The words were a statement, not a question.

'I do. I'm lucky, I know. But you'll make new ones too. It's hard not to, here.'

He seemed to think about that for a moment before nodding. 'I'm hoping that, despite the rocky start, I've finally made one.' It was the first time since I'd met him that there was anything other than utter confidence about his manner. For just one moment there was a hint of insecurity about Henry's words.

'You have,' I replied immediately, something about the brief show of vulnerability pushing me to dispel it quickly.

He smiled then and looked out of the window, the smile remaining until he once more lifted the rich, dark coffee to his lips.

The next couple of hours were spent leisurely wandering around the village, stopping to sit on the harbour wall for a while and mooching around the shops. Henry patiently listened as I told him tales of smugglers and legends of hauntings.

'You're not buying any of this, are you?' I asked, laughing as we stopped in the shade of a wonderfully large yew tree at the boundary of the churchyard.

'I'm enjoying listening to you tell the stories.'

'Hmm, you should have been a politician.'

Henry screwed his nose up. 'No, thanks.'

'I'm glad you're enjoying hearing them, but that wasn't what I asked.'

'True. Then I believe that the location of the village makes it likely that smuggling did occur in the area, but as to whether those particular events happened, I'm not sure. They certainly make good tales.'

'And what about the hauntings? Loads of people have experienced things in the pub.'

'Or think they have. Perhaps because the stories tell them they should? The mind is an incredibly complex thing and can be influenced and shaped in different ways.'

I leant on the lichen-covered stone wall beside me. 'Is there anything you believe in?'

'Lots of things.'

'Like?'

'People.'

'Really?'

'Yes.' He tilted his head. 'You seem surprised.'

'I am a little. Having come from a trauma background, I can only imagine that you saw a lot of examples of a lack of humanity.'

'You'd be right. But I also saw the opposite end of the spectrum. I saw patients rushed in with heart failure go on to survive and thrive because someone else had chosen to donate their organs. I witnessed strangers come in with someone because they happened to be the nearest person when the patient suffered the trauma, and stay until a friend or relative came, just so that person, a complete stranger, wasn't alone. You're right that every day we hear or see things that make us want to give up on the world. But then something happens to restore that faith. I left London because I was at the point where I was beginning to struggle with that restoration process, even though it was there. That's a slippery slope and I didn't want to get to the point where I no longer felt anything, where I was numb. I needed to get out while I still loved what I do and saw the people, not just another case.'

'Do you think you would have got to that? All I hear about you is how wonderful and attentive you are at the clinic.'

He gave a rueful smile, the hint of a sign that he was getting used to the fact that people were going to talk. 'Good to hear the gossip about me is good.'

'Oh, there's lots more I could tell if you'd like.'

'No!' He laughed then, holding up his hands. 'Baby steps, please.'

'Fair enough. It is all good, though.'

'Thanks. But yes, I think I was at risk of heading that way if I'd stayed where I was.'

'Then you were obviously supposed to leave when you did.'

'Let me guess, we're back to the universe leading me here.'

I shrugged, turning back to peer over the low wall of the churchyard, spring flowers nodding their heads amongst the ancient and not-so-old gravestones, their colours adding an extra layer of tranquillity to the scene. Percy volunteered for the church and kept the grass and graves neat, making sure that each one looked cared-for even if the person once laid to rest had no one to do it for them. I loved that about the village. Yes, people gossiped and were a little bit nosy, but they also made sure, even when the soul had moved on, that a person's resting place was still respected and looked after, just as important a part of the village as they had been in times past.

'I know you don't believe it, but that doesn't mean it's not true.'

'It kind of does.'

'No, it doesn't. OK,' I said, warming to my theme. 'In the sixteenth and seventeenth centuries, several astronomers claimed that the earth revolved around the sun. Some were imprisoned and at least one was burned at the stake for spouting such heresy.'

'You're not planning on any bonfires, are you?'

'Of course not.' I bumped him with my shoulder. 'My point is that we now know that to be true. Just because those in power and the majority didn't believe it, doesn't mean it wasn't true.'

'Interesting analogy, and I do get what you're saying,' Henry said as we resumed our slow walk back towards the car, having done a full circle, Spud padding along the pavement up the shady lane, off the lead a few steps ahead, content with sniffing all the interesting smells. 'I just disagree.'

'Of course you do.'

'I'm of a scientific disposition, so when it comes to auras and dream interpretation and, I'm afraid to say, many of the items in your friend's shop, I don't put any stock in it.'

'I see.' I felt his eyes on me and looked up to meet them. 'What?'

'Just wondering if you were deciding that we couldn't be friends any more.'

'No. We can still be friends. It will just give me greater pleasure when my manifestations come to fruition and I can say told you so.'

'That's very mature of you.'

'I know, but adulting all the time is very overrated, don't you find?'

Henry was silent.

'What is it?' I asked.

'Nothing.'

'Rubbish. Come on, tell me.' I caught his arm, causing him to stop.

'There's nothing,' he repeated, looking down at me with a smile. 'You know if this whole manifestation thing was true, God knows what I must have been thinking to have ended up with you next door.' His smile was wide and although his eyes were hidden behind expensive sunglasses, I knew they were smiling too, crinkling at the corners.

'I could take enormous offence to that.'

'You could, but you won't because you know now that I don't mean it like that.'

'And how do you mean it?' I asked, slowing as we came to the high wrought-iron gates at the entrance to The Vicarage.

Henry paused beside me. 'I mean it in the way that, had it been left to me, I suppose I would have chosen a neighbour in the same, or similar field. Someone strait-laced, no nonsense, and down to earth.'

I leant back on the gate. 'A mirror image of you.'

'Yes. I suppose so.' He drew in a deep breath then released it slowly.

'Sorry to disappoint.' I gave a half-apologetic smile and went to turn to face the gates, but Henry caught my arm, the large, tanned hand warm on my skin, the hold gentle. I stopped, pushing my sunglasses up onto the top of my head as I tilted my chin up.

'Don't think that,' he said, releasing my arm and removing his sunglasses. 'Please. That's not what I meant. What I meant is that, had any of it been real, that's what I would have brought into being. Instead I got quite the opposite and I'm grateful for that. Honestly. Who the hell would want to spend time with a carbon copy of themselves?'

I'd come across a few people in my time who would think that the holy grail, and I knew for sure there were several in the village and beyond who'd be more than happy to spend their time with a carbon copy of Henry Darcy, although the real thing would be preferable.

'Perhaps the universe knew better than you did.' I gave a shrug.

Henry threw his head back, the relaxed laughter making me smile. 'You're persistent, I'll give you that.'

I shrugged one shoulder and turned fully back to face the gates, each hand curled around a cool, shiny, black-painted railing.

'Isn't it beautiful?' I said, resting my forehead on the metal as I gazed wistfully down the drive at the solid, square Georgian house that sat proudly at the bottom, a large, full garden spread around it. An early-flowering rose nodded frilly-edged white blooms in the soft breeze as it scrambled up one wall of a summer house on the far side. Swathes of multicoloured tulips, late narcissi in yellow and white, and more early roses splashed the beds with colour, contrasting with the lush green of the lawn. Blossom trees were full and fluffy with blooms, and all around us the only sound was sweet, joyful birdsong.

'It is,' Henry agreed, taking a couple of steps back.

I gazed for a few more moments and then waved as the figure that had stepped out from the French doors looked up the driveway and waved back enthusiastically. Glancing round, I noticed Henry had stepped back several more paces.

'Don't worry. They don't mind me admiring the place.'

Henry nodded, his sunglasses back on.

'They saw me one time and I was so embarrassed, but Barb and Tony were so lovely. It wasn't long after I'd moved back and was desperately trying to wrangle my own garden and house into some semblance of how I wanted it.'

'So your garden wasn't always like that?'

'God, no,' I laughed. 'I wish. Although actually, no, I probably don't. It wasn't the utter wilderness yours was, but it was a bit of a mess.'

'Why don't you wish it had been perfect then?'

'Because then I wouldn't have learned all that I have. If it had all been done for me, I wouldn't have tried and failed and tried and succeeded. I wouldn't have had the opportunity to learn to grow things from seed to save money, and take cuttings, or be given cuttings to grow on from friends and made friends through it. When I look at those plants now, I think of those people. It was Barb and Tony who taught me how to take cuttings, actually.'

'Really?'

'Yeah. They were so generous with their time. Quite a few of the shrubs in my garden are ones they helped me propagate.'

'They sound like nice people. I've not met them yet. Thankfully.' He turned as he said it. 'I mean, in a medical setting.'

'I knew what you meant. I expect you've seen them in passing in the greengrocers or at the farm shop and just didn't realise,' I said, turning back to continue our walk.

Henry cleared his throat and scratched the back of his neck.

'What's the matter?'

'I probably haven't seen them getting food in the village.'

I pulled a face as we turned the corner. 'How do you know?'

'Because I've been getting everything at the big supermarket twenty minutes down the road.' He pushed his glasses to the top of his head. 'You're thinking twice about that bonfire now, aren't you?'

'Henry, where you shop is entirely your choice. I just assumed, that's all. It wasn't a criticism and I'm certainly not going to get up a posse to run you out of the village for daring to shop elsewhere. We all get stuff there at times, of course we do. But if you do fancy trying some of the local shops when you have time, I can guarantee you'll notice a difference in quality.'

'I don't doubt it. And now, thanks to the tour today, I've got more of an idea where to go. I don't know why I didn't even consider shopping here before.'

'You lived in London and worked shifts for years and barely took time off, by the sounds. It's easy to get out of the habit.'

'Yes, you're probably right. It's been nice having the time to cook again – I mean properly cook – so now I know what's here, I'll definitely be using them. Good excuse for a walk into the village.'

'Exactly.'

'It's kind of like a step back in time. Just buying stuff when you need it and having the ability to do that.'

'We're really lucky that the places here have managed to keep going. So many little towns and villages have lost their shops.'

'I know. My aunt lives in a village in Surrey and there's nothing there now. The little village post office hung on for as long as it could, but they closed that last year. There's a lot of older people there and they relied on it for banking and their pensions and so on. The bus service is pretty rubbish, so they're scuppered. It's a shame.'

'Yeah, it is. We've got the best of both worlds. Enough trade to keep places going but not so much that you're squidged like a sardine during tourist season.'

We were now back at the car, and after depositing our purchases in the boot and strapping ourselves in, we took the short but leisurely drive back.

'Ah, home sweet home,' I said as we approached the cottages. He pulled up and, as I unhooked my seatbelt from the dog's, Henry was at the car door, opening it for me and holding out a hand to assist me from the car. I popped Spud down on the pavement and then accepted the chivalry.

'Thanks for a lovely day, Henry,' I said, opening the gate for Spud to hare into the garden and do a thorough patrol.

'No, thank you. Honestly, I thought it would be a half-hour tour at the most.'

'Oh! Sorry, did you have something to get back for? You should have said, I could have—'

Henry was shaking his head and reaching for my hands. 'No.

It was great. Everything from the surfing to the stories, to the wonderful food and coffee. I completely underestimated how much this place had to offer.' He leant against the garden wall, the glasses pushed up on his head now that the sun was behind the houses, warming the back gardens. 'I came here for peace and I've got that, but it offers so much more, and I wouldn't have known about half of that if it wasn't for you.'

'So it was worth being dragged into the "woo-woo" shop?'

'Even worth that,' he said, an easy laugh in his voice. 'And now I have new reading material, which is always good.'

'I'm glad you enjoyed it. Thanks for suggesting it. I probably would have ended up working at least part of the day, if not all, if it hadn't been for this.'

'Aha, my evil plan worked!'

'It did, thank you.' I stepped through the gate and turned to close it.

'Willow?'

'Yes?'

'Feel free to say no, I mean, I know you've just got in and everything...'

'That would be lovely. Thanks.'

Henry clamped his lips together for a second. 'I haven't said anything yet.'

'Were you going to suggest dinner?'

'Yes.'

'There we are then. I was going to do the same, if you were free.'

'I've got fresh ingredients now,' he held up the bag of goodies he'd got in the local shops, 'so I need someone to test a recipe on.'

'I'm happy to be a guinea pig anytime if it means free food.'

'Good to know,' he smiled. 'Just come round when you're ready.'

'Is it OK to bring Spud?'

'Oh. Right. Yes, absolutely. I forgot about him for a minute.'

I waited. 'If it's a problem, how about you come to us.'

'No, no problem. I'm just not used to having a pet around. Please, you're both invited, of course.'

19

Henry was a surprisingly good cook for someone who freely admitted he'd lived the last however many years on ready meals. Clearly cooked breakfasts weren't his only speciality.

'A previously wasted talent,' I said, putting my cutlery together.

'Well, now I'm not working all the crazy hours, I'm trying to make sure I take the time to do more of it.'

'Sounds good.'

'I've actually invited my parents and brother down next weekend, so thanks for letting me try this out on you. Hopefully that means I won't poison anyone now.'

'If you do, they're in the right place, at least.'

'That is true.'

'It'll be lovely to have your family around you, I'm sure. I guess you didn't get to spend a lot of time together before?'

'No. I didn't make the effort I should have done. Something else I'm making a conscious effort to change.'

'I'm sure they understood.'

'You're right, they did, lucky for me but that's not the point.'

'Fresh starts and all that.' I raised my glass with the perfectly chilled Chablis that Henry had poured when I arrived. 'This really should be my last glass!'

He tapped his own crystal against mine. 'To fresh starts.'

I got up and headed out of the folding door to his patio set and plopped down on one of the chairs, tucking my feet underneath me. Henry followed, taking the sofa, his long legs stretched out, ankles crossed as they rested on the other arm.

'What a beautiful night.'

Above us the sky had turned navy and pinpricks of starlight scattered the dark canvas. As we watched, a streak of light darted across the sky.

'Wow! I don't think I've seen a shooting star since I was a kid, when Dad took us hiking and camping in the depths of Wales.'

'I hope you made a wish.'

'Then or now?'

'Either,' I said, resting my head back, the world feeling pleasantly soft and fuzzy at the edges.

'I forgot.'

'You don't believe in that either, do you?'

'Do you?'

'I don't know, but I always think there's no harm in trying.'

'Is that what the manifesting is about? That it's worth a try?'

'No.' I shifted position. 'It's more than that. That's about raising my vibrations and bringing forth the things I want in my life, the feelings I want. Aligning my thoughts and belief with what I know will come with the universe.' I rolled my head on the back of the chair. 'This is when you laugh.'

Henry didn't laugh. 'So what is it you want? Am I allowed to ask that?' The relaxing day, good food and wine had apparently softened his inhibitions.

'What everyone wants, I suppose. The right person. I mean,

I'm happy with Spud and I'm more than capable of looking after myself.'

'I don't think anyone would question that.'

'But there's something missing and I know what it is. I just don't know yet *who* it is. But I trust the universe to bring them.'

'How will you know when it's the right one?'

'I just will.'

Henry looked back up at the sky and finished the last of his drink.

* * *

The next day I set out the crystals I'd bought and prepared to cleanse them to make sure that the only energies they held were those appropriate to my purpose. Lighting the wodge of sage, I waited a few moments for it to smoke – making sure the window was open – then passed each one gently through the trails twisting up from the bundle. I studied the greeny-pink of the tourmaline I'd picked up yesterday as I did so. There were several types of this stone, but this particular one was said to help the manifestation process. Getting hold of that one had been a definite goal. No accidental manifestation this time. This time I was getting it right. Next was the labradorite, the one whose name Henry had made fun of. I smiled at the memory as I wafted the crystal through the smoke a few times. To be honest, I hadn't even expected him to enter the shop, but although it was clear he didn't put any stock in these alternative beliefs, he didn't deride them either. I wondered what he'd think of the book he'd bought. It'd be nice to talk it over with him once he'd finished.

Willow! Focus. You're supposed to be manifesting the perfect man here, not thinking about the one next door, however platonically.

Right. Back to the job in hand. Once the crystals were all

cleansed, I made use of the sage and popped round my house giving it a cleanse too. I liked to do it about once a month but, what with work being so busy, I hadn't had time. Smudging it out on a saucer, I popped them outside on the patio table to cool down completely. Back upstairs, it was time to programme the crystals. One by one, I took them between my thumb and forefinger, focusing and connecting to the stone in my hand, shutting out all other thoughts. Then, distilling my manifest wish down to one word, I exhaled, the word 'love' caught up in my breath and absorbing into the fragment of nature in front of me.

Each morning and each evening, I would stand in front of my vision board and drink it in, absorbing every tiny detail. Then I'd hold the cool stones in my hand, take a seat and hold them to my heart, eyes closed and mind open to the universe, ready to receive what was mine.

* * *

'I still don't understand why you're doing all this when there's a perfectly decent man living right next door to you. You said he even seems to be getting used to Spud now.'

I was round at Abby and Ed's, sitting in their garden with a long, cool drink of the homemade lemonade I'd brought with me along with a couple of trays of sweet peas, which Spud was 'helping' Ed plant along their fence. Abby wasn't really into gardening but enjoyed the benefits, and Ed was looking forward to getting stuck in now that he wouldn't be gone half the time. He was busy threading wire through the metal eyes he'd just screwed to the fence to train the sweet peas up. It was going to look, and smell, beautiful once they flowered.

Abby prodded me with a bare foot. 'Well?'

'I told you. It needs to be someone I share interests with, hold similar views about things with. Henry and I are about as oppo-site as you could get. It would never work, even if I was interested.'

'You can't tell me you're not. He's hardly the back of a bus.'

'I *can* tell you that and quite honestly. Yes, he's very hand-some, I grant you that. And intelligent and funny when he relaxes enough to be.'

Abby tilted forward and rested her chin on her hand, suddenly interested. 'This sounds promising.'

'It's not. Not at all. That's what I mean. I'm sure he'd be lovely for someone else, just not me.'

'Not quite the grump we thought he was, though?'

'No, I think he was extremely stressed with the renovation and the culture shock, but generally now I just think he's reserved.'

'Are you sticking up for him?'

'I don't think Henry Darcy needs me to stick up for him. Everywhere I go, I hear how wonderful it must be to live next door to such a lovely, gorgeous man.'

'You do seem to have spent a lot of time together.' Abby wiggled her eyebrows.

'Hardly. I just showed him around and we've had a couple of meals together. That's all. I'd do the same for anyone, you know that.'

'The way you two started off, I'm amazed you even speak.'

'I know. Not the best start, was it? Thank goodness we've got past that, though.'

'Despite having nothing in common...'

'Stop it, you.' I pointed my glass at her with a grin.

Abby flopped back in her chair. 'OK, fine. It's just such a shame. You look so good together.'

'Looks aren't everything. Right,' I said, placing my glass down on the table. 'I'd better be getting back. I want to try and get a coat of paint on my front gate today.'

'Are you ever not doing something to that house?'

'There does always seem to be something to do,' I agreed. 'The perks of buying an old house, I guess. But I love it. And I've learned loads with all the jobs I've taken on doing it up.'

'Would you do it again, if the opportunity or need to move arose?'

I screwed up my nose as I stood. 'Doubtful. It has been a lot of work and there's definitely a difference between doing things for fun and doing it because you have to. Anyway, I don't think that's something I really need to think about. I don't see any plans to move in the future.'

'What about this bloke you're manifesting? Perhaps he's going to whisk you away to live in Monaco or somewhere!'

'Somehow I doubt it! I'm not exactly of the Monaco set aesthetic.' I looked down at my flowing sundress with its ditsy pastel flowers and the not-entirely-clean nails from where I'd helped Ed decide how to space the sweet peas. 'I don't think that relationship would last very long! I'd stick out like a sore thumb.'

Abby stood up and gave me a hug. 'I wouldn't want you jetting off to Monaco anyway, so just as well.'

I returned the hug, gave one to Ed too, and told him to ring me if he had any planty-type questions, called Spud and began the walk home.

* * *

'Not manifested anyone to do that for you yet?' The deep voice came from behind me, making me jump and splodge my neat paint as I put the last touches to the gate.

'Damn.'

'Oops. Sorry.'

I tidied up the splodge before looking up at Henry, who was leaning on his front garden wall, looking down at me. His shirt collar was unbuttoned, his jacket was over his arm, and in his hand he carried a rather battered doctor's bag with gold initials on. I squinted at the letters.

'Have you stolen that?'

The dark brows drew momentarily together before his eyeline followed my own.

'Oh! No, I can assure you I haven't. It was my dad's. He gave it to me when he retired.'

I tilted my head to the side. 'Aah, that's lovely.'

'Your hair is in the paint.'

'What?'

'Your hair.' Henry pointed to the jar I'd decanted some of my paint into and hung from the gate latch. 'It's in the jar.'

'Oh, shit.' I kept my head still and felt around for the end of my plait in order to lift it out carefully rather than flinging paint everywhere, including on to my neighbour and his expensive suit.

'Here. Just hold still a sec.' Henry put down his bag, laid his jacket over the wall and crouched down next to me. His face was close, a hint of spicy aftershave tickling my senses. His hand moved beside me as I stayed still and waited.

'Can I use this?' he asked, holding up a bit of old sheeting I'd torn up as rag.

'Yes.'

Carefully he lifted my hair out of the paint, squeezing off the excess back into the jar and then wrapping the end in the rag, tying it carefully. 'There.'

'Thanks. I'm guessing I'm going to have shorter hair later on this evening.'

'Can you not get it out with one of your potions?'

'My potions?' I asked, laughing, handing him another rag to wipe his hands on. 'Maybe, but I'll need to discuss the best option with my coven first.'

'Sorry, I didn't mean it like that.'

'It's fine.'

'I really didn't.' His face was earnest. 'I just meant... well, you seem to have all sorts of natural remedies and tricks. I didn't know if you knew of something you could do to get it out rather than cut your hair.' He straightened and I followed, wiggling my left foot, trying to wake it up from where I'd been sitting on it. 'Honestly. I wasn't calling you a witch. I mean, I know you consider yourself a...' The word seemed to stick in his throat this time. He swallowed and tried again. 'Witch.'

'You struggle with that idea, don't you?' I grinned at him, wiping my hands on a clean bit of the rag. 'Don't worry, Henry, it's fine. I'm sure you called me much worse when we first met!'

His serious expression remained. 'That was different. We didn't know each other then and I wasn't... wasn't in the best space.'

'I was joking.' I rested a now-clean hand on his exposed forearm.

I saw his Adam's apple bounce and he gave a couple of quick nods. 'Yes.'

'Oh, God, look at the state of your hands!' His efforts to rescue my hair had resulted in paint getting all over them, despite the rag. 'Seriously, you should have left it to me. Come in and wash your hands first, otherwise you're going to get paint on your door-handle, keys and everything.'

He started to protest but I shooshed him and, showing that he was getting to know me, he realised arguing was not worth the effort and followed me around the back of the house and into the kitchen, Spud trotting at our heels.

'There. That's better.' I handed Henry a towel to dry his hands.

'Thanks. What's all this for?' he asked, looking down at the kitchen table where I had an array of veggies ready for chopping along with a bowl of lentils I'd cooked earlier.

'Dinner. I'm doing a poke bowl.'

'Looks good. Very healthy.'

'Would you like to come round? There's plenty.'

Henry's head snapped up. 'Oh, God. No, I wasn't hinting at an invite!'

'I know you weren't. I think I know you well enough by now to know that you're far too polite for that. But, if you'd like to, the offer is there. Looks like you've had a long day. I just need to sort this out first.' I pointed at my hair.

'How about if I go home and change, then come back and chop these up while you're doing that?'

'I didn't invite you over to do most of the work yourself!'

'Let's call it teamwork, then?' The smile was soft, a little tired and very attractive. My gaze slid to Spud, who was standing at Henry's feet, looking up hopefully. Henry noticed, looked down, then back at me. 'He's very attentive, isn't he?'

I crouched down and Spud sped over to me, allowing me to scoop him up.

'He's super friendly and lives for cuddles.'

Henry lifted his hand the smallest amount and, for a moment, I thought he was actually going to give Spud his first pat but instead he shoved it in his pocket. 'I'll head next door.'

'OK. Just come back in through here. I won't be long.'

'Take as long as you need.'

We headed in our separate directions with Spud charging up the stairs in front of me as I made my way to the bathroom.

Twenty minutes later I'd showered, given up trying to get the paint out of my hair and chopped an inch off instead, which solved the problem quicker. I got dressed in a vintage Laura Ashley maxi dress with a halter neck in a cornflower blue that matched my eyes. It was a recent find and I was utterly smitten with it.

'Ready, Spuddy?' I asked of my dog, who had found a patch of evening sunlight in the bedroom and was happily dozing in it. But at my words, he was up, ready to go. 'Go on, then.' I indicated the stairs and he tore down them in front of me.

'Oh!'

Henry froze, my largest kitchen knife in his hand and a tea towel tucked in his belt as a make-do apron. 'What have I done wrong?'

'Nothing! I just didn't realise you were back already. Some guard dog you are,' I said, looking down at Spud, who just wagged his tail even faster then headed over to his water bowl for a noisy drink. 'He must have known it was you.'

'Or he's a bit deaf.'

'He is not deaf, thank you very much!'

Henry flashed a grin and resumed chopping while I went to the cupboard and began to prepare my dog's dinner, scooping a handful of chopped carrot from the table and adding it to the bowl.

'Oi, that's for us.'

'There's three of us here,' I challenged, drawing myself up to my full height. In bare feet and with a distinct height disadvantage, I hardly presented much of a threat, but it was more about making a point.

'Though she be but little, she is fierce.' His smile was soft as he looked down at me.

'And don't you forget it.'

'Believe me, that's not likely to happen. These look about right?'

'Perfect. Thanks. I can take over now.' I went to take the knife but Henry turned slightly to block me.

'No need.'

'You're a guest.'

'But I enjoy it and find it relaxing.'

He pushed two avocados towards me and, side by side, we got on with the prep. Between our feet, Spud sat ever hopeful of a dropped morsel, his fluffy little tail sweeping the floor in a short arc back and forth.

20

Later that evening, once the delicious dinner had been eaten and the dishes stacked in the dishwasher and Spud fed, Henry and I stepped out onto my patio. It was somewhat smaller than Henry's, thanks to the recent makeover his side of the property had undergone, and I'd further diminished the space available for seating by filling it with plants.

'It's a little more snug out here than yours.'

'It's lovely. Very homely.' Henry handed me a glass of the wine he'd brought round. 'Very you.'

'Thanks.' I took the glass, a deep burgundy-coloured full-bodied red. 'I don't think our tastes could be any more polarised, could they?'

'They are different, that's true.'

'Does it make you feel a bit claustrophobic over here?'

'No, not at all.'

'Have you always been quite minimalist?'

'Is that what I am?'

'Aren't you?'

'You tell me.'

'Surely you know your own style?'

Henry took a sip of the wine and held it in his mouth for a moment, savouring the flavour. That was another difference between the two of us. He did have excellent taste and I was gradually learning from him about wines and what to pair with what.

'If I'm honest, I'm not sure I have a style. Moving here was a new start in many ways. I'd previously been living with someone and when that went wrong, she moved out and took all the nice stuff.'

'Shouldn't they have been split? I mean... if you'd chosen them together?'

'I have to admit I didn't participate too much in the choosing either. I'd come home, there'd be something new there, I'd agree that it was nice and we moved on.'

'Oh. I can kind of see why she took everything, then.'

'That's one of the things I like about you. Your honesty.'

I'd lit the small fire pit and I could see amusement as well as firelight reflected in his eyes.

'I don't think you were such a fan of that honesty when you first moved here,' I replied with a laugh.

'That is true. You've grown on me.'

'We've grown on each other.'

'These are great, aren't they?' he said, indicating the fire with his foot. 'There's something magical about it.' His attention turned towards the garden. 'Admittedly I was kind of livid when you were going off on one about the garden being ripped out, but sitting here now looking down at yours, I can see why you were so furious. It feels so real. A proper, living thing. The way you described mine as sterile is accurate. That's so clear now when I sit here.'

'It doesn't have to be. You could still bring life into yours if you wanted to.'

He shook his head. 'I don't have your skills.'

'I didn't have the knowledge I have now when I started, and people around here were really kind and helped too.'

'I'm not the best at accepting help.'

'Yes, I think I've already worked that out, but that doesn't mean you couldn't learn.'

'I suppose,' Henry replied with as much enthusiasm as if I'd just asked him to suck a lemon.

'What about getting a few bits for the patio? I'm sure we could find some things to make it a little more cosy but still keep your modern aesthetic.'

He tilted his head to one side just a little. 'We?'

'Just a figure of speech. You know what I mean.'

'You might be right. It would be good to bring a bit of interest to the place. I'll take a look tomorrow. Thanks for the idea.'

'You're welcome. As you might have guessed, I love anything to do with the home and garden so it's a pleasure.'

'I can see you enjoy your home. It's written on your face when you come in from walking the dog.' He paused then spoke again. 'I've just heard that out loud and realise it might sound a bit weird. Please be assured I've not been spying. I use the front bedroom as a reading room and the chair is by the window for the natural light, hence seeing you.'

'And can you really tell that?'

'Yes. You smile as you approach your home. I don't think I've ever, or would ever, feel that way. I mean I'm glad to be home, obviously, but there's a, I don't know, I'd say a glow about you but then I'd worry you're rubbing off on me a little too much.'

'Ha ha. Also "the dog" has a name.'

'I know, but it feels odd referring to a living creature as a root vegetable.'

'He likes his name, don't you, Spuddy wuddy?' I reached

down and scooped him up onto my lap, whereupon he proceeded to snuggle against me, his tail wagging madly again in delight.

'So you say.'

'Does this look like a hard-done-by dog to you?' I asked.

'Most definitely not. He's very lucky. Have you had him long?'

'About three years. I don't know how I lived without him now.'

'I'm sure it's company.'

'*He* is. Yes.'

'I meant having a pet.'

'Oh, right. I take it you've never had pets?'

'Not really. One cat, one time, but it hated me and wasn't all that struck on my girlfriend. Eventually it took off and we found out a few weeks later it was living happily with a neighbour.'

'Oh. Didn't you want to get your pet back?'

'Nope. I've come home with fewer injuries breaking up a fight in A&E than that cat gave me. They were welcome to it. Anyway, neither of us were home enough to have a pet, really. I think it was more the idea of a pet that appealed to her rather than actual ownership. I ended up being the one to feed it and try and get it to the vet and so on, which was extra sickening as the thing couldn't stand me.'

'Sounds like the feeling was mutual.'

Henry gave a short laugh. 'I suppose it was.'

'Well, like I say, I don't know what I'd do without my Spuddy.' I snuggled my dog and we all sat in comfortable silence for the next few minutes.

'How's the manifesting going?'

I looked suspiciously over my glass at him as I sipped. 'Are you actually interested or just looking for cues to take the pee out of me?'

He waggled his head from side to side. 'A little of both.'

'You're going to have to eat your words when the perfect man waltzes into my life.'

Placing his wine glass down on the small table, Henry picked up a stick that hadn't quite made it to the fire pit.

'Is that what you want?' he asked, chucking the twig into the fire, his eyes focused on it, watching as the flames licked around it and eventually caught.

'Mostly. I'm not naïve enough to think that the perfect man actually exists. But yes, the right person for me. At last.'

'You were married before, though?'

'Yes. Bit of a mistake but it seemed a good idea at the time.'

'And you got tired of city life?'

'Yep. This is what makes me happy.' I indicated our surroundings with one arm, the other resting on Spud's warm body now curled up and snoozing on my lap. 'I'm not interested in the trendiest restaurant, seeing the latest film or trying the newest cocktail bar. I just want to sit here, eat good food, watch the sun go down and the firelight dance.'

'That does sound perfect.'

'Doesn't it?'

'But it's not enough.'

'Huh?'

'The manifesting. As perfect as all this is, it's not enough.'

'I suppose everyone – or at least most people – want to be loved.'

'From what I've seen and heard since I've been here, you're pretty well loved in this village. Even when I thought you were the neighbour from hell, I didn't dare say anything against you. All I heard was, "Oh, you've moved next to Willow? She's so lovely. She's so sweet!"' He'd put on a voice, and the squeaky tone coming out of his sizeable frame together with the faces he was pulling as he tilted his head one way then the other brought on the giggles.

'They did not say it like that!' I batted him gently with my free hand, careful not to disturb Spud.

'They did!' He was laughing. 'I assumed you must have put some sort of spell on them as I already knew you to be a royal pain in the behind.'

'As well as a witch?'

'As well as a witch. Honestly, I was seriously reconsidering my life choices.'

'You were not!' I said, really laughing now.

'I was!' he replied, joining me. 'For all I knew, I'd wake up one morning, look in the mirror and find a frog staring back at me!'

'You can count yourself lucky that you haven't, then.'

'Yet,' he added.

'Yet,' I confirmed.

Henry turned back towards the fire, which was dying down.

'Do you want me to put another log on, or do you have plans?'

'For tonight?' I giggled.

'No! I mean... no. Tomorrow. Whether you need to... umm...'

Suddenly my highly articulate, erudite neighbour was struggling for words. For a doctor, he was rather adorably easy to embarrass.

'I don't have any tall, dark, handsome men due this evening to sweep me away, so feel free to chuck another log on. Unless you're expecting a booty call?'

'Very funny.' With that, he placed the hunk of wood carefully on the fire in just the right spot. I probably would have just chucked it on and let it get on with its job but that was yet another difference between the two of us. I was precise and careful in my work because I needed to be, but outside of that, if precise wasn't absolutely necessary, I was more than happy to be a bit more loose about things. Life was too short for exact plans and rigidity.

'So what do you have planned for tomorrow?'

'I'm going to go back and do some more surfing. I messaged Vijay earlier so it's all booked. If that goes well, I'm going to order a surfboard from him.'

'Wow! You really are getting into it. That's great.'

'Yeah, it's definitely time to get back to it regularly.'

'I've only ever done it a few times but it's certainly a mindful activity. You're busy concentrating on the waves and the board and your balance.'

Henry stretched his neck to the left, then the right. 'I never really thought about it like that but yes, you're right.'

'Maybe that's what you needed. To find that.'

'You think I manifested it?'

'Maybe. If you've been wanting to get out of the rat race for some time, maybe you manifested all of this.'

Henry muttered under his breath. 'Good grief.'

'I heard that.'

'Of course you did. I would expect nothing less from your special powers.' He wiggled his fingers for extra effect.

'You're pushing your luck, you know. I hope you like wearing green. Or, rather, being green!'

His laugh was all the more rich and welcome for rarely being released in the full, relaxed manner in which he did so then. It carried on the still night air and wrapped itself around me, and for a moment I wished that we weren't so different.

'I think, if that had been the case, I'd have manifested,' he made quote marks in the air with his fingers, 'a less stressful introduction to my next-door neighbour.'

I remained silent.

'Aha!' he said, suddenly more animated than I'd seen him all evening. 'I knew it! She's stumped!'

'Gracious in competition isn't one of your qualities, is it?'

'Nope. Horrible loser. Ask my brother. We're both competitive. There was a time when my parents banned us from playing all board games after they became casualties of our desire to win at all costs.'

'And you haven't improved, clearly.'

'Depends on the circumstance.'

'You haven't improved in this particular circumstance.'

'No. Sorry. I'm on the side of science. One point to me, I believe.'

There was a teasing note to his voice. Apparently the wine, combined with the easy feel of the evening, was working on those parts of Henry that had him uptight for so long. I was glad to see it. Maybe in time that side of him would come out a little more. After years of high stress and shift work, it could only do his body and mind good.

I threw him a snooty look, but he saw straight through it, sending me a smile that, had I not been so sure he wasn't the man I was waiting for, could have lit a fire inside me to rival the one in front of us.

* * *

'Did you hear there's a new doctor up at the clinic, filling in for Dr Graham while she's on maternity leave? The word is she might not come back, so he could be here to stay.' Abby was bubbling over the latest gossip as we sat in our favourite café.

'That's funny. Henry hasn't said anything about it.'

'And how is Henry?' Abby flashed her eyes at me over the top of her iced latte.

'Fine, as far as I know.'

'From what I heard, he's worked with the new doctor before. Strange he hasn't mentioned anything.'

'He's not always one to waste words. I suppose he didn't think there was anything to tell.'

'And what about you?' Abby asked, biting into a fresh Bakewell tart.

'What about me?'

'Anything to tell?'

'Nope.'

'The manifesting not working yet, then?'

'It's a process. I have to trust in that.'

'You're way more patient than me.'

'Believe me, if I could hurry it all up, I would. I just have to have faith that things will all happen as they should at the right time.'

'If I hadn't asked Ed if he was ever going to bloody well kiss me, I'd probably still be waiting!'

'This is different. You knew Ed was the right one for you, he just needed a little chivvying along. There's no one in my life right now to chivvy!'

'There is, actually.'

'No,' I said with a pointed look at her. 'There isn't. Not in a romantic sense.'

'Not yet! So let's circle back to my original question. Did you know that there's a new doctor up at the clinic?'

'No, I didn't.'

'Apparently he's super dishy.'

'Married?'

'Nope.'

'Engaged?'

'Nope.'

'With someone?'

'Nope.'

'Gay?'

Abby sat back and crossed her arms, a smug look on her face. 'Nope.'

'Well, if he's someone I'm supposed to meet, then I will. If he isn't, I won't.'

'You're putting a lot of faith in all this stuff, aren't you?'

'What choice do I have?' I held up a hand as Abby went to reply. 'Don't answer that.' I had a feeling that her answer would involve my neighbour, a large bottle of wine, preferably two, and an ironically named family-size box of condoms.

'Well, I've got a lunch date with my husband, so I'd better go and beautify myself.' Abby pushed out her chair and lifted her bag from the back of it. Her face shone with happiness at the novelty of Ed finally being home and available for such things after so many years of cramming everything into the short time they had together while he was back from deployment.

'You're already gorgeous, and frankly you could turn up in a bin bag with a face full of mud and he'd still go gaga.'

Her grin was as soppy and sweet as it had been on their wedding day fifteen years ago, giving me the same warm fuzzies today as it had then. Despite all the challenges that life had thrown at them, they had worked together as a team, even when Ed was thousands of miles away. Towards the end of my marriage, Mark and I hadn't been able to decide on what we ate for dinner, let alone anything deeper. Whatever happened with my manifesting, I knew that I wanted to be as happy and content and in love as my friend still was fifteen years into her marriage.

'You walking home?'

'No, I'm heading up to the clinic, actually. Niamh's had a patient in with me for the last couple of weeks and I've discharged him today.' I opened my bag to reveal a pale brown teddy bear resting inside, his discharge papers beside him.

'I didn't know you escorted your patients home too?'

'It's not normally part of the service, but I was coming in to meet you anyway and, as Ed was collecting Spud from the groomer's while we were here, I thought I may as well. It's not particularly out of my way, so I thought I'd extend my walk a little and take Gareth here back to his family.'

'Gareth?'

We both looked down at the bear.

'Actually it kind of suits him,' Abby said, studying the furry little face peering back up at her. 'OK.' She checked her watch. 'I'd better run.' She gave me another quick hug and dashed out of the door.

I got myself ready, waved at the café owner, who was busy pouring beans into the hopper of the coffee machine, and then headed out.

21

As I got to the edge of the village and crested the hill, the private clinic with its clean lines, surrounded by landscaped gardens, came into view. Since it opened nearly ten years ago, it had received nothing but praise from both patients and official bodies. Built at the edge of the village, some of the rooms benefitted from views of the fields and hedgerows beyond. Our friend Steve had taken a risk when he'd looked into investment for building a private hospital here, but his vision had paid off and they now offered a vast range of specialities from bunions to boob jobs. The one thing he was always adamant about though, was getting brilliant staff and the best experience for their patients. From the odd time I'd been in, there was always a calm and reassuring feel about it, and people singing Henry's praises could only add to its reputation.

The doors opened with a quiet hush and I walked up to the oak reception desk where Niamh was on the phone. She looked up and waved, a big smile on her face.

'Two minutes,' she mouthed.

I stuck a thumb up and wandered over to the noticeboard

where thank you cards had been pinned up alongside a poster for the annual village summer fayre. I was just reading the third card when Niamh called me over.

'Willow!'

I turned and walked slap bang into a solid chest.

'Oh, I'm so sorry!' I said, stepping back.

'No problem.' His smile was white but not Ross-from-*Friends* white, wide but not too wide, and backed up by a pair of dark brown eyes that were currently looking down at me. 'Hi. Umm, hello.'

'Dr Wise.' Niamh hurried over, an undisguised grin on her face. 'I see you've met Willow Haines. Willow, this is Dr Wise. He's filling in for Dr Graham's maternity leave.'

'Pleased to meet you, Willow.' He held out a tanned hand and I took it.

'And you, Doctor.'

'Calvin, please.'

'What brings you to see us? I hope you're not unwell.'

'No, luckily. I have a delivery for Niamh.' I handed over the bear and Niamh looked him over with a wide smile.

'Thanks, Willow. This is marvellous!'

She held up her bear. Calvin looked momentarily, and very handsomely, confused.

'I run a teddy bear hospital.'

'A teddy bear hospital?' The confusion turned to amusement.

'She's amazing. Don't underestimate her skills, Doctor. I reckon her stitching could give you a run for your money.'

'Is that so?' he answered, his tone interested, his focus remaining on me.

'I do have some skills.'

'So it seems.'

'Well, I'd better get back to work. I'll pop the money over on my break, OK, Willow?'

'Perfect, thanks.'

Niamh walked away, giving me a massive wink from behind Dr Wise as she did so.

'So you're new here?'

'That's right. Just temporary at the moment, but who knows?'

'Where were you before?'

'London.'

'Well, we're certainly a lot quieter down here than the bright lights of London.'

'I'm beginning to see that's not such a bad thing.'

Was he coming on to me? No. He was just being friendly. 'That's good to hear. I'm glad you're enjoying the role.'

'More and more each day.' Calvin's gaze was still on me, and his smile widened once more as he spoke.

Oh my God, he *was* coming on to me!

'I've heard that the local pub has pretty amazing food. What's your opinion, as a local?'

'Totally agree. Reggie is a fantastic chef, and the atmosphere is great. There's a beer garden too with fantastic views and lots of shade, if you don't want to cook in the sun.'

'I'm guessing you're one of those, with that beautiful Celtic colouring of yours.'

OK. He was definitely hitting on me. 'I am indeed. The Indian here is absolutely the best too, so you must try that.'

'I don't suppose you'd like to introduce me to it one evening this week?' He smiled disarmingly, his entire being confident without being cocky, relaxed but attentive, and right then, that attention made me feel like I was the most important person in the world. If this was his manner with patients, I could see that he would soon become a popular choice for the clinic.

'I seem to have taken you by surprise,' Calvin noted, his eyes dancing with amusement.

'Yes,' I laughed, releasing some of the tension and nerves that I didn't even realise I'd built up about dating. With so many other things in life, I was all about going with the flow, believing in nature, believing that what would be would be, and I'd told myself that meeting someone was the same. Admittedly I was trying to give the universe a hefty shove with the manifesting, crystals, asking the angels and everything else I could think of. But apparently none of it had prepared me for the moment when a good-looking, pleasant and solvent man actually asked me out on a date! Instead of being relaxed about it, I'd lost all sense of calm and reverted to teenage nerves. What the hell was wrong with me? Come on, Willow, get a grip!

'Sorry,' he replied, looking anything but.

'It's fine. I... I just wasn't expecting it.'

'I'm surprised at that.'

I tilted my head at him. 'Now you're flirting.'

'I'm glad you've finally noticed.'

My smile widened.

'You have a beautiful smile. When can I take you out so that I can enjoy that more?'

'You have all the right lines, don't you?'

'Only for the right person.' The smile had faded, but the gaze was more intense.

'How about Thursday?'

'Perfect. I'll pick you up at seven.'

'I can walk. It's not that far.'

'I'd rather pick you up.'

'It's only a few minutes' drive,' I said, relaxing in the face of his determination.

'That's a few minutes extra with you so it's perfect.'

'Fine.' I held up my hands in submission, still smiling. 'You win.'

'Where do you live?'

'Down near the river. Mill Cottage. Basically just drive to the other end of the village until you can't go any further.'

His brow furrowed. 'Why does that ring a bell?'

'Willow?'

The deep, clipped tones made me jump and I turned to see Henry striding towards us, his forehead etched deep with lines as he approached me.

'Is everything all right? Are you unwell?'

'Hi, Henry. How are you?'

'Fine. What's wrong?'

'Nothing. I just returned a patient to Niamh.'

'A patient?' Calvin repeated.

Henry ignored him. 'Oh, right. Good.'

'How are you?' I asked him.

'Yes. Fine. Thank you.' His face was still all frowns and seriousness.

'Willow was just saying she lives at the other end of the village. Isn't that in your neck of the woods, Henry?'

'Willow is my next-door neighbour.' Henry replied to his colleague's question without looking at him.

'How fortunate for you.' Calvin smiled at me, missing the dark look that Henry threw him.

'I'm about to go on my break. Do you need a lift home or anything? I have my car with me today as I need to pick something up.'

'Thanks, Henry, but I'm happy to walk. It's a lovely day out.'

'I'm going anyway. You may as well. We're going to the same place.'

'Maybe she just wants to walk, Henry.' Calvin rejoined the

conversation, his body language positively languid compared to the rigidity of Henry's spine and jawline.

'Was there anything else you needed, Dr Wise?' Henry faced him, the green eyes as hard as diamonds.

'Nope,' Calvin replied. 'Heading back to work now, boss.' He turned to me. 'It was lovely meeting you, and I shall look forward to Thursday evening.' With that he walked off across the clinic, saying hello to a couple of patients sitting in the serene waiting area.

'I'll give you a lift. Give me two seconds.'

I went to open my mouth to reiterate that I was more than happy walking, but Henry had already turned and strode off, his long legs crossing the distance in no time at all.

When both men had gone Niamh waved me over, her arm flapping energetically.

'Oh my God! You're going to be the envy of every woman in the village!'

'Why?'

'Uh, hello? You have a date with Dr Calvin Wise!'

'Oh. That. Yes. Also, don't you know it's rude to eavesdrop?' I giggled. Our words were low in deference to the waiting patients.

'Willow, you've lived in the village long enough to know that a secret isn't a secret here for very long.'

'Still, don't you go gossiping about me now, or I won't be doing any more emergency patient intakes for you.'

'My lips are sealed.' She made a zipping motion across her mouth. 'But that doesn't mean everyone else's will be.' She pulled a sympathetic face.

'Yeah, I know. But there's nothing to talk about yet.'

'Since when has that ever stopped people?'

She had a point.

'Either way.' She placed her hands over mine as I rested on

her desk. 'I hope it goes well, lovely. It's about time you found someone.'

'Thanks, Niamh.'

She cast a glance around before speaking again, her voice still low. 'To be honest, we all thought you and Dr Darcy would get together, living right next door to each other. Especially once people saw you out and about together.'

'We're just friends and probably best that way for exactly the same reason. If things didn't work out, it might have got a bit sticky, living next door to each other.'

'But if it did work out...' Niamh raised her brows.

'Just friends!' I repeated and quickly put my finger to my lips as I straightened from her desk when Henry appeared back into view from a corridor.

Niamh stole a sneaky glance at him. 'Shame!' she whispered back.

'Ready?' he asked.

'Yes.'

He gave a short nod and we set off towards the doors and the car park.

'I was more than happy to walk,' I said as I took two steps to his one, trying to keep up with him. 'Actually, it might have been less intense a workout.'

Henry glanced round from where he was pulling his keys from his pocket.

'Oh. God. Sorry.'

'It's fine,' I replied, laughing a little breathlessly.

'Mind was elsewhere.'

'I could tell.'

We approached his dark blue Aston Martin and he stepped forward, beating me to the door-handle and opening the door. I slid in and he closed it after me, cocooning me within the expensive cabin, the lingering scent of leather tantalising my senses before the boot opened, I imagined for Henry to drop the battered doctor's bag he was carrying inside. Moments later he was beside me, reversing smoothly out of the parking space and pointing the car towards home.

We rode in silence. A muscle flickered in Henry's jaw, his fingers tight around the wheel.

'Is there something wrong?' I asked eventually.

'Wrong?'

'Yes.'

'Not at all. Why do you ask?'

'Because we've been sat in a silence as thick as jam and there's a vein throbbing on the side of your temple that looks like it's going to explode, so I'm rather wondering what I've done.'

Henry pulled in alongside the kerb outside our houses and switched off the engine.

'You haven't done anything, Willow.'

'And yet it feels like I most definitely have.'

He flexed long fingers resting on the steering wheel before turning slightly in the seat to face me.

'I promise you, Willow. You haven't.'

'So what's up? Did you have a bad morning?'

'Not at all.'

'Henry. What is going on?'

'Nothing.' He opened the door and got out, the door closing with a quiet, solid thunk.

'Right,' I said to the empty car and went to open the door, only to find that Henry was there, pulling it open and extending a hand towards me. I took it and therefore made a more elegant exit from the vehicle than I would have otherwise, especially in the cut-off denim skirt I'd chosen to wear. As I exited, I ended up closer than expected to the broad chest of my neighbour, today encased in a pale blue check shirt, the cotton feeling soft as silk as I placed a hand on his arm to balance myself. As Niamh and Abby had pointed out several times, he really was good-looking, but I didn't need all this moodiness. I knew Henry wasn't acting this way on purpose, as some blokes did thinking it was cool to be moody and mysterious. Newsflash. It wasn't. It was childish and annoying. Since he'd moved in – and we'd started communicating in normal voices rather than angry, sarcastic ones – the one thing I'd learned was that there was nothing fake about Henry Darcy. Reserved, yes. Blunt, at times. But all of it was genuine. Which was why I was concerned.

'Henry?'

'Yes?' He looked down, his hand still holding mine.

'There's clearly something wrong, and if I haven't done anything, I don't understand what's going on.'

He took a deep breath, the soft fabric tightening across his chest, before he released both my hand and the breath at the same time.

'I wasn't aware you knew Wise.'

'Dr Wise?'

'Yes.'

'I don't. At least I didn't. I just met him today.'

'Stay away from him.'

I took a step back. 'I beg your pardon?'

'Wise. Stay away from him.'

'Why?'

'He can't be trusted.'

'In what regard?'

'In any regard!' he snapped.

I folded my arms across my chest. 'There's no need to bite my head off.'

'I didn't intend to. I'm just telling you to keep away from him.'

'In case you hadn't noticed, Henry, I'm a grown woman and, as such, I'm quite capable of making my own decisions as to who I do and don't speak to.'

'You don't know him like I do.'

'So tell me then.'

His jaw clamped as tight as a bear trap. 'I'm telling you now. Keep away from him.'

'No. You're telling me what to do which, FYI, never goes down well with me. What you're not telling me is why.'

'Look! I know him, OK? Just take my word for it.'

'I trust your judgement on many things, Henry, but surely it's only fair that we're all allowed to make up our own minds about Calvin? Clearly you dislike him, but you can't just tell everyone to avoid him without giving a valid reason.'

'I'm not asking everyone to. They can do what they like. I'm asking you to.'

'Then give me a reason!'

'Argh!' He looked to the heavens, his knuckles white as he gripped his keys. 'Can you not just do what you're told for once?'

He glared down at me and I glared back up. 'No, Henry, I can't. I'm not a child and you have absolutely no authority over me. Had you explained to me why you feel the way you do, I may well have considered listening to your reasoning, but as far as I can see, all this so-called advice is based on some personal dislike which is solely between you and him. And from what I saw, mostly you! He seemed perfectly pleasant, while you didn't even have the decency to look at him once you eventually deigned to speak to him.'

'Yes, he has a habit of seeming "perfectly pleasant", which is how he's always got on in life. The fact that underneath that slick exterior he's actually a total shit conveniently passes a lot of people by!'

'How do you know him?'

'What?'

'How do you know Calvin?'

'I've worked with him before.'

'Is he a bad doctor?'

Henry ground his teeth for a few seconds. 'No. He's actually very good at his speciality.'

'Which is?'

'Plastic surgery. He did some really good reconstructive work before he moved into the purely aesthetic side.'

'By the look on your face, that decision doesn't sit well with you.'

He was so tense that I was surprised he didn't crack his collar bone when he shrugged in reply. 'It was hardly a surprise. Wise is the shallowest person you could ever have the misfortune to meet, so the fact he prefers to concentrate on pure aestheticism is hardly surprising.'

'Do you have this problem with Dr Graham, who he's filling in for?'

'Not at all. The two of them have an entirely different approach.'

'Isn't that convenient?'

'Why are you so determined to go against my advice?' he snapped.

'Because it's not advice. You practically issued a demand with absolutely no foundation!'

'I have plenty of foundation, believe me! There's enough foundation to build a bloody office block on!'

'So tell me!'

We stood in the early summer sunshine, glaring at each other. When nothing was forthcoming, I gave up.

'I don't have time for this, Henry. I have work to get back to.

Unlike you, I'm prepared to give people a chance, which is why I'm meeting Calvin for dinner on Thursday.'

He tipped his head back, screwing his eyes closed against the bright blue sky before looking back directly at me.

'If you think that Calvin bloody Wise is the result of all your wishful thinking and incense burning, then I'm afraid you're going to be sorely disappointed!'

'It's not wishful thinking,' I snapped back, hurt at his tone. I'd really thought we'd got to a point where we could agree to disagree and still remain respectful. Apparently not. 'And actually, I'm not a fan of incense. I prefer soy candles which, if you'd taken any sort of notice at all, you'd have realised. But then I suppose that wouldn't have worked so well for your derogatory and dismissive judgements, would it? But at least I know what you actually think now. I thought all that broadening your horizons talk when we went into Crystal's shop was too good to be believed! Looks like I was right. What did you ever do with that book in the end? It wouldn't surprise me if it went straight on your fire pit!'

I grabbed hold of the catch on my newly painted gate.

'Willow, wait.' Henry put his hand on my arm. I shook it off.

'Thanks for the lift.' I yanked the gate open and pushed it shut, the metal reverberating as it clanged closed, then I strode up to my front door, jammed the key in the lock and let myself in.

22

Once inside, I scooped up my excited little dog, smelling fresh from the groomer and his walk with Ed. I hugged him to me, my throat tight and my eyes burning with unshed tears. I'd thought Henry and I were friends. I'd thought he respected the differences between us, but it turned out it was all an act. Despite saying all the right things, behind my back he was just laughing at me. I knew not everyone saw things the way I did, and I wasn't bothered by that. But something about Henry's callous dismissal of everything I was doing to try to bring the things I wanted into my life cut deep into my heart. All this time, I'd thought he'd understood and accepted me, but the truth was my first impression of him was the correct one. We were as different as it was possible to be with no chance of meeting in the middle.

* * *

Thursday evening rolled around and, as promised, Calvin was at my door just before seven. I invited him in for a minute as I grabbed my shoes and tied the ribbons at the ankle.

'Unusual shoes,' he said, watching me.

'Thanks. I got them in a market in Provence last year.'

He nodded, smiled, and we left the house. As I closed the garden gate, Henry stepped out from his car, the engine ticking quietly as it cooled. He looked from me to Calvin, and back to me again. I mentally dared him to say anything about it.

'Darcy,' Calvin said, breaking the stalemate.

'Wise,' Henry returned, his tone frosty in the summer evening.

I could feel his eyes on me and I thought about avoiding them, but then, why should I? I hadn't done anything wrong. I turned and got caught in the striking green tractor beam of his gaze.

'Willow.' His voice was softer than when he'd addressed my date, and it felt like there was a question in his eyes. For a moment, I was about to speak, to return his greeting. I'd never been one for hanging on to grudges anyway and, since I'd moved back to the village and embraced a more natural approach to life, I knew that holding onto negativity wasn't good for me. But then those words, his tone, his whole demeanour in our last meeting came back to me. How dismissive he'd sounded about what I believed in, what I was trying. At least I was attempting to move on in life, had recognised what I wanted and was doing what I could to bring that about. If his beliefs didn't align with mine, that was fine, but there had been no need to laugh at them. Maybe Calvin wasn't The One. But maybe he was, and I wasn't about to risk not finding out just because my neighbour had some sort of issue with him.

'Henry,' I replied, then immediately looked away to meet Calvin's smiling face as he leant down and opened the door to the red Ferrari he'd pulled up in. Admittedly it was a little showy for me, but he was clearly proud of it and I assumed he'd worked hard for it. As with everything in life, tastes varied, but that didn't mean they were wrong.

'Thanks,' I said, smiling back at him and lowering myself into the car. From the corner of my eye, I saw Henry turn away, grab his bag from his own car and slam the passenger door before striding up his garden path, the gate shuddering as it, too, was slammed.

'Somebody's not in a good mood,' Calvin commented as he got in beside me and closed the door, shutting us in the small, slightly cramped cabin.

'No, doesn't look like it. Did something happen at work?'

'Not that I know of,' he said as he blipped the throttle a couple of times and the engine revved loudly just behind my head before he pulled away. 'But then he always acts like an angel at work. It's just outside of work there's a problem, from what I understand.'

'You're not friends, I gather.'

'What makes you think that?' Calvin asked, then burst out laughing. 'It's that obvious, isn't it?'

'Kind of.'

'Yeah, I did worry my chances of getting the position at the clinic might have been scuppered when I found out Darcy worked here too.'

'Would he really have done that?'

'You never know with Darcy. I'm a good surgeon, though, and at least he had the sense to acknowledge that. We might not be friends, but I wasn't comfortable that our differences might be put before the care of the patients here. I knew I could help and that was the most important thing. Thankfully either Darcy saw that as well, or, if I'm giving him too much credit, he was overruled.'

'I'd like to think it was the former.'

Calvin threw me a smile as we pulled into the car park of the restaurant. 'Me too. Anyway, if it's all the same with you, I'd prefer to talk about you this evening, rather than your neighbour.' With that, he exited the car and swiftly moved to the passenger side to open my door. Thankfully the dress I'd chosen was maxi length, which avoided the possibility of flashing my knickers at either my date or the other diners in the restaurant in front of which Calvin had parked the car.

'After you,' he said, pushing the door open and waiting for me to enter.

'Hi, Willow. Oh!' Asha, manning the reception desk of the swanky, highly rated Indian restaurant, made a poor job of concealing her interest in the fact I'd walked in with a handsome man behind me. 'Table for two, is it?'

'In the name Wise,' Calvin stated.

'Ah, yes, here we are. You're not Dr Wise, are you?'

By the end of the evening, half the village would know I'd had dinner with the clinic's gorgeous new doctor, and the other half would know by the end of tomorrow.

'That's me. Oh dear,' he laughed, looking down at me, then back towards Asha, flashing both of us a winning smile. 'It sounds like my reputation is preceding me.'

'Oh, no, no, no.' She waved her hands slightly manically, the thin metal bracelets on her left arm making a tinkling sound as they touched together. 'Not at all. We are most happy to see you here.'

'He's teasing you, Asha.'

The relief on her young face was obvious as she laughed. 'I will show you to your table.'

The table in question was, I knew, one of their best. Away

from the window, so no one could peer in, far from the kitchen but not slap bang in the middle either. Ideal for a romantic dinner for two.

'Is this all right?' she asked.

'It's perfect,' Calvin said as Asha pulled out the chair for me.

'This is nice,' he said, looking around as he sat himself down.

'You sound surprised,' I replied, a teasing note to my voice.

'There's no getting anything past you, is there?' he grinned. 'I admit it. I wasn't expecting too much despite the reviews.'

'You're a London snob.'

'I am.' He held up his hands, palms towards me. 'Busted. But,' he added quickly, 'I'm more than happy to have my mind changed, and from the short time I've been here, several of those mistaken beliefs have already been challenged.'

'I'm glad to hear it.'

The waiter arrived with the bottle of champagne Calvin had ordered, along with another of mineral water.

'Just a half glass,' he said as the drink was poured into his.

'I hope you're not expecting me to finish that on my own!'

'If you don't, we can take it home.'

I gave a nod and brief smile and, as usual, my ability to keep my thoughts from being written all over my face proved an epic failure.

'By the look on your face, that's come across wrong. What I meant was, *you* can take it home. Sorry, just a figure of speech. Don't panic.'

'I'm not panicking.'

I'd totally been panicking.

'Of course you weren't,' he replied, his brown eyes amused, clearly seeing straight through me. 'So, you're the local, what do you recommend?'

* * *

'No!' I giggled as I put my hand over the top of my glass to prevent it being topped up yet again. 'I've already drunk most of the bottle myself!'

'There's only a tiny bit left. Be a shame to waste it.'

'What about taking it home, like you said earlier?'

'Hardly worth it for this bit.'

'I already look like Noddy!' I replied, touching my fingers to my cheeks and feeling the warmth.

'Not at all. A healthy glow, that's all.'

'Is that what you call it?' I giggled again, feeling decidedly squiffy.

'Absolutely. It's an official diagnosis. Seriously, you can trust me. I'm a doctor.'

'A very smooth-talking one.'

'Not really.' He rested his chin on his hand and looked across the table at me. 'It's all a bit of an act. But tonight has been great. I have to say this is the most relaxed I've felt since I got here. It's the first time I've even felt like I could actually fit in here. So thank you.'

'You're welcome.' I mirrored his posture. 'Why would you feel like you didn't fit in? And if so, what made you take the position?'

He pulled a face. 'As you so astutely pointed out earlier, I've lived in London a long time and got rather spoiled with all the amazing restaurants and other amenities within such easy reach. But that doesn't mean that I didn't want a break.'

'And you thought down here you'd get a break from the hectic life in London but at the expense of culture and good food?' I raised an enquiring eyebrow.

Calvin looked suitably abashed. 'I know. I'm a horrible, judgemental person.'

'It's true. You are.'

The perfect smile showed once more. 'You're not afraid to say what you think, are you?'

'There's not a lot of point in not doing so, so long as no one is going to get hurt.'

'And you don't think that hurt my feelings?' He put his hand to his heart, his handsome features creased in mock distress.

'For a start, I'm pretty sure your ego can take it. And secondly, it's your fault for letting me drink most of a whole bottle of champagne.'

'Fair point. I'll take that. But at least I know where I stand with you.'

I raised my glass towards him as a salutation and finished off the bubbles.

* * *

'Wow!' I let out a laugh as the warm evening air hit me as we exited the restaurant.

'Fresh air's the best thing for you.'

'That's easy for you to say. You were on mineral water all night.' I leant down to take hold of the door-handle, but Calvin was there before me, his body close, the sharp citrus scent of aftershave winding its way around my senses.

'Allow me.'

I turned my head to thank him and the dark eyes were on me, his gaze soft, the hint of a smile at the corners of his mouth.

'Thanks.' The word sounded hoarse and throaty, and I wasn't sure if it was the alcohol or the moment, but whatever it was, it felt good.

Calvin's hand brushed my neck as he protected my head as I

slid, less elegantly than before, into the car, and I felt a fizzing inside me that I hadn't felt for a long time. Too long.

A few minutes later, the sequence played out in reverse as I exited the vehicle outside my house. Calvin pushed the car door closed behind me and then we were there, together, in the quiet of the night, the only sound a soft rustle of leaves in the breeze and the haunting hoot of an owl.

'Thank you for coming,' he said.

'Thank you for asking me.'

'Would you mind if I asked you again?'

'Not at all. Actually, I think that would be lovely.'

In the light of the full moon, his smile widened, and his fingertips brushed against mine.

'I'll call you tomorrow.'

'OK.'

We stood there for a moment and then I reached up and placed a light kiss on his cheek. He turned his face, our eyes meeting. My chest felt full and my blood hummed in my veins. I wanted nothing more than to kiss this man, and from the look in his eyes, the feeling was mutual. I leant forward just enough. His lips brushed mine, tentatively at first and then—

The bright light made us both step back, shielding our eyes.

'What the—'

'Oh. It's you, Wise.' Henry was standing in his front garden with an industrial-style torch pointed in our direction. 'Had some trouble with foxes lately and thought I heard them out here.'

'Henry! Turn that sodding light off. You're blinding us!' I snapped, my hand up to my face, suddenly a lot more sober than I had been thirty seconds ago.

The light went out and my neighbour was left illuminated only by the full moon, the silvery light highlighting the sharp planes of his face.

'I'll call you tomorrow,' Calvin spoke first, the moment of earlier clearly over.

I forced a smile as I turned towards him. 'Yes, OK. Thanks again for a lovely evening.'

He bent, placed a kiss on my cheek and then strode quickly to the other side of the car, got in and drove away, the engine noise cutting through the night until, once again, everything was peaceful. Everything except me and my anger at the pettiness of my neighbour.

'Feel better for that, do you?' I snapped as Henry was about to shut his front door.

It opened again. 'Sorry?'

'Your little display back then. Make you feel better, did it?'

'I don't know what you mean. Like I said, I've had foxes sniffing around and I don't want to encourage them. How was I to know it was a rat rather than a fox?'

'Oh, for God's sake, Henry! What the hell is up with you?'

'Apart from that arse showing up back in my life? Nothing.'

'Look!' I pointed a finger at him. 'You might not like him, but that's your problem. I'd appreciate it if you didn't make it mine.'

'You have no idea what he's like, Willow.'

'No, I don't, and half of that is down to you with your ridiculous fox story! So thanks for that!' I yelled, the hangover from the champagne beginning to start early, thanks to the way the evening had ended.

'Willow, look, I—'

But I wasn't interested in listening. Unlocking the door, I quickly stepped in, picked up Spud, who was waiting just inside, and slammed the door behind me, shoving the bolt across and sliding the security chain into place. All the warm feelings of earlier – the fun, the laughter, the excitement – had been quashed and all I wanted to do now was head up to bed, take off my make-up and snuggle with my dog. Actually, that wasn't the only thing I wanted to do, but thanks to my enthusiasm for plants, I no longer had room in my garden to bury my neighbour's body.

* * *

The incessant ringing of the doorbell was exactly what I didn't need at half past nine the following morning. My head was throbbing, my stomach wasn't much better and all I wanted was a quiet day in my studio, alone with my dog and my patients.

I pulled open the door and squinted at the sunlight beaming right at me.

'Oooh! Somebody had a good night,' Abby said with a grin. 'Can I come in?'

I closed the door behind her. 'That appears to have been a rhetorical question.'

'Of course it was. Shall I make you some tea? What's best for hangovers?'

'I've had some green tea already, but a ginger tea wouldn't go amiss.' I followed her into my kitchen and slunk down on one of my pale-pink-painted kitchen chairs.

'OK. I'm hoping you have tea bags, because I don't have the knowledge or inclination to make it all from scratch.' She was already rummaging through my tea cupboard and, moments later, produced the box of ginger tea with a triumphant, 'Aha!'

Once I had a ginger tea and Abby had a coffee that looked like molasses, the inquisition began.

'Tell me everything.'

'There's really not much to tell, Abs.'

'Oh, come on. You went out with one of the most eligible men in the village and there's nothing to tell?'

'One of?'

Abby thumbed towards the party wall of the house and I gave a snort. 'Yeah, well, the village is welcome to that particular eligible man.'

'What's up? I thought you two were friends.'

'Yeah, so did I, but for all his accusations that Calvin isn't all he's cracked up to be, it seems like he's the one that's two-faced.' My throat felt raw as I snapped out the words, my stomach tight and churning.

Abby reached for my hand, the fingers clenched into a tight fist, and laid her own over it. 'Wils, what happened?'

'It doesn't matter,' I said, taking a sip of the soothing ginger tea.

'Willow. You're the most zen person I know, so whatever's got you worked up into this state definitely matters. Tell me what's going on.'

I took a deep breath, let it out slowly in an attempt to undo some of the knots in my shoulders and neck, and recounted my conversation with Henry and his actions last night.

'That's so strange. He really seemed like he was interested in broadening his knowledge about alternative therapies.'

'I know. I think that's what stung the most.'

'Really? Not the fact he ruined a moment between you and Dr Wise?' She gave a lascivious wink and I laughed for the first time since last night.

'That certainly didn't help, but all he did was make himself look ridiculous. I don't know what the hell is up with him.'

'He really seems to have a problem with Calvin, doesn't he? Do you know why?'

'Nope. He warned me off him but with absolutely nothing to back it up. Apparently I was just supposed to take his word for it.'

'Yeah, he doesn't know you very well, does he?' Abby laughed.

'No,' I agreed, smiling. 'And he's had his shot. I'm all for peace and forgiveness, but he's pushed the limit. I don't care if people don't think the same way I do about things, but what I do object to is being made fun of.' I huffed out a breath. 'I didn't think he was like that, but then I guess neither of us knew the other very well.'

'No, I suppose not.' Abby pulled a face. 'I'm sorry, hon. Just keep doing your own thing. It's his loss.'

'Exactly. Thanks, Abs.'

'Now tell me about last night!'

* * *

The next few weeks were a wonderful balance of work and play, the only cloud on the horizon being the occasional sighting of my grumpy neighbour.

'Hi,' I waved to Calvin as he strode down the lane towards me.

He waved back and Spud gave one bark, sensing that he was about get a good long walk, and promptly began dancing at my feet.

'Nice to see he likes me!' Calvin laughed as he lifted Spud up for a cuddle. 'Hello, hello.'

Spud snuggled around his face and neck, his little tail wagging madly.

'Don't flatter yourself. He's friendly to everyone.' Henry walked past, a newspaper tucked under his arm.

I rolled my eyes at Calvin. 'That is true. Spud persists in trying to befriend my neighbour, even though he doesn't like dogs.'

'What sort of person doesn't like dogs?' Calvin was ostensibly talking to Spud, but it was clear who the message was actually for.

Henry turned to close his gate and caught my eye. His hand rested momentarily on the latch, and for a second I wanted to speak to him. I wanted things to go back to the way they were. Maybe they could? But then I remembered the dismissal of my plans, the sharpness of his tone and the realisation that all the time we'd spent together had been a sham. That Henry wasn't open to anything. That it seemed he had in fact been laughing behind my back. He'd merely used my familiarity in the village to ingratiate himself with others. And apparently it had worked. Nobody had a bad word to say about him. Apart from those who actually knew him, like me and Calvin.

I looked away. 'Let's go, Calvin. Come on, Spuddy. Time for a walk.'

'Be careful, Willow.' Henry stopped, turning towards us. 'They're warning of storms coming in from the sea.'

'Bloody hell, Henry. Don't you ever relax?' Calvin snapped. 'That doesn't look like a stormy sky to me.' He pointed at the cloudless blue sky above us.

'Just be careful, Willow. OK?' The earnest, frowning expression darkening the green eyes made me bite back the retort on the tip of my tongue and pause. After a couple of seconds, I nodded then quickly turned away, Calvin taking one hand, Spud's lead in my other as we walked away from the house.

We tramped through the dry fields, the grass turning golden with the lack of rain over the past few months. The usual April showers hadn't materialised and, in the height of a scorching summer, the lawns and fields of grass were a crispy brown. Some areas had already suffered with forest fires, but so far we'd been lucky to avoid any such disasters in the village.

Rain was due, as Henry had said, but not until later according to the app I'd checked yesterday evening. My garden would certainly be thankful for a good long drink!

As we rounded the corner, two footpaths merged and we joined the South West Coastal Path. To one side, cliffs stretched towards the sky, heather, moss and a few goats clinging to its stony face. Opposite, they dropped away almost sheer until they met a glittering turquoise sea, waves washing the rocks scattered there smooth with their endless motion.

Spud stared at one of the goats and it stared back. Bouncing on his paws, he gave a playful bark hoping, as ever, to have found a new playmate. The goat peered at my little dog a moment longer then turned away, clambering up the cliff with an agility that defied all expectation, not to mention physics. Spud looked up at me.

'Sorry, sweetie.' I crouched down and kissed the curly, soft hair on the top of his head. 'You'll find someone else to play with soon, I'm sure.'

As if on cue, a chocolate-brown Labrador came hurtling along the path towards us, the owner running at full pelt behind him on a long lead.

'Sorry!' he puffed out. 'Still—' gasp '—in training—' gasp.

'Looks like he needs a bit more,' Calvin said, and I saw the man's hand tense on the lead. The dog had stopped and was happily saying hello to the ever-friendly Spud.

'He's a beautiful boy,' I said, wanting to distract the owner from Calvin's comment.

'Thanks.' The smile came back. 'He's a rescue. We only just picked him up a fortnight ago. Unfortunately the previous owners hadn't done much with him. He's house trained but that's about it.'

'Oh, that's difficult. It's lovely that he's found someone who's prepared to give him that attention now.'

'Yes. We'll get there. Luckily he's food orientated so that helps.'

'Typical Lab!' I replied, laughing. 'I'm Willow, by the way.'

'Kevin. Nice to meet you. And this is Trevor.'

At the sound of his name, the dog's ears pricked up and he turned from the game with Spud to face his new owner.

'Oh, he knows his name! That's great!'

'Yes. Needless to say, we didn't choose that particular name, but as you say he's used to it and it does oddly seem to suit him.'

'My dog is called Spud.'

'What a great name.'

'Thanks. He's fluffy now, but when he was tiny, his resemblance to a small potato was uncanny. My friend's husband said it as a joke but it kind of stuck, and now he's my little Spuddy.'

'He's gorgeous, and so friendly. It's nice to meet someone that's not afraid to play with Trev.'

'Oh, he'll always find a willing playmate with this one.'

Kevin glanced over to where Calvin was standing further along the path, looking out to sea. 'I'd better let you get on.'

I followed his glance then turned back. 'It was lovely to meet you.' I bent down to ruffle Trevor's fur. 'And you. Now you learn your lessons from your dad here and I look forward to seeing you again soon. Come on, Spud. Say bye for now. Bye, Kevin.'

I walked along the path, not hurrying, until I caught up with Calvin.

'You all right?' I asked.

'Yeah. Just don't have a lot of time for people like that.'

'People like what?'

'He should have the dog under more control.'

'He's trying. It's not his fault that the previous owners were irresponsible.'

'Then perhaps the dog shelter should train them a bit more before they let them out into the world.'

'I'm sure they would if they had the time, money and

resources, but until then they have to rely on the goodwill of people like Kevin who are prepared to take on that task and give dogs like Trevor a home.'

'The dog's name is Trevor?'

'Yes.'

Calvin rolled his eyes and turned away and began walking again. Somewhere inside me there was a nagging question that I hadn't considered before. What did he think of my own dog's name?

'Do you want to go back?' I asked.

'No.' He shook his head. 'Sorry. I'm being a grumpy arse, aren't I?' He reached out for my hand and I let him pull me closer. His arms wrapped around me, his head bent, and his lips met mine. 'Sorry.' The words were soft. 'Bloody Henry always turning up when I'm there and finding something snarky to say just got to me this morning.'

'Don't let him bother you.'

'I know. I know. I shouldn't. And most of the time I don't. Come on.'

Our hands still joined, we strolled along the path, walking single file from time to time as we came to narrower sections or passed other walkers coming the other way.

The still air of earlier had been replaced by a breeze that seemed to be growing. I pulled out a hairclip from my pocket, quickly wound my hair into a knot and clipped it up so that I could see where I was going. The bright turquoise sea had also turned more inky as clouds began to form in the previously clear sky.

'I wonder if we should start heading back,' I asked Calvin as we made our way further along the path.

'You haven't let flippin' Henry get to you too, have you? He's determined to try and spoil anything we do together.'

'No, it's not that.' I looked up at the sky.

'It'll blow over,' Calvin said. 'Come on. Forget about him and his gloom and doom.'

I wasn't convinced, but Henry had clearly got under Calvin's skin that morning and I didn't want to aggravate things any more.

'Yeah, I'm sure you're right.' I gave my positivity pants a hefty hoik up and marched on.

23

———————

An hour and a half later, I was wishing we'd listened to Henry. The cliffs were looming above us out of a thick mist that had rolled in off the sea, dragging down the temperature. The seabirds that were brave enough to battle the gathering storm struggled against the wind, their paths diverted again and again as they fought against the elements. Sounds became muffled in the sea mist and the walkers that had all been out earlier had mostly taken the sensible decision to cut their treks short and head home. Unlike us.

I pushed wet strands of loose hair back from my face as the wind chased them from my clip. The rain that had begun as fine but incessant was falling harder from the pewter sky. My companion's expression was almost as dark and ominous as the sky.

'At least you get warning in London when the weather is going to change,' he grumped. 'More importantly, there's always somewhere to dash into and warm up!'

'I thought you liked it down here.'

'I do. I just... sorry. I'm still getting used to things and I'm not really a fan of bad weather. It's why I always go to the Caribbean for Christmas.'

'Really?'

'Yes. Why wouldn't you?'

'I couldn't afford it, for a start, and secondly, I love all the cosiness of Christmas and winter in general. I find it a great time to reset and recover from the busyness of the summer.'

'Oh.'

Silence settled between us but mostly because trying to talk was being made more difficult by the wind blowing straight into our faces, accompanied by tiny little needlepoints of rain that stung the skin.

Poor Spud was soaked through, as were we. I should have taken time to look at the forecast again that morning. Henry's warning had obviously been right. The storm was arriving much earlier than expected. I knew that, had he and I not fallen out, I'd have been more inclined to listen to him. It was too late, however. Even my bones felt frozen. My T-shirt was stuck to my body, as were my shorts, and Calvin looked much the same.

Spud looked round at me.

'Not long now, sweetheart. We'll be home soon.'

'I bloody hope so,' Calvin muttered, the wind carrying his words towards me.

Suddenly Spud stopped dead, his little body beginning to shake. I bent to lift him up and try and cuddle some warmth back into both of us, but before I could do so, a huge flash of lightning darted down into the sea, immediately followed by an ear-splitting crack of thunder, the sound bouncing off the cliff beside us, surrounding us with the noise.

'Shit!' Calvin cursed.

'Spud!' I screamed as another flash and crack followed, just as bright and loud as the first, and my little dog took off along the path in fright. 'Spud! Spud, come back!' I yelled his name, my throat croaking hoarse with the effort.

'Where the fuck's he gone now?'

I spun round to see Calvin, his face pinched with anger.

'I don't know! He's frightened! Can you imagine how loud that was to him? You have to help me look for him!'

'Now?'

'Of course now!'

'I'm soaked and cold!'

'So is he!'

'He's a dog! He'll find his way home. Come on, let's just go back. I'm sure he'll be back there before us.'

'And if he's not?' I was crying now but either Calvin couldn't tell or didn't care. 'You do what you want. I'm going to find my dog!'

With that, I turned and ran as hard as I could into the wind, shouting Spud's name and trying not to panic any more than I already was. My dog was my world. I couldn't and wouldn't imagine that world without him. The fact that the man I'd believed the universe had brought me couldn't see that, or didn't care, was something to think about later. Right then, I just needed Spud. I stopped running, trying to listen, but all I could hear was the sound of my own heaving breath, the wind, waves and rolling thunder. There was no barking as Spud tried to find me, searching me out. I sucked another deep breath in against the tears and ran on, shouting Spud's name.

* * *

'Willow!'

I heard my voice being called but the sea mist was as thick as fog and I was so cold I could barely tell which way was up, but I was not going home without my dog.

'Willow!'

The sound came again and, as I squinted, I saw a light and stumbled towards it. Looming out of the mist was Henry Darcy, dressed for the weather, a heavy-duty torch in his hand and a small bundle of wet fur tucked into the top of his jacket. As I stepped closer, the bundle began to bark and wiggle.

'Spud!' The word was ripped out of me, my voice almost entirely gone from screaming his name and sobbing at the thought I might really have lost him.

I fell against Henry and took Spud's wet head in my hands and kissed him over and over as Henry wrapped his arms around me.

'You found him!' I croaked, my chest hitching with sobs. 'Thank you! Thank you! I thought I'd lost him!' The last word disappeared into another huge sob.

'He's here. He's fine. Just a bit damp but as lively as ever. See?' Gently, Henry moved me back the tiniest amount so that I could see, could focus, on the fact that Spud was indeed his wriggly, happy little self. 'Here, put this on.' With very little help from me, as all coordination seemed to have left my body, Henry wrangled me into a fleece-lined waterproof coat. I probably could have got into it twice, so I assumed it was one of his.

'Thank you.' I managed to get the words out and somehow he managed to hear them. Perhaps because he was pretty much holding me up.

'You're welcome. Now, come on, let's get you two home. The last thing Spud needs is you with hypothermia.'

I flopped against Henry's side with little energy to do much else. Knowing that my dog was safe, the adrenaline I'd been running on subsided and I felt entirely drained.

'What are you doing here?' I croaked out.

'I'll tell you later. I assume someone is going to have a nice warm bath in the sink?' He looked down at me. 'Just for clarification, I'm talking about Spud, not you.'

The laugh that I managed was weak but it was enough.

'So, does he have a special shampoo? His coat is always lovely and shiny. I didn't know if it was something you bought or something you made from your garden? You could probably bottle and sell that if it's the latter. I might try it myself, actually.'

I giggled again and Henry turned his head momentarily to smile down at me. We plodded on, every step an effort, my neighbour chatting away to me the entire time in a mostly one-way conversation, as all my energy was channelled into keeping moving.

'You all right in there, chum?' Henry ruffled Spud's soaked fur and Spud gave a wriggle and turned his nose up towards the gentle touch.

'I thought you weren't a dog person.' The words were hoarse and forced out but Henry, keeping me close, heard them.

'I didn't think I was, either. Perhaps there's hope for me yet, eh?'

I nodded in answer as relief flooded through me at seeing my house finally in view.

'Come into mine for now.'

'We'll go home.'

'Willow, you can barely stand up. I know I'm not your favourite person, but please let me take care of you both until you're back up to speed.'

I realised then that I had a fistful of Henry's coat in a vice-like grip, and that, together with his arm around me, was likely the only thing that was keeping me upright. My blurry vision did its best to focus on Spud, who, although looking cosy tucked in the front of my neighbour's coat, was still sodden and needed to be warmed and dried. I rested my head against Henry and let him lead me through the open gate and into his house.

* * *

An hour later, I was wrapped in the biggest, cosiest dressing gown I'd ever met, had drunk several hot drinks and had a washed, warm and fluffy Spud snoozing happily and restfully on my lap. The previously mentioned bath in the sink had taken place in Henry's kitchen, laughter and cooing words drifting my way as I'd curled up on his sofa, having stripped off my wet clothes and wrapped myself in the aforementioned dressing gown plus a huge weighted blanket.

'Once you're feeling better, you can have a soak in the bath or a warm shower, but right now I'm concerned you'll either sink beneath the water or collapse in a heap, depending upon which option you go for.' He'd said those words as he'd guided me gently down the stairs, having waited outside the door of the guest room where I'd had far more trouble than I should have had getting my sodden clothes off. Once I was settled on the sofa with a warm drink and he'd checked my temperature, Henry had run some water in the sink and set about warming up my little pup.

'You ready for something to eat?' Henry asked, then laughed as a previously sleeping Spud suddenly perked up at the mention of food. 'It certainly looks like someone is.'

I craned my neck a little to see the time on Henry's understated but no doubt expensive watch.

'He's got an hour to go, you little monkey.' I bent my head to meet Spud's, reaching up to mine, and nuzzled it.

'He's had a trying day. Maybe a little sustenance wouldn't hurt?'

Spud suddenly stood and clambered across my lap to Henry's. I moved to reach over and lift him back. 'Sorry.'

But Henry stopped me, letting the dog snuggle up on his thighs, resting his head against the broad chest and looking up with adoring, hopeful eyes.

'I'm afraid I don't tend to keep dog biscuits in stock here.'

Spud wagged his tail.

'Is there anything else I could tempt you with?' Henry continued the conversation. 'Perhaps a sandwich for Sir?'

I giggled from my cosy cocoon.

'No?' he asked, one hand stroking down the freshly washed and fluffy fur. 'Perhaps one could tempt Sir with a cheeseboard?'

Spud's tail whizzed into overdrive and he leapt off Henry's lap onto the floor and gave a single bark.

'You said the magic word.'

'Cheese?' Henry asked, turning to me as he stood, and Spud danced by his feet in excitement. 'I guess so.' He grinned. 'Come on then,' he said, looking down at the dog. 'Let's see which ones tickle Sir's tastebuds.'

'He'll eat cheese until he pops!' I warned, feeling a warmth inside me that had nothing to do with the drinks or the blankets.

'Ah, Madam has advised me you are a little piglet, so I'm afraid the options will have to be limited.'

Spud's tail by then was going so fast that I was surprised he hadn't actually taken off. A few minutes later, Henry was down some of his fancy cheese that I knew from previous conversations before our falling out, he'd begun to order in from the local deli.

'He'll be perfectly happy with cheddar from the supermarket. His tastes aren't as refined as yours,' I'd said, laughing, as Henry had shown him the different packets and ascertained that 'Sir's choice' was the most expensive one.

'Sir has made his choice.' Henry had nodded gravely at me before crouching down and breaking a few cubes of cheese off and feeding them to Spud by hand.

'He's going to want to live with you if you treat him like this!'

'Because you never spoil him at all, I suppose?' He'd looked up from the floor, a dark brow raised quizzically in my direction.

'Never. Not once.'

The laugh he'd let out had made me smile and excited my dog even more and resulted in a game of chase and peek-a-boo around Henry's furniture.

He flopped down next to me as Spud snuggled up and soon began snoring.

'I didn't realise it was so tiring having a dog.'

'Usually, or at least hopefully, you haven't begun by scouring the cliffs and shoreline for a lost pup.' The words were meant in jest, but I wasn't prepared for the ice that memory struck in my heart, and tears immediately filled my eyes.

Henry's hand closed over mine. 'He's here now. Look. Safe, sound and happy. Not to mention full of cheese.'

I giggled again as I swiped at the tears that had escaped.

'Thank you. I don't know what I would have done...'

He squeezed my hand. 'Don't think about it any more. You're both safe now, thank God.'

I nodded and felt the tears welling again. 'Sorry,' I sniffed out. 'I can't seem to stop...'

The arms that wrapped around me were strong and warm and, without thinking, I felt myself go soft against Henry's chest, the sobs that I thought had run dry earlier returning once more.

'I'm sorry,' I repeated, my breath and the words hitching every few seconds.

'Nothing to apologise for. It's understandable.'

'I don't know why I'm still crying.'

'Maybe because you didn't get any cheese?'

The laugh punctuated my tears and I tilted my head up to meet his eyes. 'Maybe.'

'I'll get you some, too, if you're that upset about it.'

I hiccupped.

'It's been a stressful day for you. Together with getting mild hypothermia, you were frantic about your pet. It's a very normal reaction.'

'It is?'

'Yep,' he said, cuddling me closer. 'Let it all out. No point bottling things up.'

* * *

'How are you feeling?' Henry asked, turning momentarily away from the hob on which whatever he was cooking smelled delicious.

'Much better, thanks.' I was once more snuggled into the soft, thick dressing gown following a wonderfully hot shower that poured luxuriously from a wide rainfall head. I was also sporting a bamboo T-shirt and thick wool socks, all of which were owned by my neighbour. At any other time, I might have thought the situation a little uncomfortable, but right then, after a day from hell, the exact opposite was true. The strangest thing was that it didn't feel strange at all.

'You're clearly turning something over in your head. Do I want to know?'

I screwed up my nose as I retook my seat from earlier.

'It's this room, isn't it? Or is it the whole house?'

'What? No. It's... very you.'

'Blah?'

'No! Umm... masculine.'

'I'd like to take that as a compliment but I'm struggling.'

'You should. It's reflective of your personality. No nonsense. Clean cut. No fuss.'

'Boring.'

'Not at all,' I replied, pushing myself back up the sofa in as subtle a manner as I could muster. Henry, being Henry, was not to be fooled and gave me a helping hand.

'I never really liked leather sofas. God knows why I ordered one. Slippery buggers, aren't they?'

'They are a bit,' I agreed, matching his smile. 'So why did you get one?'

'Panic shopping? Seemed the right thing to get? The sales agent was pleasant? Pick your favourite.'

'Oh, Henry. Is furnishing your house so painful?'

'No. I mean I didn't think it would be, but I don't think I've got the knack. As you can see,' he cast an arm back, 'I'm more of the "Is it functional, yes? Then it will do" school of interior design.'

'But you're saying now you're not keen on the sofa? Or any of it. Has something changed?'

'Yes. Quite a lot, actually.'

'How come?'

'I've spent time in your house, in your garden, and realised that it takes much more than just throwing money at the latest, greatest trend or brand to make a home feel like a home.'

'My taste definitely isn't for everyone, though. Décor, like anything, isn't right or wrong. It's what appeals to the individual. That's what makes a home.'

'That's the problem.' He glanced around the open-plan ground floor that had been created here, removing walls, putting in supporting joists. 'This doesn't appeal to me.'

'I think the space is lovely.'

'True. No, you're right. I am happy with that. But the furniture. It's all angles. Cold. All hard, square edges, whereas yours is soft, gentle. Welcoming. Like you.' He took another look around. 'I think you were right earlier when you said the décor reflects my personality.'

'Well, that's the biggest load of bollocks I've ever heard.'

The shocked expression on his face lasted two full seconds before morphing into a deep, rumbling belly laugh. His head was thrown back as the sound echoed around the room. Spud looked up, sleepily wagged his tail and settled down again as Henry's large, warm hand slid gently over his back.

'God, I've missed you,' he said, wiping an eye. 'You've never been afraid to say what's on your mind, have you?'

'I have actually, but I learned several years ago to not be afraid. It will probably come as a shock to you that I do always try and do it without hurting anyone's feelings. I don't know what happened when you moved in. You seem to bring out the worst in me.' I spoke the last with a smile, letting him know I was teasing.

'That's a shame because I think you bring out the best in me.'

I waited for him to smile, but he didn't. The piercing eyes rested on mine, his mouth neither smiling nor sad.

'Are you sure?'

He nodded.

'Have you forgotten the first weeks that you lived here?'

'Nope. I don't think I could ever, or want to, forget those. Finding out I lived next to a beautiful woman who was at the same time both a firecracker and able to be entirely calm and serene occupied my thoughts for many an hour.'

'It did?' I asked, shuffling my cocoon round and sliding down the sodding sofa once more.

'It did,' Henry replied, hoiking me up again.

'I thought you hated me.'

'Never. Did you hate me?'

I chewed my lip.

'I knew it,' he laughed, his words free from recrimination or accusation.

'No, wait.' I took his hand as it rested next to me. 'I never hated you. Hate is a strong emotion, and you certainly didn't warrant that. Let's just say I wasn't your greatest fan.'

'Sounds an accurate description.'

'I don't think either of us were probably our best selves at the start. I had no right to act like that and, if I'm honest, I'm rather ashamed of myself for doing so.'

'Don't be. It made me think. You made me think.'

'Think up a multitude of names for the weirdo next door.'

He dropped his head into his hands. 'I can't believe you heard that. I can't believe I said what I did that night. I am truly sorry, you know.'

'I do. And you're not the first, and probably won't be the last, to call me similar or worse.'

'Then it's probably best for them if they don't say it in my hearing.'

'Aww, Henry Darcy, are you being all protective now?'

'I am.'

I'd said it as a tease but his words were serious.

'Given the opportunity,' he added, the briefest catch in his throat.

I swallowed. Shook my head. Maybe the drama of the day was catching up with me. 'I don't need anyone to look after me, Henry.'

'I know. Having lived next door to you for some time now, that much is patently obvious. The way you wield a power tool is a sight to behold, and having seen you at work on a circular saw in your garden definitely made me think twice about getting on the wrong side of you.' He gave a little wiggle of his head. 'Even though I still managed to.'

'Oh, I wouldn't use that to chop up any bodies.' I glanced up at him. 'Dulls the blade too much.'

'Good to know.'

'Henry?'

'Yes?'

'What exactly are you saying?'

'I had a feeling you were going to ask that.'

'Don't get me wrong.' I curled my fingers over his. 'They're all lovely things, and if you're worried that I was still going to be barely civil to you, then believe me, that is not the case. What you did today… I will never be able to thank you for that, not if I live a thousand lifetimes.'

'Which I think you may believe is possible?'

'You're right, I'm pretty sure past lives are a thing.' I grinned. 'You know me too well.'

'No, see that's the problem. I don't know you well enough and I'd very much like to.'

'For someone who deals in facts, you really are being very vague, Henry!'

His hand lifted mine and took it gently to meet his lips, his eyes meeting mine as he did so, before dropping his gaze momentarily to my lips. His chest heaved with a deep breath, stretching the fabric of the Hunter green T-shirt across pecs that had been a surprise, albeit a pleasant one, when I'd first encountered them in a similar outfit when he'd helped me with the garden soil delivery months ago.

'Henry?'

'Willow?'

'Are you saying you might like to kiss me?'

24

The smile broke on his face and it felt like the sun had burst through the vile weather to warm me with its rays, burning away all the disappointment and hurt.

'I know it's not ideal, what with you seeing Wise. I probably shouldn't have—'

'Yes, you should. I'm glad you did. And believe me, I'm completely finished with him. I can't believe he wouldn't help me look for Spud!'

'I can't believe he left you!' The softness of Henry's expression just moments ago suddenly hardened. 'He's lucky I saw him out here and not near the cliffs...'

'What happened anyway?'

'I'd just got back from the gym when I saw Wise stomping up the road, soaked to the bone. He flagged me down and asked for a lift home.'

'Right.'

'I asked where you and Spud were and he said the dog had run off and you were looking for him, then repeated his request for a lift home. I said he could borrow some dry clothes and we'd go back together to look for you.' His brow darkened as he recounted the meeting. 'Let's just say that he told me that wasn't his plan, so I politely told him to find his own way home and came out to look for you two.'

'I hope it wasn't too politely.'

'Not even remotely.'

'Good!' I ruffled my partially dry hair and dropped my gaze to Spud, reaching out to stroke his sleeping form.

'I should have listened to you about him.'

'It doesn't matter. Can we just forget about him, because right now I'd really just like to kiss you.'

I pretended to think about it for a moment, but Henry pulled me closer, ever mindful of the dog, and pressed his lips to my temple, moved slowly to my forehead, the tip of my nose and finally my lips. The butterfly kiss grew into a harder, more urgent one as his hand cupped the back of my head, the fingers of his other hand tangling themselves in my hair, pulling me closer with a soft tug that ignited a flame of desire low down inside me. I let out a moan and Henry tightened his fingers momentarily before pulling back, both of us breathless.

'I wasted so much time.'

'Time is never wasted.'

'No, believe me, it is. I could have spent the last few months being with you, kissing you.' He opened his mouth to say something, then closed it again.

'What?'

He shook his head. 'Not the right time.'

As much as I wanted to grab a fistful of his T-shirt and drag the words out of him, I let it go. When the time was right, he'd tell me.

'I'm sorry Wise hurt you.'

'It's fine. Something never felt quite right. I told him we

needed to take it slowly. That I wasn't ready to jump into something, especially if he was only going to be here for a short time. But the truth was, I suspected from the beginning it wasn't right. He was nice and everything.' I frowned. 'At least, I thought he was. Today has rather changed my opinion. But I... we... didn't... you know.'

'For someone who is so free and aligned with nature, you're suddenly remarkably prudish.'

'I am not,' I giggled, giving him a playful tap on the arm. 'And just because I appreciate nature doesn't mean I'm happy to tell all and sundry about my sex life.'

'Does that mean you're still not up for dancing naked round the garden?'

'No!' I said, whacking him with a cushion.

'Shame.'

'Perv.'

'Not at all. It's called appreciation, and only when it comes to you.'

My laugh turned into a yawn.

'You should get some rest.'

'Yes, I suppose so.' My brain knew he was right, but my body wanted nothing more than to stay exactly where I was.

'Do you want to stay? And I won't be offended if you don't. Even I feel more at home in your house than here.'

'Is that true?'

'Yes.'

'Do you want to come round, then? I mean, not for... but the company would be nice.'

'It would. Hold onto Spud.'

I took the little dog off him, still asleep, exhausted from the day's events, then let out a surprised squeak as Henry swept us both up in one bundle to rest against his chest.

'Henry, I'm perfectly capable of walking.'

'Those trainers won't be dry for days.'

'Then I'll go barefoot. If you know anything about me by now, you'll know that's hardly unusual.'

'But then I wouldn't get to hold you,' he replied, kissing my temple.

I didn't have an answer for that so I rested my head against his chest and just accepted the feeling of peace that flowed through me.

* * *

'I knew it!' Abby flung her arms around me, almost bowling me over, as I answered the front door a few weeks later when they'd returned from a long overdue holiday, which had coincided with Henry and me finally getting together. 'I knew he had to be The One! I never liked Calvin anyway.'

'That's not what you said when I started seeing him.'

She picked up Spud and gave him a cuddle. 'That's irrelevant. I didn't want to hurt your feelings.'

'Fibber,' I replied, laughing.

'Seriously, though,' she said, popping Spud back down on the floor. 'Are you happy?'

'Yeah. I am. I really am.'

I went through to the kitchen and began making us a cup of tea while we chatted.

'Honestly, we seem to spend half our time at the garden centre these days, since Ed got into gardening. I blame you, you know!'

'Sorry, not sorry,' I said, handing my friend a cuppa.

'I take a book now and park myself in the café until he's ready to join me. I told you he'd started an Insta account before we went away, didn't I?'

'No!' I said, grabbing my phone. 'What's it called?'

'The Shed of Ed.' She rolled her eyes but I could see the love there.

'Love it.' I opened the app, tapping in Ed's handle. 'Ah, here it is.'

For the next ten minutes, the two of us happily sat on my patio, under a large parasol in the heat of the summer day, watching Ed's uploaded videos, liking and sharing them.

'He's already got six thousand followers! That's amazing!'

'I know. So long as it keeps him happy.'

'There's no point feigning disinterest. I've known you too long, my friend! You're as proud as anything.'

'I am!' she said with a laugh. 'Actually, it's really sweet. He seems to have quite a few female followers. Do you think it helps that he's hot?'

'Probably doesn't hurt. You know he's only got eyes for you, though, right?'

'Yeah. And he knows if he doesn't, it will be more than his eyes he'll need to worry about.'

'Don't come to me asking for it to be sewn back on when you make up, will you?' Henry's deep voice made us jump.

'God! Where did you come from?'

'Next door,' he said with a shrug and a grin, before leaning down to kiss me. 'Like always. Hi, Abby.'

'Hi, Doc.'

'What's this?' He peered over my shoulder.

'Ed's started an Instagram channel. It's really good.'

'Will you follow him?' Abby asked.

'I would, but I don't have an account.'

'Henry doesn't have any of the socials.'

'He's thinking of starting a YouTube channel as well so he can do longer content. What about that?'

'Yes, I'd happily watch that. Maybe I'll learn something.' He took one of the two spare seats and sat down, his hand reaching out to take mine, long legs resting out in front of him, crossed at the ankle. 'Do you know what the channel is going to be called?'

'His Insta is "The Shed of Ed" so I'm assuming the same.'

'Ha! Love it. That's brilliant. How's he doing?'

'Loving it. It's really helping him mentally as well as physically, I think.'

'That's great to hear.'

'Plus I get the benefit of a beautiful garden. Never thought of taking it up yourself?' Abby cocked her head, letting her gaze slide past him to look over the fence at the plastic desolation that was Henry's back garden.

Henry turned his head towards me. 'Are you getting everyone to gang up on me about the fact I have to wash and hoover my grass rather than mow it?'

'I don't need to. It's not my fault if everyone agrees that it's a crime to wildlife and the very name of gardening.'

'Maybe it's something you can help me with?'

'Really?'

'I've been thinking about it.'

I exchanged an excited look with Abby.

'Maybe Ed would consider getting involved?' Henry asked.

'Are you joking?' Abby sat bolt upright.

'It's just a suggestion. No pressure or offence taken if he wouldn't.'

Abby was already tapping out a message.

Henry flashed me a look. 'Have I messed up?' he mouthed.

I shook my head and leant over to kiss his cheek, but the gap was just a little too wide. Instead I sat back and blew him a kiss.

'Not good enough,' he said, and grabbed my chair, pulling it closer, allowing me to carry out my initial gesture.

'Much better,' he said, turning to face me, his voice low.

The sound of Abby's phone ringing brought us back to the present, Ed's Devonian accent greeting her.

'Hello, my lover.'

'Hi, babe. Isn't that great? Doc Henry wants you to redo his garden.'

Henry turned to me, mild panic in his eyes. 'Umm, is that what I said?'

I rested my hand on his hard muscled thigh. 'It's just a possibility at the moment, Ed. Nothing is decided.'

Abby turned the phone screen towards us. 'Hey, Twig. Hi, Doc. That's cool. Just give me a shout if and when you decide. All good there?'

'Yep. How's you?'

'Fine, thanks. Just getting some supplies.'

'Ed's putting a pond in the garden,' Abby filled us in.

'You are? Oh, that's great. That will bring so much more wildlife in. I've got some plants I can split, so don't worry about getting any.'

'Oh, that'd be great. Thanks! Want me to pick something up for your place, Doc?' Ed lifted up a very obviously fake lemon tree. 'This would fit in perfectly, don't you think?'

'You're hilarious, the lot of you,' he replied, struggling to maintain his unamused composure in the face of our laughter.

'Better get on. See you later, lover. Love you.'

'Love you too, babe.' Abby ended the call and pushed back her chair. 'I'll head off, too, now and leave you lovebirds alone.'

'You don't have to go, Abs.'

'Honestly, stay,' Henry said, standing. 'I have to head up to the clinic anyway for a meeting.' He rolled his eyes. 'My favourite.'

'Have you packed some food this time?'

'Yeah, it's on the bench round the side in the shade. I'll grab it on the way out.'

'Then I'll leave you alone to say your fond farewells.' Abby made a flouncy, rolling movement with her arm like some medieval suitor wooing his betrothed.

I gave Henry a flat look. 'She went to drama school. Just go with it.'

She switched to a 1940s Hollywood accent. 'I coulda been a star!'

'So it would seem,' Henry replied in his steady, reliable tone. 'You didn't pursue it?'

'Nah. All a bit cut-throat for me.'

'What she's saying is she's too nice for all that.'

'I imagine it's very competitive.'

Abby gave a snort. 'And the rest! So I came back home to teach kids and then bake cakes.'

'She may not be a Hollywood superstar but she's baked cakes for some.'

'Really?'

'Yep. Carter Harrison ring a bell?'

'Didn't he get an Oscar last year?'

'Yep. And guess who made the cake for his celebration party a week later?'

'That's brilliant. I hope he gave you a plug.'

'He did actually. My orders just about tripled from that one social media post.'

'It's very interesting how people are swayed when it comes to celebrity endorsements, don't you think?'

'I'm bloody glad they are! It's made a huge difference.'

'Are you walking home?' Henry asked.

'Yeah. Want to walk with me and we can talk about Willow behind her back?'

'Ah, see, I have to be careful about things like that, otherwise she'll turn me back into a frog and I'll have to come and live in that new pond of yours. I don't think she'll have me in this one.' He nodded at the wildlife pond that butted up against the patio.

'Too flippin' right I wouldn't. Well, I suppose it would depend on what you said.'

'All good things,' he said, wrapping his arms around me and kissing my nose. 'Definitely all good things, I promise.' He lifted his arm behind my back and checked his watch. 'Sod it. I really do have to get going. I'll see you later?'

'Yeah, just let me know when you're done.'

'Will do.' He kissed me hard on the mouth then waited while Abby gave me a hug.

'Aww, you two are so cute together. Catch up later. And don't worry, I'll report back everything he says.'

'Remember,' I said, pointing at Henry. 'She will.'

He grinned as we walked through the house to the front door to collect Abby's bag. 'Bye. See you later.' Henry grabbed another kiss, sweeping me towards him to do so, his hand on my hip, my chest pressed hard against his. Looking down, he smiled a wicked green-eyed smile that promised oh so much when I did see him later, then let go and pulled the door closed behind him.

I headed up the stairs back to work, debating whether to detour into the bathroom to take a hasty cold shower, but in the end decided to distract my suddenly raised ardour with a particularly tricky patient who needed the utmost concentration following severe injury.

'Right, Albert, let's see what we can do for you.' I took out my unpicker and slowly began to take out the stitches from a previously botched surgery to see exactly what I was dealing with.

25

An hour later, I pottered downstairs, made a cup of tea, played a few games of catch with Spud in the garden and was about to head back upstairs when a bark from Spud made me stop. I followed the sound around the side of the house and found him staring at the old bench on which sat a cooler bag.

'Oh, bloody hell. That's Henry's lunch.' Last time he'd had one of those board meetings he didn't eat until late, so I'd insisted he made something to take in this time. Having left through the house with Abby, we'd all forgotten about it.

'Fancy a walk, boy?'

Spud shot off to grab his lead and came back seconds later, trailing it along the floor.

'Good boy. I just need to lock up. Two seconds.'

* * *

'Hi, Niamh.'

'Hello, lovely. How are you?' She glanced down at her desk. 'I haven't got you in for an appointment. Is everything OK?'

'Yeah, fine. I'm just dropping something off for Henry. He's in that meeting today and managed to leave his lunch at my house. Can I leave it with you?'

'Sure, but I think I just saw them break for lunch anyway, so he's probably getting a drink. Either that or out in the courtyard. Feel free to go and find him.'

'Thanks, Niamh. Spud's outside, so I won't be long.'

She put her thumb up as acknowledgement as she picked up the phone to answer a call.

I wandered down to the courtyard, had a quick peer around, but there was no sign of Henry, so I headed back in and made my way towards the break room. As my fingers touched the handle, I heard Calvin's voice.

'How long are you going to string her along, then, Darcy?'

'What?' Henry's voice was icy. Clearly none of the love lost between those two had been made up.

'Willow. How long are you going to pretend you're actually interested?'

I swallowed hard, feeling my spine tingle with cold despite the warmth of the day.

'Shut up, Wise.'

'Oh, come on, Darcy. We're even. Is that what you want me to say? You know I'm doing you a favour. You can drop Weirdy Willow now. For God's sake, man, you can't be serious about someone who spends her day playing with teddy bears!'

'She doesn't play with them, you dick. She fixes them and provides a service that makes people happy. Her levels of empathy put us both to shame! Willow knows the items brought to her mean the world to the people who own them. They're as important to them as any breathing being and she does her utmost to ensure that they get to keep that. No, she didn't go to medical school, but she's more switched on to what people need than some of the professionals I've worked with. And a hell of a lot more than you ever deserved!'

'Bloody hell, you can drop the act now, Darcy! Everyone knows you're only sleeping with her to get back at me for sleeping with your fiancée. It was a pretty obvious move!'

My mouth went dry.

'I don't know why I got all your wrath, though. It wasn't like I was the only one she was seeing on the side. You can't tell me there's actually anything serious with Willow for you, other than sex on tap. We all know how bloody strait-laced you are, and let's face it, you're hardly going to show up to a function with bloody Willow in her dated clothes and flea market shoes, are you?'

The words I'd overheard Henry say months ago echoed around my head. The exact same thing he'd said to his brother. I froze, my hand still on the door-handle, waiting for him to deny it. To tell Calvin to shut the hell up! That he'd thought that himself, once, but had been proved wrong now that he knew me. But there was nothing. No rebuttal. Nothing! Just a deafening silence until Calvin spoke again.

'If you hadn't stuck your oar in, I'd have been back with Willow that night.'

'I doubt it,' Henry growled.

Oh, so he hadn't lost the power of speech then?

'Although I was getting a bit bored of her. Well done on getting her into bed, though. My hat's off to you for that one. Just as well I had Jenna back in London. She's always up for a booty call, thank God. If I'd known Willow was such a prude, I might not have bothered. Although it was worth it to see your face the first time you saw us together. Christ, it was a picture.'

Is that all I was? A toy to be tossed around and used to make an enemy jealous? I couldn't even summon up any tears. My fingers were frozen on the handle of the partially open door, and it felt like my whole body was numb.

I heard the slam of something heavy. As much as I wanted it to be Calvin's head, I guessed it was probably Henry's fist on the table.

'Enough!'

He was right. It was enough. More than enough. I turned away and began striding up the corridor, away from the room, my heart full of pain and fury in equal measure. As I got to Niamh's desk, I stopped, took a breath and spun on my heel marching back towards the break room and pushed the door open. I'd never possessed a poker face, and I guessed by their reactions that I hadn't suddenly gained one. Calvin's face coloured as he turned away, apparently not even interested in any sort of apology. Henry's, in contrast, paled completely.

'Willow…' He took a step towards me. I stepped back.

'Don't.'

I threw the cool bag down on the table. 'You forgot your lunch. I hope you choke on it.'

From the corner, I heard Calvin snort in amusement. How had I missed this side of him?

Because he'd shown you what you wanted to see, you idiot!

Anger surged through me. All my usual resolutions to keep my vibrations high, find the peace within and keep the negativity from piercing my bubble of calm went out the window. Which is exactly where the mug I'd grabbed and aimed at Calvin's head also went. Lucky for him, I'd always been picked last at netball because I was shit at hitting any sort of target.

'Jesus Christ. That could have hit me, you lunatic!'

'It was supposed to, you arsehole!'

Henry placed a hand on my arm, whether to spare himself or

any more of the clinic's crockery I didn't know and didn't care. I shook it off violently and glared at him.

'Don't touch me.'

'Willow!'

I turned back to face him. 'Is it true?'

'What?'

'That you got me into bed just to get back at him?'

'Of course not!' Henry snapped back, every plane on his face drum tight and sharp in anger.

'What about the other bit?'

'What other bit?'

'About being embarrassed by me?'

'No.'

'So if an important formal event came up tomorrow, you'd ask me to go?'

'What?'

'Answer the question!'

'Willow! This is ridiculous. We've been over this!'

'And yet you couldn't answer one simple question. Goodbye, Henry.'

'Willow, wait.'

'No! I've waited long enough, Henry. Waited for someone who was worthy of me, of my love! I thought that was you. Clearly the universe is testing me, first with this shit,' I pointed at Calvin, my hand shaking, 'and then you.'

'There's no bloody higher power, you daft cow,' Calvin spat back.

I now owed the clinic a dinner plate too.

'For fuck's sake!' he shouted, ducking. 'She needs locking up!'

'Just fucking leave, Wise! You've done enough damage.'

'Don't bother. I'm the one leaving.' I turned around and

walked out back towards the entrance, trying to scrape together any last shred of dignity I had to exit the clinic. I'd been made a fool of not once, but twice. Calvin I would get over. I'd have got over it quicker if I'd have been a better shot, but Henry... Henry was different. I'd thought Henry was different. I really had thought he was The One. In the end he'd turned out to be the one who had broken my heart.

'Willow!'

I kept walking.

'Willow!'

Henry caught up with me, his hand catching my arm. I snatched it away as though his fingers were hot coals. His Adam's apple bobbed as he swallowed and I stopped.

'I need to talk to you.'

'I've heard more than enough.'

I went to turn again but he shadowed my move.

'You're really going to take Wise's word over mine?'

'I didn't hear you countering his claims! And it's not about that, anyway. It's about the fact you lied to me.'

'I didn't lie to you!'

'You certainly didn't tell me he'd slept with your fiancée!'

'Funnily enough, it's not something I like to brag about!' His words were forced out through gritted teeth.

'You know what I mean. I thought we meant something. I thought *I* meant something!' My laugh was short and humourless. 'What an idiot.'

'Willow, don't—'

'You don't get to tell me what to do, Henry! In fact, you don't get to talk to me any more. I thought you were different. That, once I got through those barriers you had up, what I saw was what I was getting, but it's all just lies.'

'It's not lies!'

I took a step back. 'It was all a game to you, Henry. You and him! Who could get silly little Willow into bed. Well, congratulations, you won. But,' I saw him try and interrupt me again and poked him hard in the chest just because I could, 'people aren't toys! They're not here to be used to gain points in some twisted game with a rival or to amuse you and then be tossed away or passed on when you're bored with them!' My voice broke on the last word and I poked him again, satisfaction registering somewhere deep in my brain when he winced. I turned away.

'Willow, wait.'

I stopped. Turned around and faced him. 'Henry. My father left as soon as he knew I existed. My mother left me in my grandmother's hands and never looked back. I'm looking for someone I can trust and depend on. I thought that was you, but I see now just how wrong I was, and there is literally nothing you can say that would change that, so it's probably best if you say nothing at all.' And with that, I turned my back and walked away.

I passed Niamh without looking at her. The fact that she didn't say goodbye as I strode through the silent and thankfully empty waiting area told me that she'd heard, if not every word, then enough to get the picture. At some point I'd deal with that particular mortification, but right then it had to get in line behind a whole lot of other emotions while I decided which to tackle first.

'Come on, Spuddy,' I said, untying his lead from the wall loop and scooping my dog up, cuddling him close, breathing in the familiar smell of his fur, his soft warm body pressed against me as he gave a small whine and began to lick salty tears off my face as I walked home.

* * *

The following day Abby, having heard the whole sorry tale through my tears yesterday, messaged me to say that apparently Calvin hadn't shown up for work, merely sending an email advising that he would not be returning, leaving the clinic in an awkward situation. From what she'd heard, Henry had managed to persuade an old friend whom he knew was on sabbatical to fill in until a more permanent replacement could be found.

'Hopefully he'll find a permanent replacement for himself while he's about it.'

Abby got the message and dropped the subject. The sooner Henry Darcy was out of my life for good, the better.

Henry had spent the next ten days knocking on my door and calling me. When this had no effect, he finally seemed to get the message and left me alone. I hated that Spud still went to the fence, waiting for his friend to come and play with him, sneak him cheeky cubes of cheese when he thought I wasn't looking and vault over to scoop him up for cuddles. It broke my heart when the little dog would look round at me and let out a small, confused whimper. I'd walk down to collect him, cuddling him to me and promising to make it up to him. How, though, I had no idea. Right then my heart was in so many pieces, I didn't know where to start.

'Isn't it worth at least talking to him?' Abby asked. 'Clearly you're both miserable without each other!'

'You've seen him?'

'Occasionally, in the village buying groceries.'

Thankfully I'd somehow managed to avoid running into Henry.

'He seems to have retreated back to the withdrawn character he was when he moved here. Before you released him from his shell.'

'Don't be dramatic, Abs. I didn't release anything. He probably just feels awkward knowing we're friends.'

'It's more than that, Wils. I'm not the only one who's noticed it. Even Ed mentioned how different he seems now, and you know what men are like about picking up on stuff like that. You have to practically hit them in the face with it.'

I let out a heavy sigh and looked up from my desk to where Abby was sitting in the armchair by the window. Outside, near-skeletal branches waved and bent in the northerly gusts that blew across the land, stripping the last few red and gold leaves from the trees.

'What do you want me to do, Abs?'

'Talk to him.'

'There's nothing to say.'

'I think there's plenty.'

'Well, you talk to him then!' As soon as the words were said, I dropped my head to my chest before looking back up at my friend. 'I'm sorry.'

She gave a brief smile and nodded. 'You were happy, Willow. The happiest I've ever seen you – and we were in nappies together! He was happy too. Whatever you heard, there's no way that could all have been an act. You brought out the real Henry and you both benefitted. Isn't it worth trying to find that again?'

I snipped off a thread with far more intensity that was warranted. 'No. It's not. It wasn't real and whatever it was is done. Over. I have no intention of giving someone a second opportunity to make a fool of me, so as much as I love you, Abby, please don't ask me about him again. It's been painful enough getting over him as it is.'

'So you're over him?'

'Absolutely.'

Abby watched me for a couple of beats. 'You always were a horrible liar.'

26

The weather got colder, the days shorter and garden more bare. I cosied up inside my house, a woollen shawl wrapped around my shoulders, thick fluffy socks on my feet as I beavered away at work, repairing long-loved toys so that they could be home for Christmas. Soon it would be time to get the decorations down from the loft and pick up a tree from the local Christmas tree farm a few villages over. I'd had visions of doing all those things with Henry this year. I had many friends in the village, and Ed and Abby always invited me to their big family Christmas, which was wonderful. But the truth was, I wanted my own special Christmas with my own special person, and finally I'd thought it was happening. But it wasn't. Once again, it would just be Spud and me.

At the sound of hammering, I leant over and looked out of the window. A plain white van was parked outside the house, its green-coated owner banging a sign into the front garden next door. He gave the post a wiggle then gathered his tools and walked off, leaving me to see what it said.

For Sale.

It had been just under a year since the last board had been up and I thought of all that had happened in that time. I'd argued with my new neighbour, got to know him, fallen in love with him and finally had my heart broken by him. I suppose it was only right that the circle would eventually return to the beginning.

Pushing my chair out, I wrapped the shawl tighter around me and headed down to the kitchen to put the kettle on, Spud trailing at my feet. As I stood idly looking out of the back windows, Pepper wandered up to the fence and began braying.

'Oh, Pepper...'

The wind was bitter, its icy sharpness shocking my lungs as I sucked in a breath, my feet shoved into wellies as I made my way down the garden, my pockets full of carrots.

'Here you go, boy,' I cooed as the donkey took the treats, his friends trotting over to get their own snacks. 'Hello!' I said, stroking their muzzles and feeding them the same. 'How are you today?' Pepper leant his head against my arm and rubbed up and down. 'Excuse me, mister. I'm not your scratching post!' I said, laughing and adjusting my stance as he nearly knocked me off balance. 'Look, how about if I give it a good rub? How's that?' I scratched the side of his face with my fingers and he moved his head up and down to double the effect as he brayed in happiness.

'Looks like someone's enjoying that.'

I spun at the voice, dropping my hand, much to the disgust of Pepper, who stretched his nose over the fence and nudged me. The howl of the wind and Pepper's chatty brays meant I'd not heard, or even sensed, Henry's approach. He sent the barest glimpse of a smile before it disappeared once more, hidden beneath the stress-etched features on his handsome face. His skin, once tanned from surfing, was pale and there were dark shadows back under his vivid green eyes, the contrast making them seem all the more striking.

I turned back to the animals and watched as Henry approached his side of the fence and confidently fed them with his own treats. My thoughts drifted back to how nervous he'd been of them when he'd arrived, moaning about Pepper disturbing his peace. And now there he stood in a waxed Barbour jacket, rubbing Pepper's ears as the donkey made satisfied noises, having finished both of our offerings. So much had changed in a year.

The silence was too awkward and I finally caved in to filling it. 'You're moving, then?'

'Yes.'

'Do you know where?'

'Probably back to London.'

I turned.

'You look surprised.'

'I suppose I am.' I returned to looking out across the paddock. 'I hope the sale goes smoothly for you.'

It will be better once he's not here. You won't have to see him accidentally from the window as he goes to his car. You won't have to worry about bumping into him in the village, knowing everyone around will be surreptitiously watching to see what happens next.

I told myself all these things, but somehow it only made me feel worse.

'Thanks.'

The silence fell once more and, after a few more moments, I began walking towards the house and saw Spud jumping up and down madly at the back door. He'd had his wee and I'd sent him back inside where he'd snuggled down in his bed. But his sharp eyes had spied Henry and he was desperate to get out and see his long-lost friend. I quickened my pace but Spud was more eager to escape than I'd anticipated and suddenly the door was flying open, crashing against the doorstop as it got whipped by the wind, and my ball of fur was haring down the garden at top speed. I bent to grab him but he was too fast and nimble and dodged what he'd clearly sussed was a trap. Seconds later, he was at the fence next to Henry, barking madly and jumping with all his might in an attempt to clear the barrier.

Henry leant over and picked him up. Immediately, the barking ceased and was replaced with those wonderful deep tones of Henry Darcy's laughter. Oh, God, I missed that sound. I missed his voice, his touch, his intelligence, his humour and the solid, strong body and how he made me feel.

Stop, Willow!

Reality screeched my wandering mind to a halt. It was over and Henry was leaving. We were done. I straightened my back and walked back down the way I had come, to collect my dog.

'Spud, come here, please,' I said, having stopped at a distance from the pair.

Henry looked up at me and I bit back the pain I felt at the hollow sadness on his face as he gave Spud one last cuddle and kissed the top of his head before placing him back on my side of the fence. Spud stood there, looking up at him.

'Spud!' I called, firmer now.

He looked round at me, looked back at Henry and then back at me and let out a whine.

'Come inside, please.'

He sat down.

'Spud!' My voice was sharper now but it was the only way I could mask what I felt inside, my sad little dog's confusion, the dog that I'd once thought I'd lost, whom Henry had found for me. Whatever I felt about Henry, I would never not be grateful for that day. He and my dog had formed a bond and it shredded my heart to have to break that. But there was no other way. I marched forward and bent to pick him up as he wriggled in an attempt to escape and reach my neighbour, squirming and twisting in his effort to free himself.

'Spud!' I said, panic in my voice. 'Calm down! I'm going to drop you. Spud!'

Suddenly Henry was vaulting the fence and, as Spud began to fall, Henry was there, one arm curving behind the dog's back and the other wrapping around both of us in order to prevent Spud dropping from my arms entirely. Immediately, the dog calmed and snuggled happily between us, nosing first my face, then Henry's.

'Spud,' I said, the word breaking on a sob. I wouldn't look up at Henry. I couldn't. I'd loved him and he'd played me.

'I miss you.' His words shattered the fragile shell I'd spent the last few months building around my broken heart in the hope that, protected, it would begin to mend. But now it was once again open, exposed and raw.

'Please don't.' I spoke without looking at him.

His arm tightened the merest fraction. 'I can't help it. Please look at me, Willow.'

'What's the point? We're done, Henry!' I snapped my head up then. 'None of it meant anything!'

He stepped back then as if I'd slapped him, his Adam's apple bobbing. Carefully taking Spud from my arms, he placed him down on the ground and pulled a small Kong stuffed with treats out of his pocket and put it next to the dog.

'There you go,' he said, the briefest of smiles flashing at the dog before he turned back to me.

'I knew there had to be a reason he wanted to see you. That's called bribery.'

'It's called missing your dog almost as much as I miss you.

There's always one in my pocket, just in case.' He looked at the ground then back up at me. 'Did it really mean nothing to you?'

I tried to laugh but the sound that came out was a strangled, painful cry. 'Of course it did, Henry, yes, and I was foolish enough to think it meant the same to you. What an idiot! But luckily you and Calvin put me straight on that.'

His features darkened, brow rumpled low, and when he spoke there was a steel to his voice that I hadn't heard, even when we'd been at loggerheads back in the early spring.

'Wise is a nasty piece of work and it killed me to see you with him, that much is true. But the rest? The truth of that? You've got that all wrong. I love you, Willow! Don't you know that?'

'I don't believe you!' I shouted back over the wind that was whipping at the skirt of my dress. 'I'm not stupid, Henry. I heard you. You said it yourself right there.' I pointed at his patio. 'How I would be an embarrassment to you and that no one would ever take you seriously if you were seen with someone like me. Just like I was a burden and embarrassment to my own mother.'

'You're right, I did say that and if I could turn back time, I'd shove those words back down my own throat! I was an idiot, Willow. What can I say? I was way out of my comfort zone, and you were there, yelling at me about my own garden and looking like a wonderful nymph from *A Midsummer Night's Dream* while doing so! I didn't know what to do, so I did what I always do and concentrated on the facts. You're beautiful, but your manner and your beliefs are nothing like any of the women I've dated before or been much acquainted with. I made the mistake of assuming we would have nothing in common.'

'So just because we don't have anything in common means I'm automatically an embarrassment?'

'No!' He reached for my hand and I stepped back. 'I'm sorry. George and my family had been badgering me to meet someone else for ages, and when he started on about me seeing you, I blurted whatever I could to get him to back off. It was a stupid, thoughtless and cruel thing to say, and you wouldn't believe how sorry I am.' He ran his fingers through hair damp from the drizzling rain. 'How much I wish I could rewind time. To start all over again with you and do it properly this time so that I wouldn't be standing here now, looking at the woman I love, knowing she can barely set eyes on me.'

I bit my cheek to try and prevent the tears that wanted to flow from falling.

'If that was true, you'd have defended me when Calvin said much the same thing in the break room, but you didn't! You didn't say a word! If you love someone, you stand up for them!'

'You know why I didn't say a word?' He took my upper arms in his hands, the fingers curling round them strong but gentle. 'Because I was about to get struck off!'

'What?'

'The moment Wise said those things, things I'd said myself and hated myself for having done so, I had him up against the wall. I was so close to punching his smug bloody face, so furious about the way he'd treated you, spoken about you, that I was prepared to risk my entire career for it. All I saw was red.'

'You already had a grudge against him,' I countered, my words softer this time, less sure.

'I was over that. The moment I met you, the day we spent together when you showed me the village taught me that what I'd had before was wrong. So very wrong. This,' he tightened his hold the tiniest fraction, '*this* is right. This is how it's supposed to be. I thought I was happy before, but I wasn't. You've made me happier than I ever thought I could be. Please, Willow.' He slid one hand down my arm and curled his fingers around my frozen ones. 'You have to believe me.'

'How can I? All I know is what you're saying. There were only two of you in that room. Why should I believe you? How do I know you're any different from Calvin, saying whatever you need to get what you want?'

'Don't,' he said, his voice a low growl, expression pained, eyes blazing. 'Even if you never forgive me, please don't ever put me in the same category as that arsehole. I've been a shit, I know, but still. There's a limit.'

I nodded. 'OK.' I wasn't going to apologise but he had a point.

Spud toddled over, rested his front paws on my welly and gave a small whine. Henry looked down, one hand still holding mine as though I might flee, he reached down with his other and picked up the dog. He snuggled him close to his chest as he turned back towards me.

'I thought you weren't a dog person.'

'Turns out I was wrong.' His eyes were searching mine. 'About a lot of things.'

'Henry...'

'Oh, God. Don't. Don't say it.'

We stood there for a moment longer then he suddenly started. Popping Spud down, he held up one hand.

'Wait there.' He patted his pockets manically until he located his phone. Pulling it out, he scrolled quickly and stabbed at the screen. 'Tracey.'

'What?'

'Tracey, one of the theatre nurses. She was just coming in from the courtyard from her break when I... manhandled Wise.'

'I don't understand. If all this had happened, Henry, you'd have lost your job and the whole village would know about it!' I stepped away. 'I don't have time to listen to any more of your lies.'

'They're not lies!' he shouted, a crack in his voice as he put the phone to his ear. 'Tracey? Please, I need your help.'

27

Half an hour later, Henry, Tracey and I were sitting in my kitchen as she recounted what she'd seen.

'Frankly, Dr Wise was lucky no one else had thumped him. You know he was having an affair with another doctor's wife back in London?'

I remembered his comment about a Jenna back in London. 'Not at the time, no, I didn't. Obviously.'

'No, of course. Sorry, love.' She leant over and patted my hand. 'Apparently Denise from the dentist's nearly made a big mistake after he was swooning all over her on a night out with the girls. Thankfully she made the right decision, but to say Gary wasn't happy with the good doctor is putting it mildly!'

'But none of that changes things.'

She sipped at the cup of tea I'd made her and broke off a bit of her biscuit to sneak to Spud. 'I heard what Dr Wise said to Dr Darcy, and frankly he's lucky that I did come in at that moment. Honestly, I'd have happily cheered Dr Darcy on, apart from the fact he'd have been in serious trouble and likely struck off. He's a brilliant doctor and a good person. I wasn't prepared to see that happen. So between you, me and the gatepost, I stood in between them. Put my finger to my lips and they got the message. I left them to it and went back outside, left them to sort it out between them. Anyway, later that afternoon Dr Wise came to me and started making noises about reporting Dr Darcy, asking me to be a witness. Silly man picked the wrong woman because I knew who he was. Not that I could say anything to anyone. I mean, who's going to listen to a nurse over a doctor everyone was already fawning over? Anyway, I suggested perhaps it would be better if he didn't as I knew the real reason he'd left his last post.'

'What was that?'

'I promised him if he left quietly and never spoke of this again, I'd not tell a soul. But should I ever hear of him speaking ill of Dr Darcy, let's just say he knows his own career would be over and he'd be in a lot of hot water to boot.'

I looked at Henry.

'I know,' he said, reading my face. 'She won't tell me either. It's really annoying.'

Tracey winked at him and drained her cup. 'Thanks for this, love,' she said, standing from the table as we followed her lead and Spud dived under it to see if there were any errant biscuit crumbs to be dealt with.

'I don't know if any of this will make you rethink leaving the clinic and the village,' Tracey said. 'You'll be greatly missed if you go through with it, you know.' She shifted her eyes not so subtly to me when she said that, before looking back at him. 'At least give it some more thought.'

'Thanks, Tracey. For everything.'

'My pleasure.' She took his hand and held it within both of hers. 'Truly, my pleasure.'

I saw her to the door, opened it and thanked her for coming, more out of habit than anything else. My mind was still whirling with what she'd told me.

'Look after yourself, love. Maybe now you'll find that lovely smile of yours again.'

'I'm fine, really.'

'Don't forget, Willow. I've known you a long time.' She leant in and gave me a tight hug. 'I hope things work out. He's a good man and he loves you beyond reason. You've brought out the best in him too. It's awful to see you both so miserable now.'

'It's not as simple as that.'

'Isn't it?' she asked.

Was it?

'See you soon, Willow.' Tracey patted my arm, swung her bag across her body, the strap settling in her matronly, ample bosom, and set off down the path and back to her car. I closed the door and leant my back against it. Sucking in a deep breath, I walked slowly back down the hallway to the kitchen, my socked feet silent on the floor.

'Good boy!'

Henry's voice was soft as he held up his hand and Spud, sitting on his lap, put his own paw to it, a tiny little high five. The floor creaked as I moved and Henry looked up, meeting my eyes. The silence between us hung there, thick and awkward. He dropped his gaze back to the dog.

'I didn't know you'd taught him that.'

Henry looked back up. 'I... I was going to show you that night. We'd been working on it in secret.' His gaze dropped back to his lap. 'He's a fast learner.'

'He is.'

His broad chest heaved as he placed the dog gently onto the floor.

'Bye, Spud.'

His voice caught on Spud's name and suddenly the dam I'd built burst. All the tears I'd kept behind it rushed through and in the next moment, I felt Henry's arms around me, holding me tight. One hand moved to the back of my head, cradling it as soft, soothing words tumbled from his lips. Against my ear, his heart raced, the emotion of the moment overcoming us both. I held on to him, my hands fisting his shirt into tight knots as if afraid that, by letting go, I'd lose him forever.

Henry went to move but I gripped harder.

'Willow.' His voice was hoarse.

'What?' Mine was muffled, pressed into his chest.

'Look at me.'

I loosened my hold just enough to do so and his hands went to my face, his palms warm and gentle, his thumbs stroking gently one way then the other across my cheeks, wiping the tears away. Spud was sitting on my foot, issuing quiet little whimpers.

'I'm so sorry.' Concern crumpled his forehead, the dark brows drawn close as his eyes scanned my face.

Another tear spilled over and I dashed it away with the back of my hand as Henry bent down and lifted up Spud. The little dog immediately curled into him, nuzzling into his neck as the fuzzy little tail beat itself into a blur, his actions causing Henry's frown to disappear, replaced instead by that wonderful smile and rumbling laugh I loved.

'I've made a mess of this from the start, I'm so sorry. I should have told you ages ago that I liked you. I should have told you about Wise. I messed everything up.' His head rested against mine.

'Why didn't you?'

'Because I'm an idiot.'

'No, you're not. You're one of the most intelligent men I know!'

'I'm still an idiot. Intellectual learning doesn't automatically mean you're not a complete twit. I thought that, because we were so different, the fact that I thought you were attractive, and, as I got to know you, funny, bright and the most interesting woman I've ever met... none of that mattered. I told myself that it was a crush. A flash in the pan. That that's all it could be.'

'But it's not?'

He let out a huff of breath as he lifted his head, his hand on my cheek, the thumb caressing my skin.

'Definitely not. Entirely the opposite. I'm in love with you, Willow. With everything I have, everything I am. And I would never ever leave you or abandon you. Not ever. I couldn't!' He ran a hand across his jaw. A jaw that had missed a day or two's shave, leaving a dark stubble on the chiselled jawline. 'I thought I'd be OK after we split up. That I'd soon get over you, but I haven't. I can't, and I know I won't. Not ever. And every time I saw you, it felt like another slice to my heart.'

'That's why you're moving?'

He nodded. 'It was the only way I could think of. Perhaps if I didn't see you every day, then gradually I might find a way to get on with my life.'

'And now?' I steeled myself to ask the question. When I'd seen the for sale board go up, I'd told myself I was glad for the same reasons. But like him, I'd known it would take so much more than just out of sight, out of mind for me to get over him.

'That's up to you.'

'Is it?'

'Yes. I've done all I can to explain what happened, why it happened and apologised. But that might not be enough and if that's the case, I understand. But I'd need to try and start again somewhere new. Don't think I'll be getting over you any time soon, but at least I won't get the pitying looks and advice from the more forthright members of the community who've told me what a big mistake I've made, letting you go.'

'Did someone say that?' I asked.

'More than one! You're quite a favourite around here, you know.'

'I've just been here a long time. I'm more of a fixture.'

Henry disagreed. 'It's more than that. You're loved by a lot of people and for good reason. And I have to say I agreed with them every time.'

'Nobody said anything to me. Well, apart from Abby and Ed, but that was to be expected. They knew how happy I'd been with you, and then I was quite the opposite. They kept telling me to talk to you.'

'Why didn't you?'

'You're clearly a better person than me in being able to swallow your pride,' I said, lowering my eyes for a moment. 'I am sorry I didn't believe you initially about the fight with Calvin. I should have done. You're one of the most honest men I've ever met. As for trying to talk to you? I was nervous. What if you didn't want to talk? Or you had no interest in getting back together? That the more you'd thought about it, the more you felt that your initial instincts about us had been right.'

'Oh, my darling.' He kissed the newly falling tears away. 'You couldn't have been more wrong.'

He led me to the squashy sofa, Spud hopping up to sit with us. I looked down at my lap, my fingers intertwined there. There was one more thing I needed to ask.

'What is it, Willow?' He knew me so well. Knew there was more.

'What you said before... that I would embarrass you at functions.'

Henry dragged a hand across his uncharacteristically unshaven jaw.

'The last thing I'd want to do is make you feel out of place in a professional setting,' I said.

'You wouldn't. You couldn't ever. In any setting! In fact, I know now you'd actually be the one to keep me sane. You have no idea how boring some of these things are with everyone talking about the same thing over and over.' He lifted my hand to his lips and, eyes down, he pressed the gentlest of kisses to it before lifting his gaze back up. 'As long as I live, Willow, wherever we are, you will always be the most important, the most interesting and most beautiful person in the room to me.'

'You need to be sure, Henry. I'm not going to change. This is me.'

'And for that, I will forever be grateful. You make me a better man, Willow. I'd always hoped I was empathetic in my work, but you've shown me that that can extend much further than just within my job. Knowing that, being shown that by you has made me a better person both in and out of work. And not just that. Everything I've learned from you, everything you've brought out in me...' He shook his head. 'I'm no good at stuff like this. I'm a fact chap, as you know. But the fact is, I love you. I need you. I never knew what it was that was missing until I met you.' His head bent to mine, his lips teasing slowly at first, and then his arms tightened around me, his kiss desperate, hard and sensual all at the same time, and I laced my fingers tight together behind his neck, pulling him closer until we were almost one, and still it wasn't close enough. I knew it then. Henry was there for me. Would be there for me. Always.

'So, as it turns out, each of us is what the other truly needed. Are you a believer now?'

A slow smile spread across the handsome face. 'Are you asking if I believe that you manifested me?'

'If I did, I should have been more specific about you being less of a grumpy arse to begin with!'

'True.'

'Answer the question?'

He hesitated.

'Your answer isn't going to change my mind, Henry. I love you. And I know we're always going to disagree on things, but so long as we respect each other's beliefs and values, even if we don't believe in them ourselves, we'll be just fine.'

'I do, I promise. No, I'm not a believer in much of the alternative side, but that doesn't mean I don't find it fascinating. The mind is certainly a powerful tool and, used right, I know it can have a huge effect of our health and life in general.' He shifted in his seat. 'Actually, there's something I haven't told you.'

'Oh?'

'I've been back to Crystal's shop a couple of times since we split up.'

'You have?'

'Yeah. And got it in the neck from her for hurting you both times.'

'Ah. Yes.' I winced. 'She's quite protective of her friends.'

'That's an understatement. But the point is, she told me it didn't matter because the universe knew the truth and the way things are meant to be. She actually wagged her finger at me in front of several other customers!'

I put my hand up to my mouth, trying not to laugh, but Henry was already chuckling away.

'Crystal said that, luckily for me, this was all just a hiccup, a test for us both, and that things would work themselves out exactly how they were meant to.'

'Really?'

'Yep. She beckoned me closer and whispered something in my ear. I thought it was going to be something wise and mystic.' He pulled a hand over the shadowed jawline. 'Which I suppose it was, really.'

'What did she say?'

'Not to fuck it up again!'

My mouth dropped open. 'She didn't!'

Henry was really laughing now and I felt that once-familiar warmth wrap around me again. 'Now, I'm obviously not an expert in these things, but I'm pretty sure that isn't part of the whole woo-woo peace-and-love dogma.'

'But she was right,' I pointed out.

Henry looked at me, the smile fading, his hand tensing on mine.

'About us?' There was a rawness to his voice that made my own catch in my throat.

'Yes.'

His mouth was on mine, his hands on each side of my face, his kiss gentle but urgent.

'I swear to God I will spend the rest of my life making sure you don't regret that decision.' His green eyes were soft, diluted by unshed tears.

'I'm not sure I believe in God,' I said, laughing through my own tears. I hadn't realised until then just how unhappy I'd been, not until the moment when I knew that, however it had happened, the love that I'd wanted was right there. 'But I do believe in manifestation.'

Henry sat back, his hands sliding down my arms to hold my own, almost as though he was worried that, if he let go, I might leave.

'You think all this is because you made a wish?'

'No, it's because I let the universe know what I wanted, what I needed.'

'Nothing to do with coincidence?'

'Nope. Why do you think you got lost and ended up here, of all places? You could have ended up anywhere. Yet you ended up here.'

Henry grinned, pulled me close and kissed me. 'I've a feeling this could be the one thing we never agree on.'

'Is that a problem?'

'Nothing is a problem if you're with me.'

EPILOGUE

SIX MONTHS LATER

'That's the last box,' Henry said, plopping it down. He straightened and gave his back a stretch. 'Thank God.'

I held out a cup of herbal tea and those sharp, sexy eyes fixed on me.

'Worth a try,' I grinned, reaching up on my tiptoes to kiss his mouth before I handed him the strong black coffee I was yet to convert him from.

He wrapped his free hand around my waist as we stood at the open doors of the large kitchen–diner of The Vicarage, looking out on the garden I'd loved for so long.

'I still can't believe it's ours.'

Henry tightened his grip momentarily. 'Believe it. It's right there in front of you.'

'Do you love it?' I asked, looking up at him.

'I do.'

'You can't hoover this garden.'

'It's also possible I could kill every single thing in it unlike my previous one.'

'You'd better not. Don't forget there's plenty of room to bury a body here!'

'Excellent. At least there's no pressure.'

I laughed and, putting my tea down on the nearby dining table, wrapped my arms around his waist.

'What?' he said, following suit and holding me close.

'What?'

'You've got that look on your face.'

'What look?'

Henry gave a patient tilt of his head and I giggled.

'OK. I was just thinking that, as much as you pooh-poohed my manifestation plans and so on, everything I wanted has come into my life. I have a man I love, who loves me back, the most beautiful house and garden, and my business is thriving. Even more so since you found Elsie to help me.'

'Right.'

I pulled away a little to meet his eyes better. 'What does that mean?'

'Willow, I happened to move next door and we fell in love. It's just one of those things. Pooling our resources, we were able to buy this house when it was put up for sale. As for your business, it's thriving because you work extremely hard and you're wonderful at your job. Elsie was lonely and feeling like she had lost her purpose. The fact that she had the skills and enthusiasm to help out was just good luck.'

'Oh dear.'

'Oh dear, what?'

'You just don't get it, do you?' I said, smiling up at him.

'Get what?'

'You didn't just "happen" to move next door to me. It was arranged. I'd put it out there to the universe and then, after that house being empty for over two years, you moved in. You can't think that's just a coincidence.'

'I can and I do.'

'Have I really taught you nothing?'

'Oh, you've taught me plenty and I'm grateful for that. I also find your beliefs intriguing and interesting. But I don't believe me moving here was for any other reason than I'd had enough of my insane schedule in London.'

'And ended up here. Next to me.'

Without warning, Henry lifted me up, his hands around my backside. Automatically, my legs wrapped around his waist and I saw the light dance in his eyes.

'I did. Thank God. Or the universe, or whoever. All I know is that I'm here now, with you, and that's all that matters.'

His kiss was soft before he gently placed me down on the floor.

'Come with me,' he said, holding out his hand.

I took it and followed as we walked towards a floriferous clematis that had entwined its way through a rowan tree, creating a floating cloud of white above us.

'What is it?'

'I've got a question to ask you.'

* * *

Happy tears streamed from my eyes as I held out my hand, the diamond and platinum ring glinting as the bright sun caught its many facets.

'I wondered if you might like the reception here, in the garden?' he asked, his own eyes shining.

He knew me so well. I placed my hands on his face and

reached up to kiss him. The man with whom I'd thought I had nothing in common was my everything, and I his.

'That sounds perfect,' I replied, just as Spud came racing up to us, having thoroughly explored his new domain. His front paws rested on Henry's leg, and Henry bent to lift him up.

'And you, obviously, will have the very important job of ring-bearer. Do you think you're up to that?' he asked.

Spud gave an excited bark in answer as Henry laughed, snuggling him in between us.

'It's such a shame you're not much of a dog person.'

'Isn't it?' he agreed, leaning down to kiss me once more. 'What do you think about getting Spud a friend?'

ACKNOWLEDGEMENTS

Every time I write these acknowledgements, I find it hard to believe that another book has become real. I'd always wanted to be a writer but didn't think that it was something 'people like me' did, and I am forever grateful that dream did eventually become a reality. If you're someone who's ever thought the same, I'd like to take this opportunity to say Go For It! Write the book you want to read and keep knocking on those doors. One day one will open.

Thanks, as always, to the fantastic team at Boldwood Books without whose professionalism, enthusiasm, support, understanding and love I would definitely not still be writing. When I joined them as an inaugural writer on their launch, they claimed that they would be 'a different kind of publisher', and my word, how well they have stuck to their claim. All the team are utterly brilliant, but I must add in extra thanks to Sarah Ritherdon, my editor, Nia Beynon, who can pretty much fix any problem, Claire Fenby for her marketing genius and dynamism, and the recently appointed Niamh Wallace for the same. And, of course, none of us would be where we are without the force of nature that is CEO Amanda Ridout – her enthusiasm for Willow's lavender biscuits is unrivalled.

Thanks also to copyeditor Cecily Blench and proofreader Helen Woodhouse for all their hard work on getting the copy into the best shape. Alongside that, massive thanks to Leah Jacobs-Gordon for creating the stunning cover. I love it so much!

Thank you to Wendy at Alice's Bear and Doll Hospital in Lyme Regis, Dorset for the generous donation of her time in allowing me to visit and ask all the questions. I really appreciated this, especially in light of how busy they are (although thankfully the waiting lists there are not as long as NHS ones). The knowledge I gained from the trip was invaluable in giving depth and credence to Willow's teddy bear hospital. I do hope all your current patients are doing well!

As always, thank you to the bloggers who write and share lovely reviews and beautiful photos of my books, helping to spread the word of #readyourselfhappy. I know you have so many books to pick from, so thank you for choosing this one. I'd also like to thank Rachel Gilby who organises the blog tours and has done a stellar job from day one of launching her business.

And you, my lovely readers – thank you for the messages that you send telling me one of my books has cheered you up after a rubbish day or kept you up reading through the night (sorry, not sorry!). There's always a happy dance involved when I receive one of those notes and it will never not be amazing and humbling, so thank you. I love to hear from you, so do feel free to reach out anytime – contact details are at the end of the book.

And finally, as always, thank you, James, for National Fruiting Day and everything else. I love you.

ABOUT THE AUTHOR

Maxine Morrey is a bestselling romantic comedy author with over a dozen books to her name. When not word wrangling, Maxine can be found reading, sewing and listening to podcasts. As she's also partial to tea and cake, something vaguely physical is generally added to the mix.

Sign up to Maxine Morrey's mailing list for news, competitions and updates on future books.

You can contact Maxine here: hello@scribblermaxi.co.uk

Follow Maxine on social media:

 facebook.com/MaxineMorreyAuthor
instagram.com/scribbler_maxi
pinterest.com/ScribblerMaxi

ALSO BY MAXINE MORREY

#No Filter

My Year of Saying No

Winter at Wishington Bay

Things Are Looking Up

Living Your Best Life

You Only Live Once

Just Say Yes

You've Got This

Just Do It

Be Your Best Self

WHERE ALL YOUR ROMANCE
DREAMS COME TRUE!

THE HOME OF BESTSELLING
ROMANCE AND WOMEN'S
FICTION

 WARNING:
MAY CONTAIN SPICE

SIGN UP TO OUR
NEWSLETTER

https://bit.ly/Lovenotesnews

Boldwₒₒd

Find out more at www.boldwoodbooks.com

Follow us
@BoldwoodBooks
@TheBoldBookClub

Sign up to our weekly
deals newsletter

https://bit.ly/BoldwoodBNewsletter

Printed in Great Britain
by Amazon

46603373R00185